I have no doubt that you'll receive
RAVE REVIEWS on "UNION OF THE MASTERS"!!!

From around the Globe...
I might add.

IT is stepping out
into a New World

That – –

Could help form
the beginning
of a Distinctive Era

One filled
With More Character
Willingness
Acceptance

And Grace Itself"

—Cori Saracini
Artist

Union of the Masters

DEBORAH-MARIE DIAMOND

BALBOA.PRESS

A DIVISION OF HAY HOUSE

Balboa Press books may be ordered through booksellers or by contacting:

Balboa Press
A Division of Hay House
1663 Liberty Drive
Bloomington, IN 47403
www.balboapress.com
1 (877) 407-4847

Because of the dynamic nature of the Internet, any web addresses or links contained in this book may have changed since publication and may no longer be valid. The views expressed in this work are solely those of the author and do not necessarily reflect the views of the publisher, and the publisher hereby disclaims any responsibility for them.

The author of this book does not dispense medical advice or prescribe the use of any technique as a form of treatment for physical, emotional, or medical problems without the advice of a physician, either directly or indirectly. The intent of the author is only to offer information of a general nature to help you in your quest for emotional and spiritual well-being. In the event you use any of the information in this book for yourself, which is your constitutional right, the author and the publisher assume no responsibility for your actions.

Scripture quotations marked KJV are from the Holy Bible, King James Version (Authorized Version). First published in 1611. Quoted from the KJV Classic Reference Bible, Copyright © 1983 by The Zondervan Corporation.

Copyright Permission granted for the following quotations:
Living Buddha, Living Christ, Page 55 by Thich Nhat Hanh
Search for the Beloved, Page 42 by Jean Houston

Print information available on the last page.

ISBN: 978-1-9822-4997-7 (sc)
ISBN: 978-1-9822-4999-1 (hc)
ISBN: 978-1-9822-4998-4 (e)

Library of Congress Control Number: 2020911549

Balboa Press rev. date: 08/11/2020

To you

Contents

Introduction

Dear Friends,

Years ago, during a meditation, a golden laser beam went through the top of my head for an instant. Strong yet gentle, the beam's message was that I was to write a book about Buddha, Jesus, and Running Bear Eagle coming back to Earth at the same time to assist in our spiritual evolution. I was to show the similarities of their paths and that, in the unification of their teachings, no path was now necessary. They stood holding the Earth.

That was all I was given, and I was sure the message was meant for someone else. How could I write such a book? So, I forgot about it. Then, a few months later, I had a psychic reading.

"There is a book you need to write," the reader said, leaning back in her chair, looking up to the left, as if listening. Her colorful housedress covered her round body, which made her appear more like the mother next door than a psychic reader.

"The one I started on healing, last spring?" I questioned.

"No," she said, "that information will come through someone else."

Darn, I thought, *I waited too long. And I knew what to write for that book!*

"Another book, much more profound. You think you can't do it, and if you put one more thing on your plate, you will burst."

"Where am I to get this information?" I asked, truly confused. "Do I channel the avatars?"

"No. Go to your heart. The information is there."

She said more about the book and its impact. I listened quietly, musing at this turn of events.

I began to reorganize my office, so I could schedule time each day to write. However, with the work of managing our healing center, the *Circle of Life Center,* and my private healing practice, I did not begin.

Then, coincidentally, we had an odd number in an angel class I was teaching, so I partnered up with one of the students to receive a message from an angel. My partner hadn't held my hand for twenty seconds when his eyes popped open. "Write the book!" he exclaimed. "Write the book!"

I looked skyward and laughed. Okay, already. I got the message.

Hence, I began with great humility. I had no outline, something I used a lot in my life. I had no plan, except to be deep in my heart and activate some knowledge I trusted was there. I present this work to you as my gift. Please take what resonates with you and leave the rest.

Union of the Masters is set in the present, and real spiritual teachers and their works are mentioned in the story, so I included some references for your convenience and further study.

Presently, we are in a new age, moving out of the vibration of "religion" and into a higher vibration of "spirituality." In the past, many teachers and gurus came to Earth's school to create religions to assist us in our path back to God. Though only Buddha's, Christ's, and Running Bear Eagle's teaching are included in this story, that is not to negate the other great religions and their avatars. I honor each path with great reverence. As you will see, this story is about our connection, not our separation, and about our desperate need to find that connection *now*.

Buddha was born a prince and destined to find the path of liberation to free us from suffering. His teachings expanded on his Hindu background and developed, through the practice of meditation, the *Four Noble Truths* and the *Eightfold Path* to remove the causes of suffering. Buddha taught that the secret lay in the silence of the mind and unity with all life. Living a simple life, with neither extreme of poverty nor riches—the middle road—helps create a peaceful life.

Jesus taught us love: to love our enemy and to love ourselves. His teaching said put love first in all your words, thoughts, and actions to create a peaceful world.

Our final main character in *Union of the Masters* is Running Bear Eagle, a Native American medicine woman who teaches through *every* action in life that we are all in relationship: with Mother Earth and Father Sky and with insects, animals, vegetables, tree people, and the stone people. Realizing that we all have souls and spiritual journeys changes not only how we think, but also how we act. And *that* will change the world from violence to peace.

Union of the Masters will not only give you deeper insight into these great avatars, but also provide you with practical things to *do* to live in conscious oneness. How do we bring *spirit into matter* for the highest good of all?

We do not need a *new* religion. We have all the information and tools available to us right now. However, it is the paradigm by which we implement our tools that will save or destroy us. It is now the time for each of us to accept the inner power of God consciousness and create our lives and our world accordingly.

The Gospel of Thomas, discovered in 1860, writes of Jesus' message to us: "If you bring forth what is within you, what you bring forth will save you. If you do not bring forth what is within you, what you do not bring forth will destroy you."

My wish is that this book opens new ways of seeing and being for you, and that you are motivated to put love into action in all that you do.

Bless you,
Deborah-Marie Diamond

In Gratitude

I am forever grateful for my sister, Donna Johnson, who held the light for *Union of the Masters*. She was my *Hermit* of the Tarot Card number 9, holding the lantern to show the way. She purchased a beautiful book-signing pen when I first began to write, and I put it out on my desk while I worked. It helped buoy my perseverance.

My heart is filled with appreciation for Gigi Walton who did the final edit of the book (editor number four) with so much love and compassion. Together we went through every edit suggestion and discussed if necessary. It was a loving collaboration.

I am thankful to Kris Mease, who not only wrote a beautiful endorsement for the book, but who also pointed out some more places that needed attention!

The exquisite light that flows through Laura Marshal radiates in the painting of the cover. She has had a profound wisdom and sense of the book's meaning right from the beginning.

Blessings to Balboa Press for doing the production of the book, so it is now a reality.

And to my many teachers, friends, advisors, and encouragers who played a part in *Union of the Masters'* creation, I am deeply grateful.

I bow to each of you.

CHAPTER 1

The Meeting

Mother hadn't been feeling well for a while. The cough and vomiting were getting worse by the day, and her fever was rising. The faithful nature spirits brought her elixirs, fanned her, and even prayed over her, but no one seemed to able to stop the fast decline. She was like an out-of-control semi-truck that had lost its brakes down a mountain pass. She was spinning alone in the middle of vast space. The coughing and vomiting had become more violent tonight, and her body thrashed with pain. Her insides were on fire, and the fever distorted her mind with hallucinations. Her screams of pain reverberated throughout the land. Though the healers ran to her aid, only patchwork was accomplished.

There was no hospital to take her to, so they tried to cool her down and stop the bleeding. A cold towel on her forehead and one on her round, convulsing belly, but she heaved and moaned. Her foul, toxic breath made one aide swoon.

Finally, after some days, the convulsing calmed, at least temporarily. The devas and healers were exhausted. "We must get some help!" one nature spirit proclaimed, fluttering her wings. "We can't keep her alive much longer. We need an intermediary."

"We need beings who can shift the tide of human consciousness," Victoria said. "Let's ask Mother whom she would suggest."

Mother's answer was quick and clear, and arrangements were put into action immediately. An intervention was planned.

They gathered at the Oregon coast in early July for one of the most important meetings in Mother Earth's history. It was now the final hour to assist humanity out of the consciousness of the separate self to the consciousness of oneness and prevent Mother Earth's imminent death.

The morning of the first gathering, they prepared themselves, purifying their thoughts, cleansing their bodies, and setting intention. Each began with a familiar ritual.

A white candle flickered with the early light of dawn, illuminating the room with a golden glow. Running Bear Eagle, an Apache Indian Medicine Woman, stimulated her lymphatic system by dry brushing her naked body. Her straight dark-brown hair was lifted to the top of her head with a leather clip as she soaked in sea salt water to cleanse her aura. As these revitalizing energies began to grow, she chanted several times.

Cleanse my body.
Cleanse my light.
Cleanse my soul.
Lift my plight.
Cleanse my body.
Cleanse my light.
Cleanse my soul
that I may be pure and whole.

Her strong, stout body glistened. After her bath, she laid out her most sacred ceremonial attire. She had not worn such clothing since her last incarnation, in 1850. Remembering the ceremonies and the joy associated with them, she smiled. First, she slipped on a soft, light-brown suede skirt that hung gently to her ankles, with a traditional fringe on the hem. Then she put on a tailored cotton beige blouse. Next, she put on a special ceremonial leather vest. Below the right shoulder of the vest, in muted shades, was painted a bald eagle, her life totem.

Below the eagle, was a soft red-orange sun, radiating out, representing her connection with and veneration to Father Sky. To spiritually balance the vest, the left side represented her deep connection with the feminine Goddess. Grandmother Moon was full and radiant, and the star of Venus glistened on the vest, as if ready to speak. On the back of the vest was painted a medicine wheel, a tool of support and teaching for her people.

Looking in the mirror at her transformation, she let her thick brown hair flow down over her shoulders, brushing it gently. She stood erect and connected to Earth. The golden candlelight highlighted her strong, high cheek bones, full sensuous mouth, and radiant, sparkling dark eyes. She was truly the epitome of graceful feminine power. Encircling her body glowed a shimmering, glistening gold light.

Then she placed a delicately tooled leather headband about her forehead. Etched in the leather were scenes of a jumping deer, bushes, insects, fish, birds, and people—all children of the Mother.

Finally, she slid on a pair of brown suede moccasins with a two-inch fringe.

Whistling with renewed energy and expectation, she knelt before her altar and called in the Spirit of Sacred Fire to light the candle. She asked Sacred Fire to hold the qualities of love and transformation. Then, to cleanse her space, she lit dried cedar and sage in an alabaster shell, until it smoked. Next, she brushed the smoke with a turkey feather all around her body, ending with three strokes toward her heart.

After that, she walked around the house, fanning the smoke. The open window allowed the excess to escape. She went outside and smudged around the property, greeting the trees, flowers, and other plant life. They smiled and acknowledged her.

Next, quite exhilarated, she called in the four directions, just as her ancestors had done for thousands of years.

Kneeling to the East, humbly, with her right knee down, surrendering the warrior aspect, and her left knee up at a ninety-degree angle, representing leading with spirit, she took a pinch of the sacred tobacco and circled it through the smoking smudge three times.

Then she reached her right hand out to bring forth the energies of the East.

To the East.

To the new day.

To the Light within, without.

To Golden Eagle.

To illumination.

To the East, I call for your power and spirit to come in.

Catching the energy in her hand, she drew it into her heart, inhaling deeply. She placed some tobacco in the smudge.

Facing the South, she stretched her right arm out again.

To the South.

To trust and innocence.

To the little mouse.

To the good way home.

To the South, I call for your power and your spirit to come in.

Catching the incoming powers, she placed them in her heart and sprinkled some tobacco in the smudge, as her body began to tingle with energy.

Facing the West, she extended her right arm and said, almost in a whisper,

To the West.

To the dark waters of looking within.

To Black Bear and Brown Bear.

To Beautiful Shell Woman.

To the Medicine Path.

To the West, I call for your power and spirit to come in.

Grasping some of the surging energies, she placed her hand to her heart, inhaling deeply. Then she sprinkled another pinch of tobacco into the smudge.

Turning to the North now, she extended her right arm again and said with deep devotion,

To the North.

To the Old Ones, and those gone by.

To the Wisdom Place and the Place of White Buffalo and Snow Leopard.

To the North, I call for your power and your spirit to come in.

Her body shook with the surging power of love and wisdom, as she anchored it into her heart. Feeling a sense of protection and wholeness, she sprinkled more tobacco on the smudge.

Then she placed her face and hands on the Earth; with tears welling in her eyes, she proclaimed,

To the Earth.

To the two-leggeds, the four-leggeds,

and those who fly and crawl and swim and those who are planted.

To all the children of the Mother.

She reverently placed some tobacco in the smudge. The smell of sage, cedar, and tobacco was familiar and welcome once again. Then standing with her right arm skyward, she formed three lariats above her head and said,

And to Father Sky, thank you for this day.

And with her hand on her heart, she said,

and this one calls you.

With tears streaming down her face, she drew her mind and energy to her heart and prayed deeply that the meeting with Joseph and Sid would mark the beginning of a new time for all beings on planet Earth.

She spread the remaining tobacco around in a circle Sun-Wise, the direction of time, simultaneously creating a circle of gold light. She closed by saying, "It is a good day to die." This powerful affirmation signified that her life was in order if Great Spirit should call her to the other side this day.

Feeling full, renewed, and exuberant, she danced around the trees and sang:

I welcome Sun, the power of light.

I welcome Sun, the power within.

I welcome Sun, whose day has begun.

I welcome Sun, for we all are one.

I welcome Earth, for she is all life.

I welcome Earth, and accept her abundance.
I welcome Earth, and feel her great girth.
I welcome Earth, and know we are one.
Now she was ready for the meeting.

Joseph began this special morning with great excitement. To touch Earth again with his feet gave him such great pleasure. Reverently, he dressed in a simple beige cloth gown, similar to the garment he had worn in his last incarnation. At his waist, he tied a simple rope belt. Then he brushed his wavy, shoulder-length brown hair, as it shone in the morning light. He stroked his soft, full beard, as a reality check that he really was in his body again.

Eyes dancing, with arms swinging gently, he walked into the nearby woods. Telepathically, he greeted the trees, undergrowth, and flowers. A mushroom, one-inch wide yesterday, had grown to three inches this morning. He congratulated it on its growth. Laughing, he wished spiritual growth were that easy for humans.

The birds began to sing when they saw him. Several flew down to perch on his arm, another on his head. They chattered about their day and their excitement about the upcoming meeting. One crow, a talkative sort, said he would like to see the battle between crows and humans cease. He was tired of crows being hit by slingshots, rocks, or BB guns, by kids *and* adults.

Not wanting to miss an opportunity, the trees joined in. "We are just board feet to humans," they clamored.

"It is much worse than it was three hundred years ago," one tree continued. "No one notices or appreciates us anymore. Humans just cut us down, and the collective pain is overwhelming."

Joseph listened with his heart, nodding. He understood and expressed his hope for a change. Then they all fell silent, as if a theater director had said, "Cut." Joseph sat against a tree and breathed calmly. From his heart radiated a golden beam of love. With each breath, the golden light sphere around him grew larger and more peaceful.

More birds, bugs, and animals gathered, each stopping to be in the presence. For several moments the forest breathed together. Inhaling the universal life force, exhaling love. Inhaling the inspiration, exhaling into relaxation.

Then, as if by magic, all the birds, animals, and insects began to sing in beautiful harmony. The sound of love and its vibration permeated their cells. Joseph felt it reach several hundred miles out. With a few powerful breaths, he spread the sound of love all around Planet Earth and then through her. Mother Earth sighed in gratitude, receiving it deeply.

The cacophony continued as he beamed the stars and planets in the galaxy from his heart. The planets, reenergized with love, were excited about the eminent gathering. When the entire universe was smiling and shimmering with peace, he gently brought his attention back to the forest.

The sounds gently came to quiet, and then a silence full of wonder remained for several minutes. The world breathed as one.

He rose, bowing in gratitude for the abundance of life around him, and lightly walked from the forest.

Siddhartha was comfortable being in his body again, and he exuded a peaceful calm. His white meditation robe covered his slender frame, and he wore his thick black hair tied in a knot on top of his head. As the dawn created a pink hue across the horizon, he sat beneath a large Sitka spruce, focusing on his breath. His *ujjayi* breath was deep and throaty, and his entire body expanded on the inhale and shrank on the exhale. As his breath deepened, it entrained with the breath of the Earth. With every inhale, his energetic field expanded, until it touched the far reaches of the galaxy.

He had anticipated this human evolution for thousands of years and was hopeful the old paradigms would be set aside and the Buddha nature would be realized in every being. He had visions of a peaceful Earth, with all humans fed and disease dissolved. A world where greed disappeared and harmony prevailed. Where all people were waking up, realizing their interconnectedness to each other and nature.

Then…his mind became totally still in the silence.

From their separate abodes, each began the journey to the meeting place, deep in the Oregon coastal forest. Running Bear consciously and gently placed each foot, as she caressed Mother Earth beneath her feet. Her energy connected so deeply with Mother Earth's that there was barely a distinction between Running Bear and the ground on which she walked. Her connection afforded her great confidence and sturdy presence. And like her people before her, her posture was straight and strong.

Sid remained aware of his breath deep in his belly as he walked through town toward the forest. He was alert yet calm. Each step was deliberate, and his countenance serene.

Joseph's step was light and joyful, with a little skip. He chatted with people on the streets with excitement. "Good morning," he beamed to a young boy, whose eyes shone brightly in reply as he whizzed by on his bicycle. Then, entering the forest, he noted the shift of energy.

Appropriately, they met in the forest under a Grandfather Sitka Spruce, the patriarch of this section of forest. Trees were a symbol in each of their life stories. Joseph was a carpenter and then died on a wooden cross. Siddhartha sat beneath a pipal tree when he realized his enlightenment, and Running Bear Eagle was sister and protector of the tree people.

Once at the meeting place, they hugged in greeting, enjoying being in their bodies again. Joseph manifested his thirty-year-old body, slender and strong. Buddha and Running Eagle took their bodies from their forties.

"You look radiant, Joseph," Running Bear Eagle teased.

"And you sister, full of strength like this tree," Joseph retorted.

"Sid, finally we are together at the same time," Joseph said, embracing his spirit brother again and squeezing him tightly.

Laughing, Running Bear Eagle approached Grandfather Tree. She wrapped her arms around him lovingly. He was so huge, her arms only went about a quarter of the way around. He was a rare old growth. His grayish, thick bark was weathered from hundreds of years of coastal storms and fires. But he remained steady in stature and spirit. Like meeting an old friend dearly missed, they chatted telepathically. Joseph and Siddhartha were courteous enough not to eavesdrop and greeted Grandfather in their own ways.

When each was complete, they formed a circle. Grandfather Tree was at the north, symbolic of the direction of great and ancient wisdom. Connecting with their hands and the tree's trunk, they sat cross-legged in silence for several minutes. Upon reopening their eyes, they saw the large vortex of energy they had created in the silence. The vortex assisted them in maintaining the highest resonance possible on Earth.

Running Bear began the invocation: "Wise ones, Mother Earth, Grandfather Tree, all beings of life, Grandmother Moon, ancient ones, devas and nature spirits, please guide us to fulfill the task at hand. With courage, we come together at the same time, in body, to assist in Earth's evolution to the fifth dimension, a vibration of love and peace. We have waited a long time for this gathering. The significance of this meeting cannot be underestimated. Enough of the human race is ready to move to the next step in their evolution. The hate is finally almost played out. Ho."

"Ah ho," they said in unison.

"Now," she continued, "let's check in. Share how you feel this first day in body." Her lips curled up in an impish smile.

She brought forward her sacred talking stick, which was created in silent communion by the women of her tribe. As life, it was a dance of colors and movement. At its base, and spirally half-way up the stick, were streamers of deer leather dyed in a rainbow of purple, gold, turquoise, and red. Blessed objects from each woman in her tribe were hung from leather ribbons or glued right to the stick with tree pitch. A peacock feather hung near the base. The down feathers of a flicker donned the center of the stick, and his bright orange-rimmed tail feathers topped it. There were pieces of rose quartz crystal attached to a dangling purple leather band. Many other sacred crystals also adorned it. The rest of the stick was painted in a gold spiral, representing their spiritual movement toward the light. This stick was made in 1870, when the white man was desecrating the native people, but it held the energy of peace and hope, so appropriate for this time now.

She remembered how in sacred council, only the person holding the stick could speak, then all present listened deeply from their hearts. There was such safety and support in that. Her mind wandered briefly to the many tears that were shared holding this sacred talking stick. Life was so hard then, as they watched their family members murdered and others torn from the tribe.

Bringing her focus back to the present, she held the talking stick horizontally from the center, so as not to disturb the ornaments. As she bowed to it, her hair softly fell forward, and then gentle as a dove, she kissed it. Looking reverently into Joseph's eyes, she handed the sacred stick to him, nodding.

He began with a twinkle in his voice, "Thank you, sister Running Bear. It feels odd to be back in body, but I am sure after a while it will feel natural again."

They all smiled, nodding.

He continued with his check-in. "This is an ominous moment for which we patiently waited. It is time for love to prevail. I am glad to be here of service in this way again, and I welcome each of you. Ho." At that, he gracefully passed the talking stick to his beloved brother Sid.

Sid, seated in a lotus position, bowed deeply and deliberately to Joseph, Running Bear Eagle, Grandfather Tree, and Mother Earth in the center of the circle and said, "Namaste." Joseph and Bear respectfully bowed back. Grandfather shook his lower branches, and Mother Earth rumbled in recognition.

"I am here with great expectation and hope for the new culture of peace and love. And I am comfortable in body again." Sid smiled. He placed the talking stick at the base of Grandfather Tree's trunk and nodded to him in acknowledgment.

"Our meeting is just in time," Grandfather said. "My roots go down into Mother's belly, and as the years of depletion have continued, her strength is much diminished. Finally, the shift is happening." In recognition of each of them and somewhat playfully, he bowed his branches as he said their names. "Welcome back, Sid, Joseph, and Running Bear. We've been holding the fort down for you, so to speak, and we're very glad you're back. Ho."

Between laughter and tears, Running Bear gently took the stick from Grandfather. Bowing to him again, and with a cracked voice, she said, "We planned this gathering almost two thousand years ago, and suddenly here we are. I am excited and frightened all at the same time. But mostly, I am hopeful. Ho." She placed the talking stick in the center of the circle for Mother Earth to speak.

Everyone was listening deeply with their hearts, beholding each speaker with love.

"I am also grateful that the change of time is here just in the nick of time," Mother Earth began. Everyone nodded. "I am, as you know, feverish and quite sick. Thank you, Running Bear, Joseph, and Sid for returning together to help in this profound birthing process of consciousness. Ho."

Running Bear lifted the talking stick and raised it to her forehead. She bowed again to Earth, Grandfather Tree, Joseph, and Sid. She placed the stick in the center of the circle, as the check-in was complete, and now they would review some major issues.

Grandfather took the floor again, rustling his branches. He had wanted to express himself on these issues in person for a long time. "Most of the first tree people are gone, and many of their spirits are trapped here from improper cutting. After clear cutting whole mountain tops, the loggers poisoned the ground to kill the animals, once residents of the lumbered land. The animals' spirits also are trapped into the Earth from their violent, untimely deaths. The electromagnetic field around Mother has gotten thinner."

Running Bear flushed with a burst of anger for the suffering souls. Then, gathering her power, humbly she said, "Yes, Grandfather, I feel that, and with your permission, will free as many souls as I can while I am here. Also, I would like to personally thank you and the other tree people for helping to sustain Earth's electro-magnetic field as best you could. For without that, there would be no life here."

He bowed his branches in recognition.

Then the ground shook, as Mother Earth agreed. "Yes, thanks to all of you who have helped."

They all nodded in agreement.

"Gratefully, we each carry the collective memory," said Siddhartha, fully centered and connected to his breath.

"Each of us offered a form of worship and practices to live a fulfilled life when we were in body, to help bring humans to a higher level of consciousness," said Running Bear. "But our messages were maligned and distorted."

His brow slightly furled, Joseph added, "The greatest tragedy was humans' perception that they are separate from source, when we were trying to create unity."

"It is true that any one of the paths would take beings to enlightenment," said Siddhartha. "But no one religion is enough now to complete the evolution of all beings to peace and grace on this planet. A different kind of nudge is needed."

After a long pause, Running Bear Eagle sighed deeply, with eyes cast down on Earth. Her heart ached at the quick desecration of her Mother. Gently tapping the Earth, she said, looking at Grandfather Tree, "When life's focus shifted to the intellect and science became god, people felt separate from the unity and slowly stopped living connected, sacred lives. The downhill road was short."

They all nodded and paused to allow this reality to once again penetrate their physical bodies.

"Now is the time for all traumas," Earth said, "to be healed and lifted from the cellular memory of all beings. Every time a trauma is transformed, each of us heals a little more, for we are really just one body."

"And they must be lifted or transformed for us to move to the next evolutionary step," added Grandfather Tree, gently touching a branch on the ground. "Finally, we are at a point of consciousness similar to the leap from ape to human. We have reached another shift of time, when humans have the opportunity now to become *homo universalis* beings."

Each pausing in recognition of the significance of the situation, Running Bear gently picked up her rim drum, as her lips began to curl up in a soft smile. After stroking the top of the drum with three circles, she drummed a steady heartbeat. The heartbeat reconnected them to harmony, and the despair dissolved.

After some time of breathing in the simple rhythm of the drum, Running Bear said, "Let's have some refreshment. I brought structured spring water for Grandfather and Mother, and corn bread and vegetables for the rest of us."

"Great," Joseph said, smiling.

She spread a beautiful turquoise Apache blanket, another item from her past, down for the picnic.

Sid got up and stretched like a lithe cat. Fully present in his body, Joseph's steps barely touched the ground as he glided deeper into the forest. Telepathically, he called out for the little animals and birds to join the celebration.

When everyone had gathered in the circle, holding hands, branches, and Earth, Running Bear prayed, "Bless Great Spirit and Mother Earth for this bounty. We give thanks to the kingdoms, as we join as one. And we give thanks for the opportunity to gather together for the first time ever!" Her sparkling eyes and radiant heart were felt by all.

In deference to Sid's practice of eating in silence, they each connected their energy bodies with their food in reverent communion and ate mindfully.

When the meal was complete, Running Bear jubilantly popped up. "I think I missed the dancing the most when I left my physical body." She skipped around the circle, arms flying joyfully. "I missed the passion and camaraderie we had for life!"

Sid and Joseph jumped up and joined her. She made the circle bigger, and they danced around Grandfather Tree to the rhythm of the heartbeat. The pulse of life. *Ba-bum, ba-bum, ba-bum, ba-bum.*

Around and around. With each rotation around the circle, the vortex of energy they created grew and became more vibrant. Joyfully, the birds sang along, and the squirrels munched their snacks to the rhythm. Now, Running Bear Eagle formed a figure eight, the infinity symbol. They danced the infinity symbol with precise and connected steps, seven times around. Then they danced the symbol of the five-pointed star. Next, they danced the male and female tetrahedron. As they embedded these ancient sacred symbols into the ground, Earth's energies activated.

From joyful celebration of being back and together, they gradually began to realize the importance and impact of their work yet to come. Like the rustling of leaves in wind, their bodies shimmered and shook. The circle went faster and faster and faster, with the frenzy of a whirling dervish, until finally they fell into a pile, exhausted.

Lying quietly at first, they then began to laugh. Simultaneously, they rose and hugged each other, laughing with joy and expectation.

"Will we make it this time?" Sid whispered.

"We will, even though the stakes are higher. The cycles of patriarchy are almost complete now," said Running Bear. "We will!"

CHAPTER TWO

The Teachings

"Beat you back to the blanket," Running Bear Eagle called out as she sprang away, still a little dizzy from the dance. But when she arrived, Joseph was already there. "No fair! You used the resurrection trick," she teased, with sparkling eyes, tapping him gently on the arm.

"Actually," Joseph replied, suddenly serious, "it's not only fair, but the point. It's time for the mysteries to be known to everyone. Remember: 'On Earth as it is in Heaven.' We must stop thinking that because we are in body, we must be limited. The time and space separation does not have to dominate here any longer."

Running Bear's eyes narrowed, and her strong stance deepened into Earth, as she said, "Teaching people to transport instantly is not the most important aspect we need to focus on now. Other more pressing issues need our attention to turn this situation around." She looked at Joseph with determination, but his radiant love melted her, and her shoulders dropped as she opened to listen again for the first time.

"In Western culture, everything has turned to glitz, fantasy, or ecstasy," Joseph said, without losing a beat.

Sid was already seated peacefully, with his legs folded and his hands gently resting on his thighs. They joined him in the circle again. "Yes," he said, "but there is a *deep* undercurrent of suffering. That is what must be addressed first."

Running Bear laughed. This was an ancient discussion between the two of them. "How do we expect the people to agree, when we can't?" she said.

"Some still seek our wisdom," Joseph said, "through the books. Like Sid's work, finally translated six hundred years *after* your transition: the *Dhammapada* and the *Digha Nikaya*. And my teachings in the Bible hold truth when read for their metaphor; however, A *Course in Miracles* and the *Gnostic Gospels* come closer to the truth of my teachings.

"Even at this, there isn't time for each person to pick a path and devote his life to a particular discipline. Churches and temples still preach The Way. The Way didn't get us there. There are only a handful of enlightened masters on the planet today, and it's been thousands of years!"

"The key is in relationship," interjected Running Bear Eagle, tapping her hands on the Earth gently and leaning forward. "And relationship with all life, not just humans but also plants, animals, insects, and the Great Spirit." She waved her hands in a circle to include everyone.

"The answers are found in the quiet space within, as we know so well. Being liberated from fear, attachment, greed, hatred, delusion, temptation, and doubt has been a human challenge for all time, but when achieved, the heart opens to proliferate compassion, generosity, loving kindness, and moral integrity. And peace awakens," Sid offered as he lightly tapped his heart.

Joseph nodded. "And through forgiveness."

Earth rumbled. "When the heart and the energy of creation are interconnected with all beings, the consciousness of oneness is awakened. The heart is the key," Earth said.

"I've always wondered about that, Mother," Running Bear said. "Where is your heart?"

Earth laughed. "I am the heart: the heart of creation. I am the source of life on this planet and for many dimensions—not just the third, as many think."

"But you create volcanoes, avalanches, storms, and quakes that have killed millions of people and species throughout time. How can you call yourself the heart?" Running Bear Eagle asked.

"You create toilets to flush away your waste," Mother replied. "I do the same. It is my mechanism to keep myself cleansed. Though during the last two hundred years, I haven't been able to keep up with the destruction and pollution."

"The ice age wasn't more destructive?" wide-eyed Running Bear Eagle asked, leaning forward.

"The ice age was a repatterning of my surface to allow more growth and abundance. It also supplied the necessary water for life."

"Are you repatterning again?" asked Sid.

"Yes."

"Then maybe everything we're doing and hoping to achieve is futile. You seem to have the answer," said Sid.

"That's always been the problem," Mother scolded, and the Earth shook. "Who has the answer? There is only one answer, and that is that we work together. What I am doing is for all our survival. What you are doing is for *your* survival. We must move past survival of each species and look to what is next and how we can live *together*."

"That's not fair, Mother," said Running Bear Eagle softly. "The indigenous peoples have honored and loved you for all time."

"Not to offend, my child," Mother answered, "but your people had their share of fear, anger, and bloodshed. There is no perfect race or way. Yet you are still looking for the perfect way," she continued, rattling the stick in the center of circle. "Sid is stuck on meditation. And I must say that works. Joseph's fixation is on putting love and forgiveness first. And that works too. And you, Running Bear Eagle, focus on relationship. Which also works. But none of these paths work for everyone. So what do we do now? Millions of people are still asleep, as you say."

"But love *is* the answer," blurted out Sid and Joseph simultaneously.

"Each of you needs to go home," Mother stated firmly, "and tap into yourselves anew before we continue. The problem is the same as it was when you were here, but different. Let's end this meeting and resolve to meet again next week—same time and place. Go out into the world in physical form and see how it feels now. With a new perspective, we must transcend ourselves."

"Spoken like a true mother." Joseph laughed. "That's a good idea. We were beginning to sound like the Christ Counsel—trying to fix the problem."

"Then let's join hands again and chant *Om* three times," Sid offered, "and open to allow the new to come through us."

Their combined auras filled the forest with radiance, peace, and love. After sounding *Om* three times, they kissed each other's cheeks tenderly. This initiation was even greater than the ones each had experienced before, and more was at stake.

CHAPTER 3

It Begins

*H*ead down and mind pondering their first meeting, Joseph walked to his new Earth home. Would they be able to shift the tide of this polarized humanity in time to save Mother Earth? *Yes,* he thought, *yes. Now is the time.*

As he lifted his head, he saw a young woman heading up the stairs to his house and hastened to meet her.

"Hi, I've just arrived home from a meeting."

She jumped at the sight of his sudden appearance.

"I'm Joseph," he said, extending his hand and smiling. "What brings you here?"

"Oh, oh, um. Welcome to Deep Woods subdivision. I'm Mary, and I am here to introduce you to our area," she announced in a monotone, as if reading from a script. She was slender and attractive in her blue-and-black print dress and black pumps.

"Hi, Mary," said Joseph, smiling. *Mary, ah, that name seems to haunt me.* He could see by her energetic field that she didn't really like this job. She had a creative bent toward organizing events.

"Are you from around here?" she asked, her brown eyes rather dull and uninterested.

"I came from Israel," he blurted out before he knew what he had said.

"Really!" Her eyes perked up and her posture straightened, suddenly alert. "But, but you don't have an accent."

"I was on assignment there for a few years. I've been transferred to Oregon."

As she cocked her head, her thick black hair flowed away from her chin. "What kind of work do you do?"

"I'm an artist. I create form from nothing. I mean, I create art."

Taking a step back, with widened eyes, she said, "Oh." But she couldn't hold her distrust for more than a second. Joseph's tender gaze and radiance of love transformed her. As their eyes met, she knew him all at once and sighed. The silence lingered, but it wasn't empty. It was filled with a grace she had only read about.

Shifting from one foot to another uncomfortably, she rattled off her welcome speech and added, if he needed anything to call. She handed him a gift package and stumbled off the stoop, shaking her head, her thick black hair bobbing.

Joseph walked inside to consider this interaction. It was simple yet so complex. She was a good Christian woman doing good deeds, as she had been taught, to get into heaven. The authorities on God had told her to live a certain way, and the reward would follow…after death. All in his name.

That wasn't my message at all, he thought. Yes, do good deeds. Yes, be of service. Those are spiritual disciplines, but only when working from the heart. Never work from should or guilt or fear.

Sighing, Joseph heard Mother's words: "The problem is the same as it was when you were here before but different."

Yes, different. Many people thought they had the right answer. And the same. Transforming water into wine was much easier than transforming the human spirit. Water did not have free will, as humans did, so the change for humans must be a personal decision and come from within. Yet that was the hardest message and most threatening for most to hear. "The kingdom of heaven is within," he had said over and over again. "It is the father's good pleasure to give you the kingdom." There must be another way.

Sid wandered down to the beach before he returned home. Mother was right, he thought: their messages didn't penetrate deeply enough. The ego, the voice of fear, still won. Greed still reigned. Pain and suffering were rampant. And the wealthier people got, the more money's status grew. "Money *is* everything it's cracked up to be" was a popular saying. He had lived both sides of that story. In his life as the Buddha, he was raised a prince, with every imaginable luxury and need met. His dear parents protected him from the realities of the world by not letting him see the pain, poverty, and anguish of his human family. They believed that if he did not see it, he would not be affected. They were correct, for as soon as he saw the misery, he left his family to discover how to stop the suffering.

That search led him to deny his heritage, to the immense pain of his parents, which thus inflicted the exact pain he planned to stop. Living with the ascetics in complete abject poverty was not the answer either. Isolated in the forest, skeletally skinny, unbathed, and racked with pain, he frightened the village people. Like that, he could render no assistance to humanity, as he was in the same position as the needy—or worse since he was weak from starvation.

He shook off the memory and sighed. That was a long time ago and he was fortunate to have been able to teach into his nineties, unlike Joseph, who died so young. The Four Noble Truths were as relevant today as 2,500 years ago, and they seemed to be gaining a stronghold in the Western hemisphere over the last few decades.

"Hi," said a chipper female voice up ahead. She walked backward to face him.

Startled, Sid grounded himself and shifted his focus completely on her. Well, he hadn't lost all his earthly skills! "Hi," he replied. Oh, she was beautiful with her short blond hair gently blowing in the wind, and her dancing radiant brown eyes. But more than that, she had a strong and powerful presence. He asked if she practiced Buddhism.

"When I was only sixteen years old, your teachings opened me to vow to become one with Nirvana," she said out loud. Then laughing, "And I didn't have a clue how hard that would be or how long it would take!"

Interest piqued, he hurried to catch up with her. He couldn't help notice her slender, curvaceous body moving beneath her loose sea-foam green sweatpants suit, as she rather floated down the beach. Was this the research Mother was referring to?

"Yes!" he replied. "A hundred thousand malacopas wearing away Mount Everest with a silk scarf, little by little and a malacopa is one hundred thousand years!" He smiled, and their eyes met for a long, poignant moment.

"Yes," she responded finally, "plus a hundred thousand years of a hundred thousand malacopas! Forever! And I'm still working on it."

"If I could be so bold, you're doing quite a good job!"

"Thank you." She bowed deeply, holding his gaze.

"Do you mind sharing what brought you to the path?" Sid asked.

"Suffering of course!"

"Yes, yes, but I'd like to hear *your* story."

She tilted her head with curiosity. "Are you sure? It's really not very interesting."

"Yes, I'm sure...please proceed."

Walking side by side, she began, "For the first thirty-eight years of my life, I followed my training. Sweet, ingratiating, hardworking, and a slave to my husband and kids, just as I was trained to be by my family and society. I worked at creative jobs, but I worked twelve to sixteen hours a day for twenty years and still could not get ahead. My friends got financially ahead, and I was in their rearview mirror. But truthfully, that was not the motivation that changed my life. It was when I realized that my husband was *not* the problem. I had spent twenty years trying to change and fix him. All my focus had been on him. True, he would attest to never being happier, and his parents would always affirm that message when we saw them.

"But I was dying, rotting from the inside out," she continued, now communicating telepathically instead of out loud. "The very core of me was destroyed. I was doing everything better than most, and still I was deeply dissatisfied. Feeling empty inside, I yearned with a deep moan. Then one day at lunch, two friends were discussing the drama triangle that a psychologist discovered in the 1970s. He discovered a pattern of communication between couples and families. Each person played each of the three roles: victim, persecutor, and rescuer.

"So for example," she continued telepathically in vivid color.

Sid saw her husband as deeply driven by fear and self-hate. His every thought and action were self-destructive and thus destructive to the family and those around him. He was uniquely creative and had incredible talent in the arts, but he too suffered deeply.

"Yes," she said aloud. "You see him accurately. But at that time, I believed he lied and cheated because there was something inherently wrong with me. Remember, it was the woman's job to take care of her husband and children. *Their* happiness came first."

With this comment, Sid shuffled uncomfortably, but they continued to smoothly move from telepathic communication to speaking out loud.

"For thousands of years, there were so many struggles between the sexes," Sid continued aloud as they walked side by side. "We still see it in our monasteries and Buddhists communities around the world." He shook his head slowly.

"You kept the men and women separated, and we still do that now. As if the women were unclean, like the Christian doctrines preached. A woman to this day cannot go on the altar of an Orthodox church. Nor can she be a priest." She scrunched up her face and rolled her eyes. "The imprints are still deep."

"We separate them because of the sexual attraction between the men and the women," he said.

"Like they can't control their hormones!"

"But, continue with your story," Sid encouraged.

She telepathically flashed him her entire story in a second. He felt the pain she had lived, and then slowly, through the energetic healing of her soul, how she was able to release the pain and suffering.

"Christ was your savior," he said.

"Yes," she answered, "but not in the Christian sense. Many of the Christian religions missed his entire message. When I became physically very ill, Christ, Mary, and Archangel Michael came to me in spirit. Archangel Michael always stood in the background, guarding me.

He never said anything for the first three years, but his presence was reassuring and helped me feel safe in times of turmoil."

"But how did you know you weren't imagining it," asked Sid, eyebrows raised.

"Two years before I became ill," she continued, "I studied with a medicine woman. My first lesson was breathing and running my energy to enliven my light bodies and release traumatic trapped energy. My second lesson was to communicate with the planets—Venus, Earth, Jupiter, Sun, and Moon were my first celestial teachers.

"One day I was lying on the couch, with extreme abdominal pain from my menstrual cycle. I looked skyward and called for Grandmother Moon. 'Will I ever give birth to a healthy baby?' I cried. I'd had two miscarriages and an ectopic pregnancy. I'll never forget her tenderness as she beamed me an image of my child. The baby was whole and perfect. Then I called up to Venus and said, 'If you are really there, then take this horrible pain from me.' A violet ray shot through the sky, right into my belly. The pain stopped instantly, and the violet light encircled me in a blanket of love. I slept like a baby. That and many similar experiences that I felt, saw, and heard solidified my true knowing of the other side."

"That sounds similar to my experience under the Bodhi tree, when I woke up," Sid said.

"I wish I had awakened then," she said. "But much to my medicine woman's dismay, it took twelve years of deep healing to get some real clarity, and it still continues. She wanted me to do in six months what took her fifteen years. I was a great disappointment to her, but I am grateful to her, for she taught me the fundamentals I use today."

They walked over to a viewing bench bathed in sunlight and sat down. The sun so rarely shone on the Oregon coast, its warmth was inviting. The soft summer breeze caressed their skin, and the sunlight sparkled on the water, as the rhythmic waves enlivened their senses. Sid looked into her eyes and remembered her soul from an ancient lifetime.

Realizing what he had discovered, she said tenderly, "You know, I was mad at you for many years. Maybe hundreds, I don't know."

"I didn't realize," he said, genuinely surprised. "What were you angry about?"

"I felt you betrayed us with your isolation."

"What do you mean?"

She leaned forward intensely, looking directly into his eyes. She had been waiting for this interchange for years. "The entire guru construct only perpetuated the lie. If the information was within us, why was the guru 'responsible' for our enlightenment? That kept us just as trapped as the Christian church with its priests and nuns."

"I see your point," Sid replied. "The Four Noble Truths and the Eightfold Path were new concepts then. At that time in history, I felt students needed a guru, and in India, that fit into our cultural mindset."

"A cultural mindset you had responsibility for greatly influencing, correct?"

"In a manner of speaking," he said. "But you always had free will."

"That's the rub, Sid. You guys only intervened when it was convenient, but that really left the power with you and not us," she continued. She began to walk again to move the energy building in her. She hadn't realized how angry she was at him.

Trying to catch up, he touched her shoulder to turn her around, and looked into her piercing eyes. "What do you mean?" he asked, truly confused by this show of anger.

Now walking backwards and gesturing empathically, she said, "I mean, you said go inside, but you made someone *outside* responsible for what went on *inside*! Don't you see the idiocy in that?"

"Go on."

She spun around to walk forward and beside him. "Christ did the same thing," she said, punctuating with her right hand. "'It is the Father's good pleasure to give you the kingdom.' As if to say, it is not yours until you earn it, and then Daddy will give you the prize!" Her face was red and her voice reached a fever pitch. She stopped to face him.

"It was just another way to keep us under control." Her eyes narrowed. "Well, it didn't work. The entire thing backfired. We have a world of people who are victims and waiting for the approval of their

25

parents or spouse or child or God before they are worthy! Or maybe it did work. Is that what you wanted?" She burst into tears.

He paused, stunned, then instinctually approached her and ever so gently wrapped his arms around her and held her, as she cried hard for her own suffering and the suffering of the world. She calmed some as their breaths entrained.

She looked up at him and collapsed into the sand. With her head in her hands, rocking back and forth, she softly said, "O Sid, I am SO sorry. How could I be mad at you? Your teachings changed my life in such profound ways. I guess it's apparent that I suffered deeply from the need for approval—not your fault." Digging her bare feet into the sand, she kept her face hidden.

Looking at her with compassion, he kneeled beside her on the sand. Gingerly, as if lifting a wounded bird, he raised her head and gazed into her eyes. So much suffering. As he tenderly took her hands in his, he said, "I am sorry too." And they both wept.

After a long pause, still holding his hands, she popped up, bringing him with her, and said, "Race you to the water!" She sprang forth with gusto and zeal, leaving him in a spray of sand.

Then, holding hands and laughing, they jogged down the beach awhile, letting the sound of the lapping waves and the negative ions clear and calm them.

Looking right into his eyes with great esteem and love, she said, "So now you are meeting with Joseph and Running Bear Eagle to figure out how to give us the power back?"

"How did you know?" Sid said, eyes wide.

"It was all over your energetic field." She gestured in a circle.

"You can see."

"And hear and feel. It is different down here now. Some of us have polysensory awareness."

Another pause followed. These were the very issues the Christ Council and the Galactic Council were discussing.

"You were always a challenge for me," Sid said, smiling. "And you have not lost any of your vigor. I must say I was a little hurt when you picked Christ over me to seek your path this time."

"Another problem with you guys, still ego. As above, so below."

"You are harsh with me. That was not ego. It was fact: I missed you."

They both laughed and embraced. Twenty-five hundred years had passed since they had been in body at the same time. They recalled when she had been one of his first students and how she stayed with him as his righthand man through his long life of teaching and creating monasteries across India. It was an exciting and fertile time.

With the air cleared, they glanced again at the water, only to realize that dusk was upon them and the horizon was ablaze with streaks of deep reds and oranges. They found some driftwood to lean against to be present for a spectacular Oregon coast sunset. They sat side by side, gazing out at the water.

"Did you give birth to the baby you saw in the image?" asked Sid.

"No. I thought for a long time I would, but I finally realized the image of the baby was a healing of the loss of the other babies and a healing of myself as an infant. We adopted two children. I believe our children are the same souls who tried to come through me, so I am grateful." She affably pressed her shoulder against his as she said, "Sid, why did you use the guru structure of teacher/student relationship? Was it to keep us in control?"

He paused again, giving this question full attention. "I think after the fall of Atlantis, we were afraid humans weren't ready for the full power. But my teachings are all based in the cessation of suffering so you can be free within yourself. The practices raise the consciousness of the individual, so you are not so 'I' oriented. We did not anticipate such dependency."

She nodded. "That makes sense. Who could have known what we would do with the teachings and ourselves? Even today, it is rare that people truly dedicate themselves to the work, though the number is growing."

Flooded with the radiance and love she had known as his student and senior monk, she kneeled before him and bowed very slowly and deeply. A palpable sigh filled the space.

He smiled. It was different now. He was not a monk, and he was very drawn to her. His eyes called her to rise and sit beside him again.

Looking out at the sunset, with their arms around each other's waists, they sat in a circle of love—two ancient souls reunited.

Running Bear Eagle, always so sensitive to what Mother said, was frustrated by the meeting. She had said earlier that she missed the emotional breadth one could experience in body, and realized frustration was part of the package. She, however, did not miss that piece. Knowing the law of polarity, she knew she would experience calm and joy with as much intensity. Soon, she hoped, the joy would return.

She walked deeper into the woods, where she always found her solace. Spotting Grandmother Tree, she approached.

"I've been waiting for you," Grandmother Tree began.

"May I sit with you?" Running Bear Eagle asked.

"Yes, my dear, wrap your legs around me. We will hold each other, like the other days."

Running Bear Eagle sighed and pressed her body against Grandmother Tree. They melted into each other, and Running Bear could not distinguish her body from Tree's. As Running Bear breathed deeply, activating all her chakras, she dropped energetic roots from the base of her spine and through her legs and out the bottoms of her feet into Earth. She breathed the roots deep and wide into Earth. Like fine fibers of shimmering life force, their roots intermingled and brushed each other in awareness. They were one. One body, one mind.

As they sat so intertwined on all levels, nothing needed to be said. The richness and love of silence said it all.

Finally, Running Bear broke the silence. "Ah, such peace I feel, Grandmother Tree. Thank you."

She shook her branches ever so lightly.

"I wish other humans could connect like this with you—and to each other, for that matter. Then there wouldn't be such widespread abuse and disrespect. How could anyone disrespect trees or any life, after being in such communion with another being?" Running Bear Eagle said telepathically to Grandmother Tree.

"Most humans do not interconnect with this depth and with no barriers. Real intimacy is frightening for most. You see, we must totally trust each other in this union. This is true vulnerability, total surrender. Isn't it grand?" she said, with a tickle in her voice.

"Yes." Running Bear whispered. Then a squirrel climbed up to sit on Bear's shoulder, munching a nut. Totally safe and content, he listened with interest.

"Caw, caw." From a distance three crows were approaching. They were drawn by the energy Running Bear and Tree were creating. Above, they flew three lariats, acknowledging and welcoming Running Bear. Squirrel looked up, and Running Bear bowed her head to them in reply. "Thank you," she called out, smiling. I am glad to be here again." And they flew off as quickly as they had appeared.

"Grandmother, I missed you so much. Being just in a spirit body, I couldn't feel emotions or touch sensations, like I can now in a physical body. It is so wondrous! But I am worried about our mission." The joy drained from her body.

Grandmother Tree, of course, heard her thoughts and felt her mixed emotions and deep love for Mother Earth and all her inhabitants, including the tree people. To soothe her, she extended her energetic field around Running Bear even more deeply, in a comforting hug. Then she whispered, "I wish I had the answer, but we will find it together."

Bear wept. It seemed this battle was taking forever. On the other side, she could distance herself from the feelings, but being in body now, she felt the despair all over again.

She sweetly kissed Grandmother Tree and thanked her. Reluctantly, they unwrapped from each other and said goodbye.

CHAPTER 4

Alchemy

No meetings with the group today, so Joseph was doing some household chores. He was beginning to like the modern conveniences, but was still rather shocked by all the noise everything made. Television was really a stunner. How all that action came out of that screen was beyond him. There really wasn't anyone he could ask about it, so he just watched with amazement. Shaking his head in disbelief as he viewed the movie *Jesus Christ Superstar*, he was startled out of his trance by a knock on the door. Clicking off the television, he leaped up to answer it and found Mary with a friend.

Mary's hands shook ever so slightly as she straightened her dress and primped her hair. Just as he opened the door, she caught a reflection of herself in the glass. "Oh, hi, Joseph!" She jumped. "I, um, brought a friend to meet you," she said, tugging at her dress. "I hope this is a good time."

"Perfect," Joseph said, smiling and swinging the door wide open. He knew it had begun.

Mary's head tilted toward her guest as she introduced him. "Joseph," she said, nodding, "may I introduce Reverend Bill Sunderland."

Bill's belly jiggled as he extended his right hand and looked up at Joseph, without making direct eye contact.

Joseph took his hand with both of his and smiled warmly. "Welcome, Reverend Bill, please come in." He gestured for them to come in and have a seat.

Pulling on the tie that was pinching his puffy neck, Bill shuffled uncomfortably to the couch.

"Would you like something to drink? I don't have much yet, but I can offer you tea or spring water." Joseph had learned quickly the need for fresh water, as the tap water, though acclaimed to be clean, had chlorine in it. He was shocked when he first tasted it; he thought it was poisoned.

They both declined refreshment, and Bill jumped right in. He was on a mission to learn who this strange man was in a little coastal Oregon town. "Mary tells me you are an artist who has just arrived in Oregon from Israel," Bill, began, his eyes glancing a little to the left, avoiding Joseph's eyes. "What's your medium?"

Hum, thought Joseph, *right to the point*. "My art takes many shapes. I'm an alchemist of sorts. How long have you been preaching?"

"Twenty years," Bill replied, straightening his shoulders, and with volume up, said, "Mary is an active volunteer in our church and wanted me to meet you. She has belonged to our congregation for over ten years and is highly respected in our community." He glanced at Mary for reassurance.

Joseph smiled and radiated such love that he began to fidget.

Bill glanced at Mary again, but her eyes were unfocused and there was a whimsical smile on her lips. A comfortable silence prevailed. After a few moments, the damn burst, and Bill began telling Joseph about all his problems at the church and his difficulties and squabbles with the parishioners. The words gushed out.

Keeping eye contact, Joseph leaned forward intently, surrounding and filling him with love.

"So, how do I stop the bickering?" he said in a fevered pitch, throwing up his hands, looking right into Joseph's eyes for the first time, frustration overtaking him.

"Let he who has never erred pick up the first stone," Joseph said.

"Oh, we *know* that!" Bill said, shaking his head and pounding on the coffee table. "I've said that dozens of times. But nothing changes."

"Knowing it is not enough," Joseph replied calmly. "We know lots of things, but unless we apply them, they are useless to us."

"What do you mean?" Bill asked, exhaling deeply.

Joseph looked past his eyes into his soul. "First," he said gently, "the problem is not your parishioners. They are just a mirror of what is going on inside you. You have confusion—maybe not about the management of the church, but about the power and role of God in your life. That confusion comes alive for you through your parishioners. If you create harmony within yourself, it will be reflected in the actions of the parishioners."

"How?" Bill asked, his jaw dropping. "I spend time in prayer. I have asked for God's help, but until today I never felt the love spoken of by Jesus."

"It is often that way." Joseph continued. "Those who seek the hardest can be the farthest away. You search for the answer in your mind, but it isn't in your mind. It's in your heart." He leaned over and placed his hand on the center of Bill's chest and tapped twice.

"But I pray and pray," Bill's voice tightened and rose to a crescendo. "I practice loving acts. I just can't *feel*." He pinched the top of his nose and squeezed his eyes to control the escalating emotion. "I've never admitted this before," he said, shaking his head. "But it is the heart of my despair. I so long for the joy of which the Bible speaks." Fists clenching, he continued, "But, I am *so* far away from it." Unable to bridle the mounting pressure of anguish any longer, he threw his face into his hands and wept uncontrollably.

Joseph walked over to the couch and sat beside him. Putting his hand gently on Bill's shoulder, he held him in the presence of love. Grace once again filled the room.

After several moments, Bill relaxed. He looked up, like Eeyore from *Winnie the Pooh*, and said, "Oh bother!"

Everyone burst out laughing.

With a twinkle in his eyes, Joseph continued, "You make the mistake so many make. You believe the opening is in the giving. It is. But it is not the first step. The first step is being able to receive. Somehow the message got turned around. You can never *truly* give until you can *truly* receive."

"What do you mean?" Mary interjected; her head tilted like a curious dog. "Giving is the source of service, the highest contribution we can make."

"Yes," Joseph said, nodding. "But giving is not pure, even in service, if it is not filled with love and there is no expectation for any return." Picking up the Welcome Wagon packet she had left him, he continued, "Mary, you are in service to Welcome Wagon not because you love to meet new people, but because you think you should do *something* and that fits your schedule. Your real bliss would be organizing gatherings, bringing people together for special events and classes. Am I correct?" He paused as she sighed.

"Oh Yes," she said. "How did you know?" *How could he know?* she thought. *I haven't said anything to him except that ridiculous welcome speech. My husband doesn't even know!*

Her imploring look softened his heart. "Oh Mary," he answered ever so gently. "Because I see and hear you with my heart. Service cannot be done to prove you are good. If it is, it will backfire."

"Yeah! I've experienced that in my church," Bill said. "People say they will do something in service, but then they complain about it through the entire project: 'It took too long.' 'It was too hard.' 'Someone else should do it.' All that complaining drains the energy out of the project."

Joseph nodded. "When service is done in love, there is a clarity to it," he said. "It is transparent and it flows with love. Service done to get acknowledgment or any other reason has a mucus-like film over it—energetically, that is. It wouldn't feel right. Hurt feelings or anger or resentment may result. But you can't work in love if you can't receive love. There's the hook."

"My *Course in Miracles* teacher said to give what we did not get," Mary said. "And in that giving we will receive the love we *didn't* get. The giving came first."

Ah, mused Joseph, *she has read it. This is good.* He went into the kitchen to get two glasses—one filled with water and the other empty—as well as a strainer and a piece of wood. He brought a large decorative bowl from the fireplace and placed it on the living room table.

"This glass," he began, "is full of water." He placed the piece of wood over it and tipped it upside down. "When it is covered with this piece of wood, nothing comes out. This represents the giver who gives from duty, not heart. Nothing really flows out, but a whole lot of shaking is going on inside. Now, this glass is empty, so it cannot give anything either." He turned it upside down to demonstrate. "So both glasses, representing people, are in the same situation."

Mary and Bill nodded in agreement.

"Now, on the other side of the coin, take people who are being given to like mad. They ask and they receive. The flow is tremendous, but they still feel needy. It is never enough. It is like the woman who mourns the fact that her daughters did not have children, therefore she is bereft with no grandchild and grieves. Then a new neighbor moves next door with a three-year-old boy who falls deeply in love with the woman. They become best friends, and the little boy dashes to her door daily and calls, 'Sue! Sue! Let's play pirates!'

"But still the old woman grieves the loss of her grandchildren. So, what happens? The neighbor has another baby! God listened and worked hard to answer her prayers, but she is not receiving the gift. What happens next? The woman's best friend, her daughter's age, has a baby! So, Sue cares for all three children; she advises the parents on how to raise them properly, just like a grandmother! But, she can't accept that they are not her bloodline, and she still grieves that she has no grandchildren."

Joseph poured water through the sieve. He poured and poured, realizing Mary and Bill were so engrossed in the story that they failed to notice there was far more water flowing from the glass than was in it. He kept pouring.

"This represents the would-be grandmother. She is receiving and receiving but she cannot retain it, so it flows right through. She never feels it but remains needy and a victim of her childless daughters. She can't see that she has *three* grandchildren who dearly love and adore her and run to her when she visits. Her prayers were answered, but not the exact way she wanted, so she can't accept the gifts deeply. It will never be enough for her because she has no foundation or ability to receive.

She complains about the children, for she can't fully love them. Though she needs them desperately."

Bill leaned forward, eyes wide. "So, how does one learn to receive?"

"The first step is to clear the blocks that reside within you that keep you from receiving. Those blocks deal with past hurts in this and past lives. The times you didn't receive enough love when you needed it still live in your cellular memory. When your parents weren't there for you, your subconscious mind registered 'not worthy.' When it happened enough times, a belief system formed. The belief system—just like a magnet—continually gathered proof that the statement was true and interpreted personal events as 'See, I'm right. I'm not worthy.'"

"So, a vicious cycle formed?" said Bill, eyes blinking. "Because she believed she wasn't worthy of receiving, she couldn't truly allow the gifts to penetrate? Oh boy, I know that one. I see that in several of our parishioners."

Joseph smiled tenderly and nodded. "It is easy to see it in others, but the challenge is to see it in yourself. That is where healing begins. When you truly begin to receive, your example will teach others. You won't have to preach about it."

With both eyebrows up and jaw dropped, Bill said, "Oh!"

"Take the situation at your church," Joseph continued, "with all the bickering. The confusion stems from you not being able to receive the love and joy you preach about. I bet you even talk about opening your heart so Christ can come in. But as you said yourself, you didn't feel the unconditional love until today. So how do expect your parishioners to be able to truly give in service?"

"So, I must be able to receive the unconditional love," Bill said, scratching his head, "before I can give it? That makes sense now." With his hand on his chin, he looked off and up to the left, nodding slowing as the thoughts penetrated. "Thank you, Joseph."

"What about giving what you did not get?" Mary probed, relentless.

"When you give what you did not get, you are really giving to yourself. You're actually in the receiving mode. For you have made the intention to give unconditionally what you never get. The gap or void is being filled with your own love because it is coming from within you, going out, and returning to you. Now here is the key: *with your own love.* Your perspective is different now because you've realized how you can heal."

"I'm not sure I get this," Mary said, shaking her head.

"What we give," Joseph reiterated, "we get back tenfold. It is a universal law. When you give unconditionally, you get it back the same way. Everyone loves a puppy or kitten. When we see one, our hearts open and love just flows out. Puppies and kittens are safe to love. Their natural instinct is to just love us back. And do they. They pour it on. Notice how people coo and giggle with puppies and kittens. It is a mutual exchange. But when it comes to other people, we have memories of being hurt, so it doesn't flow as easily. There's risk involved, so the flow is blocked."

"I get it!" Mary said quickly straightening up. "When we realize the void can be filled with our own love, we can allow it to flow and give what we didn't get!"

Joseph nodded. "The only reason you can finally give it is you are finally ready to receive it. And it takes practice each day. Because we're used to blocking the flow in both directions. We actually have to retrain our energetic system, so the stream remains open."

"So, when my parishioners complain, it is really a call for love?" Bill asked, as he leaned forward to listen more closely.

"Yes," Joseph replied. "Complaining is always a call for love. Sometimes just holding the space for listening is all that's necessary."

His cell phone rang and Joseph walked away from his guests to answer it. He chuckled at the mechanism of the telephone. Before he reached it, he knew it was Running Bear Eagle. "Excuse me a moment," he said to his guests, "I'll be right back."

"Hi, Running Bear. What's up? Why did you use the phone?"

"No offense, Joseph. I've been trying to get your attention for the past hour, but you have been too engaged with your guests."

"Oops. Sorry. What's up?" he asked again.

"I guess I am frustrated and maybe a little lonely down here. Want to meet for lunch tomorrow?"

"Okay. Where?"

"Hillstreet House. How about noon?"

They made arrangements, and he walked back into the room.

Looking at her watch, Mary said, "Joseph, I didn't realize how late it's gotten. I need to go home. Thank you so much for visiting with us. May we stop by again sometime?"

"Anytime, Mary, and you too Bill. Good luck at church this Sunday."

"I think I have something to say this Sunday," Bill said, smiling. "I'm inspired. Thank you!" he added, shaking Joseph's hand vigorously with both of his. Their eyes connected and they knew each other completely.

Mary and Bill practically floated off the porch, smiling broadly, as Joseph waved goodbye.

CHAPTER 5

A Miracle

Running Bear Eagle was walking to meet Joseph at the Hillstreet House Restaurant, when a gunshot sounded as she passed a Plaid Pantry. Screams filled the air, and the energy pattern in and around the store was filled with fragmented red lightning bolts.

She quickly gathered large amounts of universal life force energy from the center of Earth, then beamed a violet ray from her hands around and through the store.

The screaming stopped instantly.

She walked in calmly. A stocky young Black man with a shaved head, about eighteen years old, held a gun and shook all over. A dog lay dead in a puddle of blood on the floor. Running Bear quickly put a gold shield of light around the dog to postpone his transition. Standing directly in front of the boy, she extended her hand for the gun.

Without hesitation, he handed it to her, as he looked down at the floor. He stiffened to control his shaking hand.

Now, meeting his gaze, she said, "How much money did you get?"

"I don't know, I haven't had time to look."

Shoppers were frozen in their tracks. You could hear a pin drop.

"Give it to me," she said firmly. He did, and she handed it to the store owner. "Did you mean to kill the dog?" she asked the boy.

"No! It jumped at me! I got scared! I shot it."

Running Bear took the boy's hand and bent down to the dog. She placed his hand on the dog's heart. The boy's big brown eyes filled with anguish, then tears. The dog's heart was still. He hung his head in despair.

Running Bear then asked the dog's soul if this was his proper time to transition, as the soul had not completely left the body yet.

"No," the dog's soul transmitted to Running Bear. "I have much more service to render to my master. I am teaching him how to love unconditionally."

At that, she drew in a powerful Earth Sky breath and escorted the soul back into the dog's body.

The dog's body jerked, and he gasped for breath.

"He's alive," the thief stammered and jumped away from the golden retriever. "He's alive! I felt his heart beat!" With mouth and eyes wide open and hands outstretched as if to protect himself, he backed away. Running Bear Eagle was quickly at his side and held his arm.

Forgetting his fear, the tear-streaked store owner ran around the counter and lifted his loving dog into his arms. Kissing and stroking him, he murmured through his tears, with his face buried in the dog's neck, "Thank God. Thank God. He's alive." He sobbed violently.

The people in the store started to get up off the floor and out from under the counters. Everyone was talking at once. "Did you see that?" "I can't believe my eyes." "What happened?"

Nonchalantly, Running Bear linked her arm in the dazed young man's and led him out of the store.

Someone yelled, "STOP! He's getting away! Call the police!"

Running Bear turned to the screaming person and said in a soft strong voice, "He doesn't need more anger and punishment. This boy needs love."

She walked out with him. "Keep walking at a steady pace," she advised the youth. "Stay next to me."

They walked like this for a while, and when he finally came out of his astonishment, he pulled away and faced her. "Hey, what's going on? Why did you save my ass?"

"Son," she said with eyebrows raised, "if you could have anything in the world, what would it be?"

"All the money in the world," he said, eyes darting and fists pounding in the air. "Then I could get out of this stinking hole. I'd be free." He puffed up his chest and quickened his step, fighting back the tears.

"Money, eh?" Bear replied. "Have you eaten lately?"

"Nah. That's why I was robbing the store, until you came along. Now I don't have no money. Thanks, pal! If you hadn't come along, I'd be sitting pretty now."

"How much money did you get?" she asked for the second time.

"One hundred, maybe two or three hundred. Yah. I bet it was three hundred." His arms gestured larger with each increment.

"If I give you three hundred, would you come to lunch with me and a friend of mine?"

His dark eyes opened wide. "Now?"

"Yes, now. It's lunch time."

His eyebrows rose. "Do you really have three hundred dollars or are you bluffing me?"

"I never bluff." She looked into his eyes, her brows narrowing. "Turn right here," she said and nodded her head in the direction of the restaurant. "The restaurant is up ahead."

They walked in and saw Joseph already seated, looking up at them. Joseph smiled warmly and stood to kiss Bear on the cheek. He shook the young man's hand and motioned for him to sit down.

"I'm starved," Joseph said, picking up the menu. "What's good here?"

The young man, half out of his seat, looked around for an escape.

"You're safe here, son." Joseph said, coaxing him back into his seat. "We aren't the police."

"How'd you bring that dog back to life?" the young man asked Bear, twisting in his seat, eyes darting around the room.

But the waitress arrived. "What would you like?" she asked, looking at the restless boy.

"I'll have a buffalo burger with fries and a cup of peppermint herb tea," replied Bear.

"I'll have a chicken salad," Joseph said and turned toward the boy. "What would you like?"

Somewhat hesitantly, he ordered a hamburger with fries and a Coke.

"I would have come to the store," Joseph said, "but it looked like you had it under control."

"Thanks, Joseph." They both looked at the boy, who shrank in the booth. "Joseph," she said, "meet my new friend—"

"Bud," he answered, "Nice to meet you... I think."

"Bud, I'm Bear." She smiled.

Bear looked at Bud's energetic field and saw and felt the many beatings and arguments he had endured from his father. She saw Bud as a child in the crib, witnessing his father beat his screaming mother unconscious. Bud at that moment vowed to be tough so he would not get beaten up. But of course as a small child, he was defenseless against his father's rage. Bear saw the teachers in school giving up on him, labeling him a hopeless case. Bud believed he was dumb and destined for a rough life. Bear wanted to sweep those traumas away, to free him of the pain. But she didn't. She knew the boy would have to participate in his own healing to really become strong.

"The dog?" Bud said, breaking the silence.

"I used life force energy from Mother Earth and Father Sky," Bear answered. "The force was so strong that his soul reentered his body. But more important, it wasn't the dog's time to die. You almost took him out early. He wasn't finished with his life's purpose."

"Give me a break. The dog has a life's purpose?" Bud said, shaking his head. "A dumb dog? I should have really killed him. I probably missed. He probably wasn't dead at all."

"You felt his heart," Bear answered, realizing how frightening the entire event was for him. "It was not beating."

Bud pursed his lips. "Then it was . . . So, how'd ya do it?"

Joseph and Bear smiled. She beamed the scene to Bud's mind, this time the way she saw it.

"Bud fell silent; he was barely breathing. After a pause, he said, "Can anyone do that? Or is it some sort of gift or something?"

"Anyone can do it, with some practice, and yes, it is also a gift," Running Bear said.

"Do ya think someone like me could learn? Nah, I'm too dumb," he replied, answering his own question.

"Rub your hands together like this," she said, demonstrating. "Now put your hands about three inches apart and feel the heat going between them."

He rubbed his dirty hands together—hands that had known much violence in his short, but seemly long, life of eighteen years. Living in terror seemed to lengthen time. "I can feel a little heat!"

"Okay, now breathe with your feet," Bear instructed.

His eyebrows reached up to meet each other. "Get real!"

"I'm serious. Pretend you have two noses, and they are at the bottoms of your feet. Take several deep breaths from your feet."

Focusing hard, with a little grimace, he attempted to breathe with his feet. Then his dark eyes popped open with amazement, and he exclaimed, "My feet are tingling!"

"Good," she said, watching him with a pleased smile. "Now, breathe deeper and bring it up your legs into your heart."

Bear watched the trickle of energy flow up his legs and into his heart.

But Bud kept breathing, and pretty soon the current was larger. "I feel heat now, like I did with my hands! This is incredible, man!" he exclaimed, and took an even deeper breath.

"Now bring the energy from your heart down your arms, out your hands," she explained. "Now put your hands together. Do you feel any difference?"

"Do I? Wow!"

"Now pulse your hands back and forth," Bear continued. "See how far apart you can get them and still feel the energy."

He pulled his hands apart quickly.

"Not so fast," Bear warned, "or you won't be able to feel it. It's very subtle."

"What's sud, sud—what did you say?" Bud said, never losing a beat. He picked up the technique as if he had been doing it for years.

"That's all there is to bringing the energy through. Now, you add sacred intention," Bear said.

Lunch arrived. Bud was so engrossed, he barely noticed. Joseph and Bear cupped their hands over their food. Breathing with their feet, they brought up Earth's nurturing energy to bless and thank the food, the cooks, the kingdoms, and Earth for the abundance. They finished the blessing by making three circles over their food with their energized hands.

Bud saw them from his peripheral vision. "Whacha doing now?" he questioned.

"A sacred prayer of thanks," Joseph answered. "We brought the same energy up from the Earth, through our hearts and then sent it into our food."

"Like this?" Bud cupped his hands, now streaming with energy, and filled his food.

"Now, to yourself, give thanks. It's that easy," said Bear.

Bud placed his cupped hands a few inches above the food, filling it with life force energy, his eyes wide with wonder. A few bites later, he remarked rather softly, "I've never had a better hamburger."

Joseph and Bear laughed. They ate in silence. Everyone was pretty hungry by then.

When lunch was finished, Bud glanced suspiciously at Joseph and Bear. But no questions or recriminations followed. "What's next," Bud asked bravely.

"Oh, I forgot," Bear said, reaching into her pocket. She handed him three hundred dollars. Then Joseph and Bear got up, waved goodbye to the stunned Bud, and paid the bill on the way out.

Bud shook his head. He looked around and then smiled, with a little chuckle.

Outside, Joseph took Bear's hand, swung it high into the air, and laughed. "It's not so bad being back."

They skipped down the street and disappeared.

Tonight Bear and Joseph watched the local television news to see how the Plaid Pantry story was portrayed. The report was a headline story of how an American Indian woman stopped a Plaid Pantry robbery singlehandedly, with no weapon.

"An armed Black man, about eighteen years old, shot and killed the owner of the Plaid Pantry's golden retriever. And then after returning the stolen money to the owner, the American Indian woman brought the dead dog back to life!" read the television evening news anchor. Then the camera zoomed in to the owner of the Plaid Pantry, who was holding and petting his dog. "I'm so glad he's alive," he wept. "I don't know if I'll ever let him out of my sight!" His dog gave him a nice big lick on the face and seemed to smile like only a dog can do.

The police forensic artist had sketched a drawing of Bear from the descriptions given by people in the store. It was a good resemblance. Not much was said about Bud. The story continued: looking right into the camera, a heavyset man of about forty said, "We were all screaming, and suddenly I felt a calm come over me. Then in walked the Indian woman. The boy just handed her the gun. After that, he gave the money to her, and she gave it to the storekeeper." His voice was excited and unbelieving. "*Then* she put the boy's hand on the dog's heart, and the dog came back to life right before my eyes."

"If anyone sees this woman," concluded the sexy brunette news reporter, "please notify the police. They want to speak with her."

Head tilted to the right, with a slight smile and tender eyes, Joseph said, "Great, Bear, second day back and you got the news media and police after you. What are you going to do next?"

"I don't know. How do you bring a culture full of fear and anger to love? I can't keep holding down Plaid Pantries."

They both laughed.

"I guess that's the question we're here to answer, isn't it?" Joseph replied. "But the Creator will probably have us just stumble into it."

CHAPTER 6

Separation

*B*ud didn't know what to think. Walking home in a daze, he bumped into a man coming toward him. He heard himself say, "Oh! Excuse me." The man nodded. Normally, he would have said something smart and given him a dirty look. But with a simple apology, there was no conflict. That was different.

He reached his street and heard a scuffle up ahead. He couldn't see who it was yet. Two young men were beating up a short, stocky old man. Bud ran over to get a closer look. He knew the guys. "Whacha doin'?" he shouted.

"Come on!" they invited him to join, as they pushed the old man again.

Bud rushed between them and blocked the next blow coming down on the old man's face. "Stop!" he shouted. "Stop now!" He pushed the boys away and lifted the old man off the ground. His nose was bleeding and his eye bruised.

Bud looked up and saw the two guys coming at him.

"So, what's with ya?" one cried, his fists up, inviting Bud to strike him. "Come on, tough guy," he taunted, hopping from one foot to the other.

Bud's glare caused the boys to slink away as he steadied the old man. "Where were you going?" Bud asked the old man soothingly.

"Home," he whispered, bent over in pain.

Bud helped the old man up, allowing him to lean on him as they went along in silence. When they reached the man's home and Bud finally got his voice back, he asked, "How badly are you hurt?"

Exhausted, bruised, with hardened blood on his face, the man burst into tears. He muttered between sobs, "Thank you son," and walked into his house, his head bowed in defeat.

Bewildered, Bud headed toward home. On the way, the same two guys ambushed him.

"Whacha trying to do back there, ruin our fun?" The skinny one nudged him.

"Huh?" The guy with four rings in his nose knocked him down and grabbed his wallet.

"I told ya he was just doin' it to get the old man's money!" The ringed-nose boy exclaimed. "Look! Three hundred dollars!" Triumphantly he waved Bud's wallet in the air.

Bud yelled out, "That's mine! I didn't take it from the old man!"

"Right!" the other exclaimed, leaping into the air and waving the wad of cash. Then off the two ran.

Bud picked himself up, wiped his bloodied nose, and shook his head, muttering "What a day!"

CHAPTER 7

Healing

A s Joseph approached his home, Mary was waiting for him on the front stoop. She waved and gave him a big smile. She was with a short, plump woman in her late sixties.

"Joseph, I would like you to meet Thelma. She is a friend of mine from church."

Thelma was dressed in all black, with straight brunette hair streaked with grey. She walked with a slight wobble, bent forward at about a thirty-degree angle. She looked as if she would fall over at any moment

"Blessings, Thelma." Joseph took her outstretched hand with both of his to steady her. He saw her fear and loneliness and the abyss of pain she carried within her soul. "Come in," he offered, "and join me for some tea."

Mary began apologizing for coming unannounced and so late. But Joseph's eyes were filled with so much grace, she paused in mid-sentence. With a soft sigh, her shoulders relaxed, and she and Thelma followed him into his colorful, artistic living room.

The brown textured couch stood on a jute area rug, flanked by soft leather-tone walls. Splashes of orange and yellow were on the throw pillows. The honey-toned wood floor had a calming effect, and abstract art flowed with oranges, browns, yellows, and a hint of turquoise. Joseph felt that art was an expression of God. When creativity was woven with innovation and clear vision, spiced with passion, a new form emerged. That was art *and* creation. His place was a metaphor for the creative transformation happening on Earth. Taking all the highest thinking, principles, love, and actions, humans would evolve to a higher species: the universal human. All humans must rise in consciousness to the level he reached over two thousand years ago. Realizing humans' divine potential, he was a prototype of the future human.

Thelma drank in the beauty of the room and sighed with pleasure. As an interior designer, she knew this room was a masterpiece of balance, harmony, and beauty. Then she caught a small flaw and wobbled over to straighten a painting. Now everything was as it should be, and she sat down on the couch.

Joseph fetched a steaming pot of tea. Mary looked stunned when he returned so quickly.

"How do you like your tea, Thelma?" he asked, ignoring Mary's surprise.

"With a little sugar," she said, leaning toward the tea eagerly.

He scooped some out of the sugar bowl for her, stirred it gently, all the while blessing it with love and safety. As he handed it to her, he looked into her eyes, sending her the message that she was safe here, and he was glad she had come. The room was filled with a peaceful silence.

As a result, Thelma began to speak as if something deeply internal was moving her. "I can't stop crying," she burst out, looking down at her tea. "Ever since I had acupuncture, I have been crying about everything. I see little children who are neglected, and I cry. I think of my dogs who have died, and I cry. I cry during the news broadcast. I've just become a crybaby, and I hate it." She gritted her teeth and glared at Joseph.

Joseph embraced her eyes again. "Yes," he said, nodding.

"The acupuncture helped me quit smoking, and I've been crying ever since. It's been two years!" Her voice cracked, and she was almost in tears again. "So, this week, I called the acupuncture clinic and told them my problem. I asked them to close me back up, so I'd stop crying. They said they had never heard of anything like that, and they couldn't close me up." She choked back the tears, swallowed hard, and looked defiantly at Joseph.

Scanning her energetic field, Joseph saw a life totally unfulfilled, with unrequited loves; numerous disappointments; and deep, unresolved grief. "You believe that crying is bad?" he asked gently.

"Bad?" she replied, her eyes narrowing. "It's terrible. Things happen in life, and you swallow and move on. I'm not a crybaby. I lived through the Depression! Nobody's going to take advantage of me."

Joseph felt her anger but also the fear beneath it, which was hidden from her. He gazed into her soul and felt her insatiable longing for connection. But he also saw that she wanted the connection in a particular manner. She wanted the storybook doting husband so she could live happily ever after. After several unsuccessful marriages, she still blamed her husbands for the failures. Even with that history, she clung to the fairytale of living happily ever after—as if that gave her life.

"There is a deep yearning in our society today," Joseph began. "A yearning for love. We often think love must come from a partner, but the truth is, it is our search for ourselves."

Thelma wagged her forefinger at him. "I've heard that before. I know who I am. I was raised in the Chicago ghetto and was beat up every day after school. No one is going to take advantage of me!"

"That made you tough and helped you survive your childhood. You did a good job."

She nodded, puffing up her chest and sitting straighter.

"But, Thelma, you're not just crying for the children or the bad news, you are crying because *you* are filled with grief and pain," Joseph said lovingly.

"That's what my daughter tells me. But I've resolved my life. What is, is. I have risen above it. However, I can't stop crying; *everything* makes me cry."

Mary glanced at Joseph with pleading eyes.

To add to the deep grief she was carrying in her energy field from her own wounds, she had the pain that had grown in her since she stopped smoking. Now that her smoke screen was gone, she had no boundary sphere to protect her spirit, so everyone else's emotions went directly into her. It was like a double whammy. No wonder she was crying all the time.

He took her hand, and she melted like butter. "Let us pray," he said softly. Mary, Thelma, and Joseph joined hands. "There is one power and one presence in the universe, and that power and presence is God. God is all around us, through us, and in us. Feel the presence now. I pray that Thelma realize the wonder of God within her now, and be filled with the power and the grace that is her birthright. I ask that she be filled with peace forever more. Amen."

After a short pause, they opened their eyes. "The room seems lighter," Thelma blurted out. "*I* feel lighter."

More silence. Thelma started to laugh, then giggle like a little girl. "Thank you," she said to Joseph, catching his eye shyly. And, as if on cue, Mary and Thelma stood up, said goodbye, and floated out.

Overlooking the ocean, under a magnificent Sitka spruce, Sid and Victoria sat endlessly talking. As the water glistened and danced under the sun, the tree branches swayed gently, carrying the ocean scent to them. The sky was azure, as it can only be on a sunny day in Oregon. Warmed from the sun, they stretched out on the beautiful Mexican blanket, with the remnants of lunch strewn about. They both breathed deeply and paused in the wonder of the moment.

Leaning on her elbows, Victoria said, "I lost my train of thought. Where were we?"

"Discussing the fundamental teachings of Buddhism," Sid replied.

But neither of them seemed interested in anything but each other. He scooted over and kissed her gently on the lips. His fingers stroked her high cheekbones, then caressed her strong, angular jaw line. Breathing together, their gentle embrace suspended time and space. With each kiss, their bodies came closer together, until they could not feel where one ended and the other began. They lay intertwined for eternity... or so it seemed.

Bud's mother, Faith, was singing, "God watches over his sparrows, I know he's watching over me," as Bud walked past her in the kitchen. She was a large-boned woman about five feet six inches tall and weighing in at about 180 pounds. Her large, bare forearms wagged as she washed pots and pans and sang with a strong, bold voice.

Bud tried to sneak by and conceal his bloody nose, but as always, she seemed to smell a rat with no warning.

"I thought you were going to look for a job today? How'd ya get your nose bent in?" she asked.

Not knowing if the truth would even be believed, he muttered, "Not a good day, Ma," and walked into the bathroom.

With more passion and zeal, she sang. "God watches over his sparrows; I know he's watching over me."

She set the table and called out, "Dinner's ready!"

Sullen and a little frightened, Bud joined her for a simple meal of pork and beans. The old olive-green counters were warped and faded but so clean one could eat off them, and the floor was spotless as well. Faith had found the chrome table at a garage sale. It had witnessed many family conflicts *and* resolutions.

They served themselves in silence, and Faith gave the evening blessing, plus asked for strength. About mid-way through the meal, Bud got up and put on the television. Much to his dismay, the news broadcast of the Plaid Pantry robbery filled the airways. The forensic team had made a sketch of Bud and Bear. Just as Bud attempted to turn the television off, his mother looked and saw the artist's rendering of her son. Reluctantly, he left it on, so she could hear the story. Bud was grateful they stressed the miracle of the dog coming back to life and not him.

"Come sit down, Bud. What happened today?" she asked softly.

"I didn't mean to shoot the dog, Ma. Really, I didn't. I got scared with all the confusion, and the gun went off."

"You're lucky the dog's alive. Remember the law of God, Bud: 'Thou shalt not kill.' And what about 'Thou shalt not steal?'"

"No one will hire me, Ma. I'm just no good. I wanted to bring home some money today. I got three hundred dollars. I was gonna surprise you!"

"I don't need them kind of surprises. Why can't you work like everyone else? Get a job at a Plaid Pantry, don't rob it!"

"I can't earn enough. It's dumb. Everyone will laugh at me."

After a while, the silence felt like a pressure cooker, and Bud blurted out, "I couldn't believe it! The dog stopped breathing. She put my hand on his heart, and it was still, and suddenly he was breathing again. Everyone started to yell, and we just walked out of the store together. Then the woman invited me to lunch with her friend and showed me how she healed the dog. You won't believe this: she asked me how much I stole from the Plaid, and she gave me the three hundred dollars to replace what I gave back."

"Sounds like the work of the devil," exclaimed Faith, shaking her bowed head.

"The devil? Ma, she saved my ass in that store. I gave the money back to the storeowner. She brought the dog back to life, and then she paid for lunch and didn't even read me the riot act. How could that be the work of the devil?"

Faith's eyes sternly linked to Bud's. "That's what the devil does. He appears to be doing good, but it's for evil. You better be careful. You not only have the law after you, but now the devil. Lord save us!"

"Ma!" Well, he figured, at least the heat was off him and on the Native American woman.

They ate the rest of the meal in silence.

Faith fought back her tears. "God watches over his sparrows. He must be watching over me." Her voice quivered as she rose from the table. "Just don't end up like your dead brother, okay?" Rustling his hair lovingly, with tears streaming down her face, she sang softly as she walked to the sink.

CHAPTER 8

Cancer

*A*s Victoria glided into her small healing room, filled with vibrant, healthy plants and flowers that basked in the sunlight streaming through the spacious windows, the phone rang. She dashed to it before it clicked to the electronic voicemail.

"Hello," she said, breathless.

"Hello, is Victoria there?" a woman's voice asked.

"Yes, this is she," Victoria answered, not recognizing the voice.

"This is Beverly from Home Health. I received your name from Rita, who has done several healings with you. She thought you may be able to help."

"Yes?" Victoria replied.

"We have a client on hospice care who is dying of cancer. She is close to the end, and she is open to some hands-on healing. Can you help possibly relieve some pain?"

"I may be able to assist her," Victoria said. "What is her first and last name?"

As soon as Victoria received the patient's name, she began to energetically scan her. The woman was filled with cancer and suffered great pain in the abdominal region. She was weak, frightened, and despondent. Aware of her impending death, she was terrified of going to hell.

"Beverly, first you must understand that I do nothing; it is the spirit within me and through me that does the work. From what I can perceive, the best I can facilitate at this stage—she *is* terminal—is to help prepare her soul for the transition. If that would be of service, how do I reach her?"

After receiving the information, Victoria phoned and set an appointment for the next day. Something churned in her stomach after she made the appointment. There was something scary about this situation. Was she in over her head? Often Spirit brought her new lessons through clients, but this one made her feel uneasy.

Victoria arrived at Martha's right on time. Greeted by the nurse, she stepped into a stuffy, dark, and ominous apartment. Hardly able to breathe, Victoria felt a rush of anxiety. She had facilitated many cancer patients before, but somehow this was different. Martha was lying in a morphine stupor on a hospital bed in the main living area.

After the introductions, Victoria set right to work opening the windows and drapes.

"Ruth," she said to the nurse, "this room is like death itself. We need some air and fresh flowers. Throw these dead ones away." Then, with permission, Victoria began to smudge the main room, then the kitchen area. Next, she smudged Ruth, Martha, and herself. The room began to feel lighter.

Taking her cue from Victoria, the nurse went outside with clippers to cut some fresh flowers.

Victoria pulled up a chair next to Martha and sat down. Filled with love, she gently took her hand. "Martha," she said soothingly, "tell me about your pain."

Martha stroked her abdomen, as her wide, frightened eyes pleaded. "The drip helps," she offered weakly.

"Whatever we do today, Martha, we do together," Victoria reassured her. "I do nothing; it is the divine within me that does the work. And all the healing is done with the love of Christ."

Martha sighed and closed her eyes. "Am I going to die?" she whispered.

"Do you want to live?"

"Yes, I want to live."

"What do you want to live for?" Victoria asked.

After several seconds' hesitation, she answered, "My grandchildren. I don't see much of my grandchildren."

"Have you healed your relationships with your children and ex-husbands?"

"What do you mean?"

"I mean, have you forgiven them for whatever hurts they caused you in this life?"

"Well, they came over last week, and they brought me a gift, and I got to see my granddaughter. She played right here on the floor."

"Have you forgiven them?" Victoria probed. *There's not much time left for this woman to remain in denial*, Victoria thought.

Then Martha began to pour out the story of all the hurts and betrayals. All the things her kids had done to her.

Victoria held her wrinkled, lifeless hand and channeled in the loving, universal life force energy. "One of the most important things we *all* must do before we die or transition is finish all of our emotional business. That means forgiving every hurt and letting it go. That does not mean you condone the betrayal or that it was right. It does mean it no longer hurts you. Do you understand?"

"Sort of."

"Can you forgive your daughter for all the things she has done to you?" Usually this process took several more steps to reach the forgiveness piece, but a much bigger window seemed to be about to open up here. Eminence hung in the air.

"Yes, I think so."

"Then, *it is so for all time past, present, future, parallel and in-between lives. Let all the wounds be lifted,*" she continued the sacred incantation at barely a murmur. "Now, souls of Martha's daughter, son, and granddaughter, can you forgive your mother for harm she has done to you, perceived or not perceived?"

The souls of Martha's family had gathered around the bed. Martha's son blurted out, "Hell no!"

Victoria had a telepathic conversation with him to convince him that what his mother had done was not right, but if he could forgive her, it would no longer eat at him and affect him in subtle yet poisonous ways.

After some thought, the son agreed. "Okay, I forgive her, but just barely!"

"May she be forgiven for all time past, present, and future," Victoria incanted, swinging her pendulum in a circle. She proceeded like this through the entire family, blessing each with the new freedom they would experience when these burdens were lifted.

Then Victoria stood at the foot of the bed and placed her hands on Martha's feet, so she could look deeper into the situation. When she shifted her vision to see what other spirits were in the room, the real problem became apparent. The room was suffocated with demon angels. Every square inch was filled with demons. They were swarming around Martha's head. "We have been waiting for you," the spokes-demon said to Victoria.

"What do you want?" Victoria answered, also telepathically, as she dropped light force energy deeper into the Earth and energized Martha's field. Victoria had dealt with demons many times before, and they did not intimidate her. "Are you responsible for destroying this woman with cancer?"

"She sold her soul to the devil many years ago. We're just doing our best work. Not bad eh?"

Victoria could see that Martha's gut was distended to twice its normal size. Her weak, pale body twitched in pain. "What do you want?" Victoria repeated, feet firmly planted.

Suddenly Lucifer appeared, standing eight feet tall. He loomed behind Martha's head, overshadowing the other demons. "I'll get to the point, for as I remember, you aren't much for small talk. Many thousands of years ago, you made a contract with me, and I have come for my payoff."

"What contract?" Victoria asked, nonplused. She stood straighter with eyes piercing Lucifer.

Cloaked in black, with piercing red eyes, he said, "I can't tell you now. But I'll make you a deal. I'll clear this woman's soul from all evil karma before she dies, if you will fulfill your end of the obligation."

"I don't know what you want me to do, Lucifer, and I don't remember what our original agreement was. How can I concede to anything?"

"Okay," he said. "You always did drive a hard bargain. I will clear her soul if you promise to meet me in your healing room this evening at 8:00 pm."

My healing room is well protected, she thought. "Okay, eight tonight." And he disappeared.

Chanting a powerful incantation, Victoria sent the demon angels back from whence they came. Trailing out with a sinister laughter, they left one by one. When the room was completely cleared, Victoria chelated Martha, a process of balancing and running the energies through the main chakra system and acupressure points. Victoria repaired her major chakras, which were very damaged from the cancer and hard life she had lived. This would relax and relieve some of Martha's pain and allow her the strength to finish her inner personal business.

Several minutes lapsed. Martha, still in a trance, whispered again, "Am I going to die?"

"Yes," Victoria whispered back, "but your soul will be lifted from its pain. You must find it in your heart to love everyone in your life. In your mind's eye, lovingly hug your ex-husbands, your kids, and your grandkids. It is love that heals. Do you feel the spirit of love that I am filling you with now?"

"I feel it," she sighed.

Victoria finished the energy work and sealed Martha's aura in gold light. Consequently, the room glowed in loving, simmering gold light. Her transition would be peaceful.

In closing, Victoria prayed aloud, "I give thanks for the opportunity to be of service in this way. Now I encircle you with gold light to seal in this healing, and I pray for a continued miracle of healing." With her hands in a prayer position at her heart chakra, she continued, "Now I return your healing and your spirit to you. I call back my spirit to rest in my heart that I may be fully present." And with a small gesture, she opened her hands toward Martha's heart to return the healing. This disconnected them energetically, allowing the tortured woman to use her own spirit to complete her forgiveness work.

Finally, she took Martha's hand and thanked her for the opportunity to be in service.

The nurse, who was back from the garden, took her aside angrily. "Why did you tell her she was going to die? I spend all my time trying to keep her hopes up!"

"Because she is, and she needs to take my counsel seriously and not procrastinate, as she has done her entire life. She knows she is dying. Look at her. Right now she needs the truth and lots of love. Your job is to keep this place open, with fresh air and fresh flowers and plants. Remember you are *living* here also. Death doesn't have to be mean, dark, fearsome, and ugly. It can be a transition into the light, filled with love."

Shrugging, the nurse nodded. Then she wrote Victoria a check for her services, which Martha, although weak, signed.

Before she left, Victoria hugged the nurse and squeezed Martha's hand one last time. "Bless you," she whispered. "May God be with you."

Martha died peacefully a few days later.

CHAPTER 9

We Create the Global Mind

From extensive logging of the Sitka spruce, the central Oregon coast was now filled with mostly Douglas fir, red alder, and Western hemlock. Rhododendron bushes grew out of rocky crannies and moss crept up the trunks of the Douglas fir. But Grandfather Sitka, tall and strong and over a hundred years old, remained a proud guardian over his tree people.

Sword ferns, salmon berry blossoms, and moss, danced across the coastal forest floor, creating not only a beautiful sight, but also lots of food for the birds and animals.

Running Bear donned a pair of blue jeans and a crème blouse and a plain brown leather vest, and of course, her moccasins. Her stride was light and long, and her posture straight and strong, as she approached the location of their second meeting under Grandfather Sitka. She spotted Sid, as he rounded the corner, coming toward their sacred circle. They dashed toward each other, and she beamed him a delicious smile and gave him a huge hug. "Welcome brother!" she exclaimed, truly glad to see him. "How has your first week back in body been? Things have sure sped up since I was here last."

"You can say that again!" He hugged her back. He was more demonstrative than she ever remembered.

"You look comfortable in those loose beige cotton slacks—I see you found organic ones. Way to go, Sid!" She gave him a high five.

Joseph, a twinkle in his eyes, was happily humming as he approached the circle, comfortable in his new surroundings and sweat suit. He sure liked these comfortable clothes with the soft fabrics. Nothing like he had two thousand plus years ago.

As they joined hands—including Grandfather Sitka to the north— Running Bear Eagle pronounced the invocation: "Great Spirit, we call on your wisdom to guide us in love and pure intention for the highest good of all. I call forth the spirit of Earth Mother to join us." After a pause, she continued, "Welcome, Earth Mother. I call forth the spirit of the East, of the new day, to join us." After a pause, she said, "Welcome spirit of the East. I call forth the spirit of the South, to the good road home." After another pause, she added, "Welcome, spirit of the South. I call forth the spirit of the West, of the dark waters of looking within, to join us."

Suddenly the skies darkened and an audible groan arose. The pause elongated into several minutes. Running Bear continued when she knew the energies of the West were present.

"Welcome, spirit of the West. I call forth the spirit of the North, the wisdom place and place of White Buffalo, to join our circle now." After a pause, she continued, "Welcome spirit of the North. I call forth sacred fire to help us burn to the truth. I call forth sacred water to keep our spirits clear. I call forth sacred air for our divine inspiration. Thank you for joining our circle."

A gentle breath caressed them as the elements entered.

Next they sat in silence, holding hands, breathing in the inspiration of Creator.

After the richest silence, Grandfather spoke. "Welcome, humans, to our wisdom council. There is a matter on the table that we need to discuss as soon as we complete our check-in."

Sid took the talking stick Running Bear had put in the center and began, "My finger tips are sensitized to soft skin and tender flower petals. My nose so tantalized by the fragrance of roses and daises and fresh-washed skin. My tongue and mouth so alert to tingling sensations of taste, and my eyes so filled with the beauty all around, that I wonder how I got so stuck on all the suffering down here last time."

Everyone burst out laughing.

"Sid," Joseph said and smiled, remembering Mary Magdalene. "You're in love!"

Turning a bright shade of red, Sid grinned. "Love. Yes. I had forgotten how wonderful it feels. It shows?"

Again, laughter abounded. Sid handed the talking stick to Running Bear, with an embarrassed grin, and bowed his head.

"I remember the confusion," she began. "The love, the fear, the hate, but mostly the neglected souls. There is a vast emptiness out there, a black spiritless hole. Grandmother Tree helps me stay grounded. She consoles me."

She handed the talking stick to Joseph.

"My neighbors have discovered me, and the welcome lady brings her friends by," he said, with a big smile and his brown eyes sparkling. "The loneliness here seems deeper. I get a real sense of despair and disconnection. I see so many transfixed by their cell phones. But still, I am hopeful for peace and love to reign," Joseph concluded and gently set the talking stick back in the center of the circle.

"I feel better." Mother Earth shook the talking stick slightly as she spoke. "At least I feel better at the spot where you danced the sacred symbols into my body. I'm hopeful again too. Having the three of you in body at the same time and place is no less than a miracle. Thanks for answering my call." The talking stick rattled. "There are high spiritual teachers alive today on Earth, but many are still preaching 'their way or the highway.' Have you noticed how ominous the skies are today? I think sacred wind and sacred water have something in store for us."

"You speak of the confusion, Running Bear," Grandfather said. "There is a universal law that a void will always attract something to fill it. Space does not remain empty."

"Yes?"

"I believe," Grandfather continued, "that the confusion and anger have resulted from several things. One aspect is that a huge void was made when spirituality and daily life were separated. Humans created such a secular society that the miracle of being alive, the very miracle of breath, is not honored or recognized in their daily lives. The void created by secularism filled with fear. The untamed ego and the devil archetype fed on fear. So, the more we stepped away from the sacred, the more we filled the global mind with the lower vibrations."

"I feel," Joseph answered, "we need both new and old. But the old must be cleansed of its past. The dogmas must be shed, and only the richest and purest of ceremonies practiced. Ceremonies are needed that apply to today's needs, like cleansing Earth and ourselves. Like reenergizing Earth and rebalancing her energies. Like revitalizing the soil, cleaning the water, and purifying the air physically and energetically," he said, rocking sideways and taking a deep breath. "I'm stunned at the pollution humans have created from their waste."

"Thank you, Joseph. I sure could use some intentional loving care!" replied Mother Earth, and the talking stick rattled again. "Many people from all over the globe are making an effort. Some folks are working individually, some in groups. But is your point--not enough, not fast enough?"

"I think my point," Joseph replied, "is that the religions, like everything else, must evolve according to time and need. Humans got stuck thinking one way was the only way. In 200 BC, it was appropriate to sacrifice the fatted lamb. We don't need that any more, though some ancient religions still practice it. It isn't that Buddha's message is outdated, but rather that, combined with mine and the Native American messages, all the messages become richer. Even our perspective of what God is must be transcended. Our social group must be all life, not the clan or even just humanity. Imagine a quiet mind with an open heart that respects all life, even the germ-spreading fly, the ant over there, and the biting flea."

Smiling tenderly and nodding reflectively, Bear said, "I believe some people are attempting to live in harmony and love. But most either don't feel a sense of urgency or are too overwhelmed by the enormity of the crisis. Hmm—what is our role?"

"Let us energetically go into the global brain. There may be a clue there for us," Grandfather suggested.

They joined hands and began to synchronize their breath. Sid began to chant a sound that drew them into themselves. "No need to go out anywhere," he said softly. "The global mind is right here within us. Ask to perceive it now."

Like a glowing sun, their circle lit the forest. After about twenty minutes, Sid said, "Now ask what our next step is."

The birds quieted, the wind hushed, and the gray clouds lifted. After another few moments, the group members gently opened their eyes.

Bringing their awareness to the center of the circle again, Bear declared, "The global mind is, at its essence, a void. Formed by thought and feeling, it is constantly creating itself. We are shaping it right now, as are the kids playing in the park over there or the businesswoman on her computer or the couple arguing. There seems to be a mass of energy, like a reserve bank account, as it were, filled with the most prevalent emotions and thought forms—with pockets of particular thoughts or emotions—and fluid at the same time."

"Let us project fear into the global brain and see the response," Grandfather suggested.

As they closed their eyes again, Sid projected fear of losing his relationship with Victoria. Joseph projected Thelma's fear. Bear sent fear from the Plaid Pantry incident. Tree was afraid for the survival of his species. Earth tuned into a massacre that was happening simultaneously on another part of her body. Moreover, each watched to see what happened next.

In a dramatic display of power, a huge vortex of fear welled up in the sky and shot rays of dull black energy right down into and through Bear, Joseph, Sid, Tree, and Earth. Then, playing out like a movie, dozens of scenes of the horrors appeared one by one in no particular sequence. Hitler marched across the screen, exciting the crowds to feel the superiority of their Germanic race. Droves of Jews were pushed into the gas chambers and murdered. Bombs exploded, devastating Hiroshima, Pearl Harbor, the Persian Gulf. Battles arose between the Indians and the cavalry, the Spanish and the Aztecs. The caribou were slaughtered. A man shot his wife, then himself. A young boy killed his drunken father and hysterical younger sister. Angry battles ripped through bar rooms, court rooms, bedrooms, living rooms, and kitchens.

The Pope ordered the genocide of women in the 1300s. Mass shootings took place in schools, mosques, churches, theaters, concerts, subways, and shopping centers.

These movie-like image seemed endless. Now, a young Italian smashed the car window of innocent tourists as they drove through Florence, Italy, and he grabbed the American woman's purse.

Simple conversations arose against the government, against the next-door neighbor, the coworker, the spouse. When Mary had critical thoughts of Thelma, a beam of negative energy went from Mary's second chakra and attacked Thelma. The incidents were endless, and new ones were being created as they watched. A man slapped his wife, while a dog growled in fear at a thief breaking into his master's home. A Wells Fargo bank was held up. The more they saw, the more it grew.

Some negative thoughts were as simple as a judgment against someone: "Look how fat she is." "You're bad." "All they think about is money." "I wish she were dead." "I'll get him back." You can't do that to me." Each drew energy *from* the fear vortex and pumped more energy *into it*. The fear thoughts and actions fed the vortex like gasoline to a fire.

Then the vortex moved on its own, with no apparent thought form directing it. It had become an entity unto itself. Now the black rays struck people down in the street. A child was hit by her father. A dog was kicked and tossed into the street and killed by a car. A wild cancer perpetuated itself from the food of fear. Every fear thought activated itself like yeast in a culture.

Bear gasped and grounded her energy further into the Earth. But she found no solace, for she tapped into Earth's fear and rage and began to shake violently all over. Blood drawn from her face, she was sheet white.

Sid called out, "Enough! Show us now what drains this mass."

They each knew instinctively what to do. They shifted their energy into their hearts and felt great appreciation and love for God and each other. They projected the love into the vortex. At first nothing happened. They remembered the many charitable acts people had bestowed upon each other. The Red Cross went into a war-distressed area. Meditation groups were praying for peace. On World Peace Day, millions on the planet prayed for peace simultaneously. A daughter was helping her mother. A father jumped into the river to save his son. Angels saved people from various perils. They kept seeing and feeling the great abundance of love and sent it into the vortex.

The dark streaks slowed down, then stopped all together. The vortex started to retreat, but a drunken man began raping his five-year-old daughter. She screamed with terror. He gagged her and thrust his penis into her little bleeding body. The vortex was fed again. And so it went for a seemingly endless time—the love counteracting the violence, only then to be counteracted by more violence. A vicious cycle ensued.

Exhausted, Sid disconnected their minds from the vortex. They lay dripping with sweat on the ground, gasping for breath.

Finally, Earth spoke. "As of late, I cannot disconnect myself from the scenes, for I feel them in my body, and they are more prevalent than the vibrations of love. The fear is frenetic, and I am worn."

"It is an energy loop, caught in its own web." Joseph panted, out of breath.

"Does it seem bigger now?" asked Sid.

"It feels more desperate, more determined," Bear responded, still breathing hard.

"More mature," Joseph added. "The fear thought form has grown, as has the consciousness of love. Very interesting. I don't quite know what to make of it."

"It is feeding on itself," Bear continued, "like an autoimmune system disease. No wonder so many humans are afflicted with AIDS, rheumatoid arthritis, chronic fatigue, Crohn's disease, and fibromyalgia. Those diseases are created from anger and fear thought forms turned against the body. Most of the thought forms are not even conscious to the individual."

"A good example of why mindfulness is so necessary," Sid interjected, managing a slight smile.

Bear continued without pause, "Individuals' fear thoughts and traumas get trapped in their energetic fields and eventually fall into their tissues and therefore their organs. The thoughts and emotions literally become matter. And because the thoughts are toxic, the matter is toxic also, so disease is the form it takes. Caught in a fear loop, they continue to feed the fear messages into their bodies, *and* therefore the global brain. The negative vortex of the global brain is strengthened and subsequently feeds it back out into the individual consciousness, and the cycle continues. Phew!"

"But does it have a life of its own? Like its own consciousness?" Sid asked, half talking to himself. "Do souls then manifest from this form? Is it generating life?"

A long silence ensued, as each pondered these ideas.

"If that were true, then..." Sid was interrupted by a woman's voice: "Help! Help! Heeelp!"

Grandfather tuned in and said, "Her son has fallen into the river and is caught by the current. She can't swim and needs help."

They ran to the scene. The boy fought against the current, but it was too strong for him, and he was swept down the river, crashing into rocks.

A young woman hiking in the forest also heard the call. Swift as a gazelle, she flew down the trail adjacent to the river, moving ahead of where the boy was tumbling. Maneuvering through the rocks into the water, she reached out to catch him, but he swished by. He resurfaced again, but his struggle was silent and his limp body floated down the river ahead of her. Without hesitation, she lay down on the water, in the fastest flow.

"Ouch!" she cried, as her hip hit a sharp rock. "Dear God, please help me save this boy."

The boy was snagged in an eddy.

She stroked hard to reach him and lifted his unconscious body over her shoulder. Using all her strength, she swam quickly to the shore. Blood flowed from his forehead. Climbing over the shore rock, she found a flat place to lay him on his stomach, with his face to the side, and pressed firmly against his back. A rush of water poured from his mouth. She repeated this until all the water was released. Then she rolled him over and checked his pulse. She began mouth-to-mouth resuscitation, then palpitated his heart. "Come back!" she cried. "Come back!"

Above her, his spirit floated. Her spirit joined him, as she kept resuscitating his body.

"What's going on?" her spirit asked his.

"Life isn't worth living," his spirit replied. "The planet's dying. Adults keep talking about saving the Earth, but we continue to kill each other and our home. Give me one reason to live."

"Because it is people like you, who are aware, who can change the trend. There are almost enough people *acting* environmentally to produce the hundredth-monkey effect."

"No, it's all talk. I see it all the time. Even with my parents. They talk environment, and then they go to McDonalds and eat food that is full of preservatives and hormones and genetically engineered, and throw their paper plate, paper cup, and plastic ware into the trash. No, nothing is changing; we're a convenience society. It's all talk. There's no future for us kids."

His spirit began to rise further. A bright white light drew him upward. Turning toward it, she pleaded, "But if *you* give up and others like *us*, then we don't just lose the battle, we lose the war. It's more than just the children who are at stake. It's your dog, your sister, your parents, and that robin in the tree. You can help. In your body, you can help by *doing*, not just talking. You can show people how to bring talk into action with integrity. It's all about the physical and how we manifest the spirit of love through our every thought and action." But he was fading.

Finally, Bear and Joseph arrived at the scene. Bear stood to the side listening to the woman and boy's conversation. Joseph relieved the woman from the physical resuscitation. Nodding a thank you, she sat on a nearby rock.

"Don't you understand?" the woman's spirit pleaded with the boy's. "If you give up, we lose the spirit world too. There is no difference between the two. We need each other!"

His advancing spirit stopped. As the white light drew him, he turned to her, then back toward the light.

"Ask God if it is your time?" she offered.

"What God?" he sneered.

"Ask the light, then. You can feel it call you." She prayed, *God, angels of the light, speak the truth to this boy. If it is his contract to transition and the contract is still viable now, I let him go in love. But if not, let him know the truth.* Her field was a brilliant gold as she prayed.

A beam of shimmering gold light radiated into his spirit body. The message was clear. "Go forth and be not a *spokes*person but a *model* of living, caring action. Your contract is to assist in bringing the spirit of love into matter. Go now and begin your work. And leave your wailing victim archetype behind. Leave him here in the white light. Go now."

Joseph called out, "He's breathing!"

Just as his mother and Sid breathlessly approached, the boy's spirit body returned to its physical body. Simultaneously, the boy gasped for air.

Throwing herself on the ground, the mother lifted his head into her arms, kissing his face over and over again. She held him tight as tears streamed down her face.

Sid reached the bank and ran over to the hiker who saved the boy's life. "Victoria, it *was* you! Are you okay?" he asked with the love only a man can have for a woman.

They embraced. Sid's entire body flushed with energy.

"Yes," she said, holding him tight.

Joseph, looking on, nodded and smiled.

Bear called the ambulance on her cell phone. She thought it best to stay clear of any more miraculous happenings. Joseph and Sid carried the boy to the road. When the ambulance came, they each hugged and blessed the mother and squeezed the hand of the young boy. He would be safe now.

Victoria leaned over him a bit longer. Gazing into his eyes, he recognized her and nodded.

Running Bear, Joseph, and Sid walked back to the site of their original meeting, as Victoria waited on the outskirts of their circle. They performed a closing ceremony, thanking Earth Mother and Grandfather Tree. After setting the next meeting time, they met Victoria and walked out of the woods together. Sid introduced Victoria to Joseph and Bear. They were all talking at once about the event, and Victoria reluctantly excused herself, and with obvious hesitation, parted from the group.

CHAPTER 10

In the Light Again

Victoria arrived at her healing room at 7:50 pm, just enough time to energetically ground herself before Lucifer came. She sat in her healing chair and took several deep abdominal breaths—inhaling through her nose and exhaling through a small opening of her mouth. With this relaxing yogic breath, her field immediately regenerated with shimmering gold light. A calm swept over her. Each breath brightened her being. After filling the room with shimmering gold light, she felt the spirits of her guardian angel, Archangel Michael; Christ, the radiant one; and blessed Mother Mary.

"Thank you for coming," she said to the spirit essences. "Have you come to assist me with my meeting with Lucifer?"

"Yes," they responded.

Lucifer spoke from a distance. He had not entered the golden room. "No," he said empathetically. "Victoria, you must do this alone. Send your friends home. This is our contract, and it must be done alone, as we agreed. I promise, no harm will come to you. Now send them away."

Nothing further needed to be said. Christ, Mary, and Michael lifted off, moving out of range but not too far.

"Have you cleared Martha's soul?" Victoria demanded.

"Check it out yourself."

She tuned into Martha. Clear as crystal. "Thank you," she said, meeting his eyes.

"Now to your part of the bargain," Lucifer quipped, approaching her.

"I don't remember any bargain," she said, holding out her hand to stop his approach.

He beamed her a time when they were both angels in God's court. Lucifer, God's favorite angel, was the most radiant and talented and loving of all the angels. Victoria and he were dear friends. Victoria's whole being filled with compassion for Lucifer. Their love flowed freely, and her memory awakened.

"We used to play, and you teased me mercilessly. Oh how we loved each other. So free we were, and happy." She remembered many such times. But quickly her sweet smile faded as she saw the scene of Lucifer leaving the court to build his own kingdom. "What happened to you?" she said. "Why did you leave? It broke my heart to see what became of you. We all died some and heaven's light diminished."

"When I went to the other side, you contacted me and pledged that when the time was right, you would assist me in coming back to the light."

She gasped and her heart skipped a beat. Could she have agreed to do that? She was just a lower-middle-class kid from Chicago. Slowly she said, "How do I do it?"

"If I knew, I wouldn't need your help! *You know.*"

She sat quietly for a time, breathing softly. "Like you do each day with the shadow aspects of the souls of your clients," her inner voice reminded her.

Gently at first, then louder as the notes released from her, she sounded ancient clearing tones. Several notes harmonized simultaneously as she moved her hands in a mysterious manner to draw out the darkness that had filled Lucifer's soul. For several minutes, she pulled black energy from his field. With each release, she toned deeper. The room was filled with swirling energy. A gold light vortex, created for such purposes, lifted the darkness up and transformed it into the light of love. After about twenty minutes, the entire room was radiant and standing in the center was the most glorious archangel of them all: Archangel Lucifer. Oh, yes this was the angel she had known and loved so long ago. She was filled with tears of joy.

Archangel Lucifer gently caressed her cheek and said, "Thank you. We have much work to do now. I will see you again soon." And he was gone as quickly as he had come.

She burst into tears.

CHAPTER 11

Another View

*V*ictoria's bright, plant-filled healing room was alive and vibrant, full of grace. The sun shimmered through the large floor ferns potted in huge turquoise pots, making intricate patterns of shadow and light on the adjacent walls. On the right wall was a five-foot palm tree that gave the room a regal look. Not only were the plants vibrantly healthy, but they were in service to help keep the healing space in a high vibration. The plant devas, specific to each plant, in Victoria's healing room, as in her house, loved to be part of work that was saving the planet. Sometimes when Victoria needed extra energy or encouragement, she tuned into the plants and expressed her deep love and appreciation for their assistance. They beamed her back vibrant universal life force energy. A sense of refreshed calm came over her.

The brownish gold pine paneling added to the sunny feeling. At the far end of the room was a small altar with the four sacred elements present: earth, air, fire, and water. There were fresh flowers, a bottle of holy water from Greece, and two healing crystal spheres that encircled a pink candle in a spiral brass candlestick holder. Sacred fire breathed sacred air. These divine objects rested on a beautiful pink, green, and white summer floral cloth.

The crystal spheres were very special to her. She purchased the rose quartz crystal when she was recovering from a serious blood disease. And beloved friends and clients gave the clear quartz crystal to her for her birthday one year. She used the clear quartz crystal sphere for lifting cancer, candida, rheumatoid arthritis, and other autoimmune system diseases.

Each morning before the sacred work began, she cleansed the room with the smoke of burning sage and cedar, called in the four directions, and thanked the angels for guarding the space. A powerful gold vortex over her property and a large part of the neighborhood kept the vibration high and full of love.

The light blue massage table was set against the wall. Beside it, a large wicker chair faced an oak chair where Victoria sat. A doctor's stool stood next to the massage table, and next to Victoria's light oak chair was the sacred altar.

For several months now, Victoria had been receiving clients with past-life histories in wars. Each of the clients carried the past wars in their energetic fields, and it affected their present lives. One man had chronic pain in his right shoulder. After every imaginable medical test, the cause was still unknown. Victoria regressed him to the past life where the original wound occurred, so that it might be healed. He had been killed in battle; however, the guilt of being a warrior lay heavy on his soul. She helped him let that go and filled the guilt energy with love.

This morning the trend continued. The clients were a young man, Ralph, and his wife, Miria, who were being hounded by federal agents. Their house had been ransacked, and their phones tapped.

After the opening prayer and invocation, Victoria listened to their tale. As they were describing the men who were harassing them, Victoria could sense a past-life connection between the husband and the wife and the federal agents. Ralph lay down comfortably on the massage table, and Victoria chelated him. Afterwards, returning to his feet, she tuned into the cause of the conflict. It was the Vietnam war. Ralph went into a deep trance, as his wife bore witness.

Victoria saw Ralph as a Vietcong who had gathered a group of young kids to fight. He had armed them with weapons. Ralph's present-day wife was his little sister, whom he had the responsibility to keep from harm. Their village was being attacked, and he rushed to its defense. Three of the Americans he shot were the same souls who were harassing them today. Ralph was killed, and so was his sister. In the scene, the Americans vowed revenge. Much blood was shed in the village, and Victoria called forth all the souls who had died in this battle and lifted their trauma to the light of love. She proceeded to cleanse the village's energetic field.

Then her healing partner, the spirit of Christ, the radiant one, said: "Before the Earth can heal, all of the wars must be cleansed from the planet, and in so doing, they will be cleansed from the global mind. The global mind must be cleared of the wars and the lesser conflicts that consume human daily life, before the Earth can reach peace, for it is the mind of each individual that continues to create war. You are clearing an aspect of the Vietnam war now. So, let us continue. Call forth all the souls who were killed in this war, and we, with the assistance of the healing angels, will transform this energy into the light."

With an incantation, Victoria summoned the souls who were killed in the Vietnam war. Downtrodden, sullen, bent over in grief over a life missed, they paraded across the center of the room. One soul still wept for her baby. Some spirits carried their maimed bodies with them. Other souls were jubilant of their victory—Americans, Vietnamese, French, and even some English.

As the souls came through, Victoria, the angels, and other spirit guides cleared and blessed them, lifting the trauma of the war from their light bodies, souls, and consciousness. The dark energies of the war rose and were guided by angels through a powerful gold light vortex that raised their vibration to love.

Then the spirit of Christ guided her to begin the cleansing of Earth where the battles had occurred. First they energetically swept the land with a vibrant violet light to cleanse the fear and hate from the buildings, soil, plants, and animals. Next, Victoria chanted ancient cleansing sounds into the Earth. Many war victims' souls were stuck in the ground. As she chanted, the souls rose up and were cleared of the war trauma. Then they were released from this dimension and went to their right and perfect place—the next step in their evolutionary journey. From the sky came beautiful gold rays of light that penetrated deep into the Earth's surface, raising the vibration to love. From battlefield to battlefield, they combed the land, purifying and blessing it. With each new section, Victoria could feel the global mind lightening and brightening. Earth sighed with relief.

When complete, Victoria smiled and the spirit of Christ said, "Your work is not over yet. Now call in all the souls of the bereaved families and friends."

At his command, the souls began to gather, eager to be freed of their pain and suffering. Again, Victoria and Christ lifted their grief, smoothed their light bodies, and blessed them. By this time, Victoria was gently crying. She felt the tremendous grief and the relief of each soul.

Finally, she brought her attention back to her clients. She smoothed Ralph's energy field and encircled him with gold light.

"I give thanks to the spirit guides and angels who assisted in this healing. And I pray for continued healing and wholing of Ralph and Miria. This healing will continue for several days. Now I return your healings and your spirits to you."

Stillness filled the room, as Ralph sat up slowly and Miria blinked to focus. As they returned to full consciousness, they looked around the room wide eyed and sighed.

"I feel lighter and deeply rested," Ralph said, still a little dazed.

"After you cleared our souls in Vietnam, I felt many other entities enter the room. What happened?" Miria asked.

Victoria briefly described the healings. "You see, we must cleanse the collective unconscious before we can truly reach peace on Earth. Your healing allowed us an entry point into the war so we could help transcend it."

"But how could the souls get caught in the Earth? When they died, why didn't they go to the other side?" Miria probed.

Ralph sat quietly, eyes staring blankly.

"Often in war or some other violent death, such as getting hit by a car, the soul gets trapped in the body. Wherever the body is placed or thrown, in the case of road kill or war victims, the soul gets stuck. If it does not get released within three days, it, or at least an aspect of it, may stay on this plane. It can also happen if a soul hasn't finished its spiritual business on the Earth plane. If it stays too long, it can get stuck. There are literally hundreds of thousands of stuck souls down here called discarnates."

"What do you mean by soul fragment?" Miria queried, leaning forward in rapt attention.

"A soul is like a hologram, so if a fragment or an aspect of the soul is trapped somewhere, it appears as if the entire soul is there. Other aspects of the soul can still incarnate. Your soul is living several lives simultaneously. It is in this lifetime that many of us have chosen to ascend. That means we must gather all of our soul fragments from past, present, future, and parallel dimensions into our present soul body. As we do this, each of these lifetimes must be healed and cleared, so that the soul returns to its fullest vibrancy. Only then can the soul fully ascend. Which, by the way, does not mean going up and out, as previously thought, but rather becoming a radiant spirit that is integrated into the physical body. Spirit into matter, as it were. With this then, the soul can truly be one with God and radiate at the golden vibration of love. Christ modeled this for us, and it is now time for us to step into the light in this powerful way. We must become the light of love." Victoria was getting excited as she spoke. She had spent so many years clearing herself and working through the dark night of the soul, and now she was excited about the prospect of ascension actually happening.

"So you were clearing the soul fragments of the people who suffered a death in the Vietnam war?" Miria asked. "How do these fragments know where to go? Do they go to present time or another time in the past or some parallel life?"

"Good question. They go to the most dominant essence that can carry their particular vibration. For example, *my* soul fragments would come to me in this lifetime, because it is this lifetime in which I am healing all of my lifetimes. If I locate a soul fragment in a healing session, we heal the issues it is carrying and then physically integrate it into the person's soul. Sometimes it feels quite strange for a while, like a close friend you haven't seen in a long time who has come home. You feel fuller, yet lighter, all at the same time."

"So," Miria continued, "will the thugs stop bothering us?"

"I hope so, unless there is more to the story. It appears you have agreed in a previous life to practice a deeply spiritual life this time. The thugs are your wake-up call. If you listen, your chances are good that they will leave you alone. If you ignore the signal, your trouble will continue."

"What do we do?"

"I've introduced you to the angels today. Come and participate in my angel class, and you will learn how to communicate and allow the angels to actively help you, as well as how you can actively help them. There must always be an energy exchange, for all energy goes in a circle. What goes out comes back magnified to the intensity of the emotion it is carrying. For example, if you are in love and loving someone, you will get love back, hopefully from the person you want it from!" Victoria laughed. "As we are nearing the end of our session, do you have any other questions or comments?"

They both shook their heads. They hugged each other, and Victoria gave them a flyer for the angel class as she saw them out.

Hues of orange, yellow, and pink blended into the horizon over the ocean as the sun set on a beautiful warm July day. Sid and Victoria were entwined like sailors' rope in a deep discussion of Buddhism. Their energetic fields were glowing rays of purple, yellow, and blue as they passionately expressed their views of the dharma, or the way to enlightenment.

"I find it curious that your entire premise to enlightenment was through eradicating craving," she said, "when it was *your* very craving to eradicate suffering that brought you to enlightenment."

"As I look back on it," he responded, "I was so shocked by the suffering I saw outside the castle on the streets and in the town. I remember the pain searing through my body like a hot sword when I saw the decrepit old man that first time outside the grounds. My father attempted to hide all the sick and suffering from me, but some unaware old man wandered into my view. Stunned, I couldn't believe my eyes. The sense of helplessness was overwhelming. I had been raised a prince with nothing but youth, beauty, and splendor all around. When I reached sexual maturity, I had the pick of the women on the court and I chose a beautiful wife. That was my reality. That was my *entire* reality. Old age, disease, suffering, deformity, and death were not known to me."

"Funny you should say that, Sid. Did you mean it to be a pun?"

"What do you mean?" he replied.

"Well," she said, "you left the palace to figure out how to end suffering, and you *really* made it an illusion of the mind through rigorous mind-control techniques of the Eightfold Path. But in the meantime you white-washed life."

"What do you mean, once again?" Sid asked, now pensive and open to listen. "Are you being unduly hard on me, Victoria?"

"Okay, look at it this way," she said. "Your premise was that there was suffering because we crave continual existence, sensual pleasures, fame, and power, etcetera. Deep desire for these life aspects produces actions that cause more karma, which in turn will cause another rebirth, which means another life of suffering. How am I doing so far?"

He nodded. "Go on."

"Cravings produce attachment, which starts the whole cycle again," she continued. "The belief that our soul is permanent became a source of attachment for people, so you taught that we are all of one universal soul, held together by five aggregates, or *skandhas*: matter, sensation, perception, predisposition, and consciousness." With a stick, she began to draw a human figure in the sand. When the rather lopsided form was complete, she smiled and said with an Italian accent, "Okay, so I'm no da Vinci!"

They both laughed.

She then drew seven circles on the body, indicating the seven chakras. "It's interesting to me," she continued, "that if you place each of the five aggregates on the chakras, there is quite a startling revelation." She etched into the sand *matter* beside the first chakra, *sensation* beside the second chakra, *predisposition* beside the third chakra, *perception* beside the sixth chakra, and *consciousness* beside the seventh chakra.

"Matter," she continued, "is the first chakra. It is our most intimate connection to Mother Earth. The first chakra draws life-force energy up into our bodies. We are made of carbon-based molecules, just like Earth. In essence, we are Earth in a human shape and experience. So matter is the first chakra.

"Sensation is our ability to feel. Our senses come alive through the full spectrum of emotions: love, anger, fear, jealousy, resentment, glee, hate, and so on. These emotions and our issues around control are centered in the second chakra. Also in the second chakra are our opinions of ourselves that we learned from our parents. Codependency and addictions reside in the second chakra. So, sensation is a second-chakra issue.

Sid's eyes glistened as he listened to her. Victoria's aura was sparklingly with excitement of flashing gold, purple, green, blue, pink, and yellow.

She felt his distraction. "Are you with me?"

"Yes, yes, go on. I'm fascinated."

"Okay, predisposition is the personality, our predisposed character, and ego. It is in the third chakra, where self-esteem also resides." She paused, staring into the azure sky. "It just occurred to me," she said, taking an excited leap into the air, "that fear is also in the third chakra. That's probably why we are so afraid of who we really are, and why we're so entangled with the ego, who is our voice for fear. What a web we weave!"

Sid watched with interest.

"Anyway, perception is the sixth chakra; it includes our thoughts, our house of wisdom, etcetera. Finally, consciousness is the seventh chakra. Sid, look at the drawing. Doesn't something stand out to you?"

"Yes. That's very good thinking," he said with a little grin.

"Yours or mine?"

"Mine. I, I, I, mean yours."

They both laughed.

"Sid, the fourth and fifth chakras are completely missing from your soul aggregate. The fourth chakra is the heart, the chakra of love, forgiveness, and relationship. The fifth chakra is the throat. It is the first connection to the divine, or the spiritual realm. The fifth chakra is the chakra of spiritual creativity. Sid, there is no love or relationship or forgiveness or creative rapture in your model."

Sid gazed at her sand drawing. "Yes, you're right," he said. "How interesting. I must have closed my heart to block the suffering." He stared off into space, deep in thought. After a long pause, but still with that far-away look, he said, "At first, I was overwhelmed by the suffering and no way to help. Then, when my mind became involved in the eightfold path, I was focused away from the suffering and on the solution of right speech, right action, right livelihood, right effort, right mindfulness, right concentration, right views, right intentions."

"Yes," Victoria replied in her teaching voice, "and there again, if you categorize the eight disciplines into three segments you get moral conduct, mental discipline, and intuitive wisdom. Moral conduct is first chakra, along with the tribal laws; mental discipline is third chakra; and intuitive wisdom is sixth chakra. Totally negating the heart again. I think this is why I've been so upset with you for thousands of years. For me, you missed the entire point of life. Life is to love, to be in relationship, to feel the vibrancy of living, not escape it."

"Yes, that's why you followed Christ. He was the teacher of love," Sid mused.

Her compassionate, loving eyes gazed at him. "Your whole being was so shocked by the suffering. And there was really no one to share that pain with, was there?"

"No, my life was cut out to be kind and rule, but it didn't fit. May father was a kind and generous king, and still so much suffering, disease, and death existed. I had to make a new path."

She nodded.

"Please continue."

"Are you sure?

"Yes, yes go ahead. I'm interested."

"Okay then, later in Buddhist history," Victoria said softly but with intention and strength, "the heart aspect was integrated into the philosophy of Buddhism. The dharma had to become easier if more people were going to join. Later, Mahayana taught that the Buddha nature is in everyone, not that enlightenment is reserved for the elite few and only one Buddha can exist in an eon, as we see in the Theravada teachings. So, though you left your princedom," she continued cautiously, "rambled about the country side starving yourself for the first several years of your impassioned search, you still incorporated elitism and exclusivity into your belief structure to enlightenment. I remember that *really* irking me."

"I see the contradictions in my early actions. You're right: I never would have strived so hard if my heart weren't breaking from witnessing humans' slow self-destruction. And sometimes not so slow." Sid bowed his head and wept. After a moment or two, he took a long breath. His eyes fluttered and closed. He drifted off into the emptiness of peace, that place of solace and safety.

She realized all at once his deep sensitivity, and her heart beamed him love. What courage he had to face the plight of suffering and to resolve to offer solace. His teachings changed the world, and she was grateful for a fuller understanding. Her long-held anger completely melted away.

She sat softly beside him, gently placed her hand on his chest, and kissed his cheek.

With quivering eyes, he squeezed her hand and said, "I love you Victoria. I love you." Then he released a long sigh.

CHAPTER 12

The Miracles of Angels

B ud wandered around the neighborhood, trying to avoid everyone. As if for the first time, he noticed the worn-down houses and the litter scattered on the street. The low ceiling of the gray clouds seemed to press on him. Kicking an empty beer can, he wondered what to do, where to go. He was so lost in his thoughts that he almost walked right into a telephone pole. Regaining his balance, from the corner of his eye, he saw a flyer: ANGEL CLASS. His neck whipped around. SATURDAY at 10:00 am.

That was in half an hour! He had to go. Double-checking the address, he calculated that if he caught the next bus, he could arrive on time.

What luck: a bus was coming down the street that very moment. With a mighty spring of anticipation, he leapt onto the bus.

Victoria had just finished setting the energy in the classroom, when the students began to arrive. She wore golden embossed linen pants and a vest, with a beige silk blouse. The pants were very wide and loose fitting. Though casual, the outfit was elegant, and flowed when she moved. The small seminar room was set in the quiet woods at a Presbyterian retreat center. The wall of the fireplace was covered by beautiful golden cedar paneling. The other walls were a soft texture, with hues of yellow orange like the sun, warm and calming. She had set a gold light vortex over the little building their class was in, to raise the energy to the level of the Christ light.

The morning sun shone through the east window and glistened through the clear crystal ball she had on the altar on the eastern wall. While daisies danced on the altar in the sunlight, her iPad chanted "Om Namaha Shivaya," recorded by Robert Gass, in the background.

"Good morning," exclaimed Victoria as Aaron and Melissa walked in.

Exchanging hugs, they took a breath of relaxation. After signing the register and paying the tuition, Aaron got some hot tea and Melissa got a glass of lemon water. They had been to Victoria's classes and knew the routine. They would need plenty of water during the day to help their bodies process all of the cellular changes.

After greeting each participant with a loving, radiant smile and hug, Victoria guided them to the drinks and a comfortable chair. She wanted each person to feel safe and welcomed.

Next Ralph and Miria arrived, still glowing from their recent healing.

"Good to see you, and bless you." Victoria hugged Bill and Mary, who were both new people. *How had they heard about the class?* She wondered.

Several other people sauntered in and got settled.

As everyone nestled into their chairs and relaxed, a shuffle sounded at the door, then a knock. Must be someone new. As Victoria opened the door, Bud started to turn away. "May I help you?" she asked, realizing the boy's confusion.

"Is this the place for the angel class?" he blurted out.

She could feel his embarrassment, and reached out her hand to his and said, "Yes, you found us. Come in. We're just ready to begin, so you are right on time."

He sighed in relief as she showed him to the one empty chair in the circle. The participants welcomed him with smiles and bright eyes. He nodded self-consciously, and he slouched in his chair, as if trying very hard to disappear.

Before Victoria could sit down, someone else knocked.

The boy she had pulled out of the river several days earlier timidly entered. Their eyes met and acknowledged each other. Her smile assured him of his safety, and Melissa pulled up a chair for him.

"Welcome," Victoria said, "and good morning."

"Good morning," everyone said in unison.

"Let us open with the song 'Morning Has Broken,' by Cat Stevens. Please stand and hold hands. You will know when to let your partners' hands go when you feel a squeeze come around the circle."

Several of the new people were obviously uncomfortable holding someone's hand. They looked down, hesitated, closed their eyes, and then very lightly took a person's hand on each side. As everyone sang along, "Morning has broken, like the new dawn," they began to sway to the music and soon lost their uneasiness in the safety and love that filled the room.

When the song ended, Victoria prayed, "Mother Father, God, we give thanks for the opportunity to come together and share your grace, power, and presence. With each breath, let us be filled with your love and know that your love is all that is or need be. I now call in the angels of light to join us and assist us in learning about you and your beautiful mission on Earth. Thank you, God. Blessed be." She squeezed the hand on her right and then on her left. As the squeeze went around the room, people let go of their partners' hands and were seated.

Bud nodded to the person next to him and even managed a little smile.

"It is our tradition to do check-in, but first let me review the guidelines we follow to keep this space safe enough for each of you to share the truth about yourself and your feelings. To ensure that you feel safe to explore your inner self, with as much depth as you wish:

> Speak from the 'I' center. That means use the pronoun
> 'I' instead the commonly used 'you.' This gives you
> powerful ownership for your thoughts and feelings.

No judgments. Things aren't good or bad here, they just are.

Give no advice. Giving advice disempowers people and cheats them out of an opportunity to grow. Now, if someone asks for advice, answer with, 'Are you sure?' Nine times out of ten, with some thought, the person will reply, 'No, actually. Thanks anyway.'

Listen with your heart. As others speak, open your heart to them and focus entirely on them. Don't think about what you will say when your turn comes. Planning your speech is living in the future. Practice being in the present while you're here.

Respect each person for the divine being he or she is.

No cross-talk. That means, when it's your turn to speak, no one will interrupt you or ask you questions. You have the floor for one minute, max.

Everything said here is confidential. That means it does not leave this room, and we do not talk about it among ourselves. You may share your personal experience with others outside the group, but not another's experience.

Are there any other guidelines you would like to help you feel safe?" Victoria paused for a response, and several students shook their heads. "All right then, during check-in, please state your name and how you are doing today. If you have something on your mind that is blocking you from being fully present, place it in the center of the circle, and we will help you lift it off into the cosmos to be transformed into love. Also, tell us what your expectations are for the day. Remember, you have one minute. Now, close your eyes for a moment and bring your energy down to your heart and into the ground to the center of the

Earth. Now, ask yourself, 'What are my expectations for the day?' I will give you a moment." Victoria paused for a few moments, allowing the group to clear any mental chatter and decide what they were going to say.

"Now," she continued, "you all know what you are going to say, so you can give your full attention to the person speaking. Who would like to start?" She held up the rose quartz crystal used as a talking stick, fondly called Rosey.

Melissa took the crystal and began. "I'm Melissa. I feel great and full today, and I'm excited about meeting my guardian angel and whatever other angels I may encounter." Smiling broadly, she passed Rosey to the person on her right, going clockwise around the circle.

Bill held the stone for a moment, choosing his words carefully. "I am Bill." He paused, holding his breath. He crossed his legs and folded his arms tightly across his chest. "Today I am grateful for the position I have on the food chain."

Several participants gave knowing smiles.

"I have been a minister for fifteen years," Bill continued, "and I have never met my guardian angel. I can't even believe I never thought of it until recently, but today I break that barrier." He passed the crystal to the right.

"I'm Val. I've been sick to my stomach all morning, but I wouldn't miss this class for the world. I am already in communication with my guardian angel because I took this class last year, but I love being in the energy here. And something wonderful always happens. So here I am," she giggled.

When it came time for Bud to speak, his face turned bright red. Breathless, he blurted out, "I don't know what to say!"

"Start with your name," Victoria nodded.

After some hesitation and a shallow breath, he said, "My name is Bud, and I saw the flyer on this class this morning and something in me said go. So here I am. I have no idea what this is even about."

Everyone laughed knowingly, and Victoria said, "Then you're in good company, Bud. No one else knows what to expect either! Thanks for listening to your inner voice."

Taking the crystal from Bud, sixteen-year-old Jerry rolled Rosey in his damp, sweaty hands and pondered it in silence. Then he took a deep breath and looked up at Victoria with beseeching eyes.

Victoria nodded encouragingly to him.

"I am Jerry. My life really changed recently when I drowned in the river," he said, bowing his head and looking up tentatively with only his eyes. "Thanks to Victoria, I am alive today." He paused to search for words. "When I died, I was hopeless, despondent. There was nothing to live for. Everywhere I looked, I could only see the destruction of our planet, broken promises from the adults in charge. As my spirit hung above my body, it looked so meaningless and helpless. There was a strong pull from a brilliant white light, but Victoria helped me see that I *did* have a purpose, much bigger than my present self-pity.

"Things changed when I returned home from the hospital," he continued, now making eye contact with the others and breathing more calmly. Everyone's focus was on him, in rapt attention. "I began to see all the vibrant life around me. Grass pushing up through tiny cracks in the cement, just for an opportunity to live. Little squirrels burying their winter store. Flowers blooming. Life was everywhere. I don't understand how I missed it before. Today I am going to step into my commitment to help the planet. Today I will receive help from the angels to do my work." He exhaled, deeply relieved, and passed the crystal to Victoria; she always went last.

"Thank you, Jerry, for sharing that story. I am *very* glad to see you here, and that goes to all of you." Her loving gaze went around the circle personally acknowledging each person in the room. "I am Victoria."

Everyone laughed.

"Today," Victoria continued, "it is my pleasure to help you connect with your guardian angels and other helping angels. The spirit world is as organized as our physical world. We have kingdoms here: the plant kingdom, the mineral kingdom, and the animal kingdom. There is also an angelic kingdom, which is as well organized as every other kingdom. Today you will be introduced to your personal guardian angel. Now, just imagine for a moment," she continued, "what it would be like to have the perfect devoted friend—someone to help you out when you are in trouble, sick, or worried. Plus, this best friend, your angel, has far more power than you can access now.

"My favorite angel story is about a plane crash. A full passenger plane was flying to its destination, and one of the engines blew up and then caught fire. One side of the plane blew open, causing tremendous suction, like a tornado. Several people were sucked out of the plane to their deaths. A woman reached to a man across the aisle and grabbed his hand. He was in the next row from the people who had just blown out of the plane. Holding onto him for dear life, she thought, 'This may be the last person I ever see or touch. God, if you are out there, help us now.' And in a holy instant, from the open gap in the plane, she saw a huge, magnificent angel fly under the plane, level it out, and bring it to a gentle landing." Victoria's voiced choked, and tears welled up in her eyes. Though she had heard hundreds of heroic angel stories, this one always touched her deeply. She paused to let in the power of the story.

There was a murmur throughout the room.

"Wow," burst out Bud. "Really?!"

"Yes, really." Victoria laughed. "And there are hundreds of similar stories. Angels are here to assist us. But you have a responsibility also."

"Oh, I knew there'd be a catch!" Bud blurted out.

Victoria cocked her head. "Not like you think. It's not a catch. The angels help everyone, the so-called good and bad people. Each person has a guardian angel who watches over him or her. But think of it this way: wouldn't you want to give something back in return? Isn't the greatest gift you can give, service without any expectation to get anything back?

"Just like the angels!" Jerry said, with a little leap, as if he'd caught a fly ball.

"Maybe the highest purpose of working with angels is to teach us how to be one," said Bill, with a huge smile and twinkle in his eyes.

"Yes! You got it!" said Victoria, laughing."

"How do we start?" Bill asked.

"Well, first understand how the angels work. They do everything with unconditional love, without judgment. They do everything for the highest good of all. They practice what I call high courtesy. So do the same. Always thank your angels for coming to speak with you. Always thank them for their help. Always send them back to their right and perfect place when your meeting is complete. Pretty simple, isn't it?"

"Does meditating help?" asked Val.

"Yes, as you learn to meditate and practice it regularly, your mind quiets and you can hear the subtle voice of your inner knowing or higher self, and your guardian angel. Those voices are on a spiritual channel. Quieting your mind attunes you. Meditating is a spiritual practice, so are daily prayer, chanting, sacred dance, and so forth. It's like when you begin a weight training program: you start out with light weights and build to heavier ones as your muscles grow. The same principle applies to spiritual practice. Hence, when we perform spiritual practice regularly, we build spiritual muscle."

"Also, repetition of anything builds chi around it," interjected Melissa. "Be it a breathing exercise, meditation, weight lifting, reading, or prayer."

"Precisely." Victoria continued. "Thank you, Melissa. The more chi, or energy, surrounding an activity, the stronger it will get. That is why it is best to mediate or pray at a regular time each day and in the same place; you create a force field that holds the energy of prayer or meditation. This field supports your prayer and raises your vibration to assist you in connecting and communicating with the angels."

"My football coach," Jerry said, "taught us the principle of the three P's. Practice. Practice. Practice."

"Exactly," said Victoria. "Each time you practice, three things happen: First, chi is built around and through the activity, giving it substance. Second, new neurological pathways are myelinated in the brain, actually forming new circuitry. Third, you build muscle memory. So, like Jerry said, practice, practice, practice!"

Everyone laughed.

"What if I ask the angels to do something bad? Will they still help?" asked Bill, the minister.

"The angels work for the highest good of all. Their mission is to keep you safe, not satisfy your every whim," Victoria answered. "Humans battle with two wills: the divine will—which is God's will, or your soul's plan for you—and your ego or little self's will."

"The ego will is mostly the voice of fear," Melissa said, "whereas God's will is for your highest good."

"But how do we tell the difference?" asked Bill. "I think I hear God's voice talking to me, but sometimes what is said doesn't sound right."

"That's where the practice of meditation helps quiet the ego voice of fear and judgment, good and bad, and the should'a, could'a, would'as," Victoria said. "It is the practice of surrendering your ego will to God's will."

"You make surrendering our ego will to the divine will sound so easy," Bill said. "I've been trying my entire life and have rarely accomplished it."

"Well, Bill," inserted Aaron, who had not spoken yet this morning. "It takes PRACTICE. PRACTICE. PRACTICE."

Everyone laughed again.

"Let us continue this discussion after we meet our guardian angels. But first we'll take a break. Fluids in; fluids out. Be back in ten minutes," said Victoria.

There was plenty of fruit, tea, and juice to choose from for their snack. Jerry was unusually hungry, as was Bud. They met at the table, both diving into the fruit bowl.

"My brain must be burning up a lot of energy," Bud said, grabbing an orange slice. "I'm starved."

"I still don't understand the practice, practice, practice part," said Jerry. "Why can't the angels just do what we tell them, if that's their job anyway?"

"I don't know," said Bud. "Let's ask Victoria. Isn't she something else?"

"Yeah, *really* something else." Jerry said, nodding vigorously.

Victoria sounded a chime at the end of ten minutes, and everyone reconvened.

"Time to meet your guardian angel," began Victoria. "Close your eyes and take several deep belly breaths. Feel yourself being supported in your chair. May all the thoughts of our discussion wash away, leaving a beautiful calm. Keep your eyes closed." While angel music played softly in the background, she began the incantation.

"Blessed angels, we thank you for your time and service.
We thank you for your patience and love.
We know that you are here to guide and protect us.
And we are grateful for your loving care.

"I call forth the angels of light to join us now," Victoria proclaimed. As she paused, she saw several participants feel the gentle flutter of wings and warm loving glow.

"I thank you for coming," she continued. "And now take several deep breaths. Breathe your energy deep into the center of the Earth to ground and quiet you. With each breath, sink deeper into relaxation.

"I now call in the guardian angel," she continued, "of each participant to stand at his or her left side. Angels, make yourself known to your charge. Now, students, from your heart, extend your energetic field to your angel. Next, sit quietly and listen and feel. You may feel the fluttering of the angel's wings. Or you may feel a temperature change. You may hear something. You may smell something. I will give you a moment to connect." She paused for several minutes.

"Now, ask your guardian angel its name." She again paused a moment. "Ask it what message it has for you." She gave them time to listen. "Now ask it any questions you may have. You may receive your answers through visible symbols or words or feelings." She let several minutes pass.

"Thank your angel for being in service to you all these years. Now, ask the angel what *you* can do for it." She hoped their angels would ask for something so there would be a return on the energy, to complete the circle. "Next create some sort of code to communicate with each other. For example, the angel may tap you on the shoulder if it wants to communicate with you or gently call your name. You two decide." She paused. "In closing, give thanks for the meeting and the information and love shared. You may visualize hugging your angel in gratitude.

"Now, gently bring yourself back and feel yourself in your chair. Lightly wiggle your fingers and your toes, bend over and touch your toes, and say hello to someone in the room."

The music faded out, and the participants slowly came back. Some obviously liked the peaceful place they were in so well that coming back was difficult. After several minutes, everyone had said hello.

"Stand up and stretch, and then we will share our experiences," Victoria said.

Everyone took a moment to stretch. Some sighed, others blinked as they returned energetically.

Victoria held Rosey up. "Who would like to share first?"

Bud took Rosey. "I can't believe it. I saw her! She was beautiful. So bright. Her wings were this big." He stretched his arms out as far as he could reach. He was shaking with excitement. "She said her only job was to watch over me and make sure I was *safe*. She said she *loved* me. I've never had anyone say those things to me before." And he exploded into tears.

Victoria waited a moment, but the dam had burst and Bud's floodwaters would gush for a while. Astute to the potential miracle at hand, she gently went to him and sat at his feet, wrapping her arms around one of his legs. She signaled the other participants to gather around and gently touch or caress him.

Soon the entire class had surrounded him. His tears continued with as much force as they had begun. The angels gathered too.

Bill stood behind him and stroked his head. Victoria saw how love flowed from Bill's eyes and filled Bud with such great tenderness that Bill also started to cry. Loneliness rose up in him, and the unconditional love present in the room refilled him. Victoria smiled knowingly.

Then she turned her attention to Mary, who was crying openly with Bud as she felt his and her own grief well up and get washed away by the intense presence of love in the room.

"God," Mary whispered, "forgive me for my closed heart. I did not know of this love before." Crying harder, she whispered, "Thank you, God."

With tears running down her cheeks, Melissa stroked Bud's arms. Her aura was a glistening, shimmering green ray of love that penetrated into Bud's body.

Jerry sat beside Bud's other leg. Victoria saw him hesitate and draw back slightly. Bud *was* a Black kid from a gang and definitely from the "wrong side of the tracks." But, once Jerry felt Bud's leg, he knew no separation. As he held Bud's leg, he was Bud: a confused, angry, lonely kid. Victoria watched as their two energetic fields merged into one—no borders, just oneness. When Jerry looked up, his eyes brightened at the sight of his own guardian angel, luminous white light, wrapped around *his* leg. Bursting into tears, he understood. "Thank you, God. Thank you, God. Thank you, God," he muttered. "Thank you, God."

Now Victoria's attention went to Aaron. One of her jobs as a facilitator was to make sure each participant was safe and not becoming overwhelmed by the energy or emotions. Aaron was standing behind Bud, with his hands on his shoulders. Victoria saw Aaron's energy ground into the Earth and move out around the circle. He was always helping others. She heard his angel say, "Let go, Aaron, you don't have to do anything here. You don't need to support. You are being supported. You are being supported. You are being supported." The whisper faded out. With that, a rush of heat flowed through him, and his muscles went limp. Reaching for a chair before he fell, he looked around and saw his guardian angel unbelievably magnificent. She smiled at him, and he broke down in tears. All those years of being the provider, the strong one, were washed away in an instant. *He* was being supported. "Wow," Aaron mumbled through his tears, as he recalled Jesus' saying, "Let me carry your yoke… I will make your burden light." A wondrous ray of gold loving light surrounded him, and his shoulders slumped, as he sighed in relief.

The room glistened with shimmering gold light. Angels encircled the group, radiating unconditional love. In each student, cellular changes were being made. Deep holes of neglect were filled. Crevasses of hate were replaced with love and hope.

After several more minutes, Victoria began a prayer: "Divine love, so present in this place. Thank you for filling us with grace. May we remember these moments and bring them with us throughout our days ahead. Blessed Be."

Slowly each participant left Bud's side, each saying thank you to him in his or her own way. Victoria kissed his knee and muttered yet another prayer. Jerry caressed his leg with loving gratitude. Bill kissed the top of his head, blessing him. Melissa squeezed his hand and whispered, "Thank you. Praise be to the power and presence of God."

Once they were back in their chairs, Bud made eye contact with each person, nodding in gratitude. His checks were stained with tears, and his eyes full of wonder. He looked lighter and clearer as they sat in profound silence.

Victoria waited several minutes before she suggested they take a break. Trance-like and smiling, they got up and walked around. Soon everyone was talking and laughing, shaking their heads in wonderment. "Wow" was repeatedly heard throughout the room.

Finally, Victoria called them back into the circle. "Let us now continue with the grace of love prevailing. Please be seated. Would anyone else like to share?"

Aaron shared his experience of the weight of responsibility being lifted. "I feel like a feather allowing the light breeze to drift through. And it feels safe!" he said and laughed.

"I've prayed for this moment my entire life," Bill said, shaking his head in wonderment. "Never have I felt grace like this before!"

Everyone nodded. As they went around the circle, they each shared their amazement at the experience. Bud began, carefully formulating his words. "I have never experienced such love and connection. I think I felt what 'we are all one' means. It was like we were only one body, one energy. Thank you, each of you."

After a polite pause, Jerry returned to his earlier question: "Why do we have to commit to a spiritual practice? Why can't the angels just do what we say?"

Bill jumped in. "It shows respect and gratitude."

"Yes," Victoria added, "but it's even more than that. It is true we need to respect and honor the celestial beings and God. But many people get confused about this very point. The angels and your other spiritual guides don't want to live your life for you. If you think about it, that wouldn't be fair. But they do want to *assist* you. If they did everything for you, you wouldn't develop your potential or spiritual muscle, which leads to authentic power. When you learn to work with the angels, your life does become much easier.

"Gary Springfield, a spiritual teacher," Victoria continued, "told a story of a deeply spiritual woman he knew. She had a very close and loving relationship with her angels. She really motored on angel power. As the story goes, it was time to pay the rent, and she was ninety dollars short. She sat down in prayer and told the angels she was ninety dollars short, and she needed the money by the end of the day. She gave thanks, and then didn't give it another thought. She went about doing what needed to be done by her that day. At about noon, the doorbell rang. There was a man standing there she had never seen before. He was holding an envelope, and said, handing it to her, 'I was told you needed this.' She thanked him, and he left. There were ninety dollars in the envelope."

The class stirred, and Jerry was the first to speak. "It doesn't sound like she did much to get the money!"

"There are two levels to the story," Victoria explained. "First, she *asked*. That's important. The Bible says, 'Ask and you shall receive.' Many people are afraid to ask. They feel they don't deserve it or they don't want to bother God about it or it really isn't that important anyway. *For God, no request is too large or too small.* So, asking is first. Second, after many years of practicing the spiritual principles of prayer and meditation, she had the spiritual muscle not to worry. She didn't say the prayer and then spend the rest of the day worrying, 'Were they out to lunch? Did they hear my prayer? Did they lose my file? Oh, I really need the money.' Instead, she asked, then truly gave it to her angels and didn't think of it again. She knew they heard, and they would respond. The important aspect of this is on the energetic level. Doubt thoughts conflict with the angels' ability to act. Doubt thoughts throw up energetic barriers and can actually block the miracle from happening. But she let it go and went about her business and the money rather magically appeared."

"But,' Bud said, with a dazed looked, like someone who had woken up in a different universe, "how do you explain what happened today? We don't know nothin'. Well, I don't!"

Everyone laughed.

"All our energy together and holding the intention for miracles allows it to happen," Melissa replied, her black chin-length hair bobbing and her hands gesturing. "We were so much in the presence." Her right open palm swept across her body. "And in the wonder of the presence, there was no *time* to doubt!"

Everyone nodded in recognition.

"Plus," Victoria said, glowing from the angel visit, "the first wake-up call is always a veil-breaking episode that deeply etches your mind. That one memory can propel you through an entire lifetime. If you plant an acorn, you get an oak tree. You can pray, rant, and rave all you want for a lilac bush, but if you planted an acorn, you're going to get an oak tree. So, plant the seeds whose harvest you want to enjoy. The spiritual practices of prayer, mediation, self-healing, and energy medicine reap a more cooperative, peaceful life. Now, listen up. That doesn't mean that when you start to meditate, everything will be all right. What it does mean is, if you are serious, your life is going to change. You will experience new relationships, new jobs, maybe even moving to a new state or country. *Source* will guide you to meet your challenges of spiritual growth and will give you the situations to stimulate that growth. But we are getting beyond the scope of this class now. There will be other classes. Let us get back to our beloved angels! But first, it's time for lunch. Be back at 2:00 pm."

Everyone got up and began discussing where to go for lunch and with whom. After lunch, they had a brief check-in period. After check-in, Victoria opened the floor for questions.

Bud was first. He certainly had lost all his inhibitions. "Is this angel stuff a religion?"

Tilting her head to the left, with a wisp of a smile, Victoria said, "Many religions believe in angels. Angels come in all colors—white, yellow, brown, black, just like our human races. The Judeo Christians communicate with angels. The American Indians are especially attuned to the plant kingdom angels, called devas. Did you know there is a specific deva for each type of plant? They protect the plants, as our angels protect and befriend us. The Buddhists focus primarily on becoming awake or living in the present moment, so fully that the past and future have no relevance. That is also the Christ journey: to live fully in the present. The angels assist us in that, as they help teach us trust, so we can let go of the past and future. They help show us that we really are safe and cared for. Remember, they are messengers from God *but* should not be confused with God.

"Psalms 91 is a protection prayer. The story behind this prayer is that a platoon of soldiers all memorized the protection prayer and went into battle saying it. None of them were killed or injured, yet many of the soldiers around them died or were injured in battle. I will read you this protection prayer. Close your eyes and listen with your hearts:

He that dwelleth in the secret place of the most High shall abide under the shadow of the Almighty.

I will say of the Lord, He is my refuge and my fortress: my God; in him will I trust.

Surely he shall deliver thee from the snare of the fowler, and from the noisome pestilence,

He shall cover thee with his feathers, and under his wings shalt thou trust: his truth shall be thy shield and buckler.

Thou shalt not be afraid for the terror by night; nor for the arrow that flieth by day;

Nor for the pestilence that walketh in darkness; nor for the destruction that wasteth at noonday.

A thousand shall fall at thy side, and ten thousand at thy right hand; but it shall not come nigh thee.

Only with thine eyes shalt thou behold and see the reward of the wicked.

Because thou hast made the Lord, which is my refuge, even the most High, thy habitation;

There shall no evil befall thee, neither shall any plague come nigh thy dwelling.

For he shall give his angels charge over thee, to keep thee in all thy ways.

They shall bear thee up in their hands, lest thou dash thy foot against a stone.

Thou shalt tread upon the lion and adder; the young lion and the dragon shalt thou trample under feet.

Because he hath set his love upon me, therefore will I deliver him: I will set him on high because he hath known my name.

He shall call upon me, and I will answer him: I will be with him in trouble; I will deliver him, and honor him.

With long life will I satisfy him, and shew him my salvation. (kjv)

She let the prayer of divine protection settle in and then proceeded.

"Let me reread the part about the angels: 'For he shall give his angels charge over thee, to keep thee in all thy ways. They shall bear thee up in their hands, lest thou dash thy foot against a stone.'

"This literally means that we are protected from the slightest things. But the agreement is that we honor God with faith, love, and devotion. 'He who dwelleth in the secret place of the most High shall abide under the shadow of the Almighty.' Or keep God in the upper most consciousness of our thoughts, actions, and words, and he will keep us. It is a give and take.

"Now be careful with this concept," she warned. "You have a guardian angel, if you believe or not. But the truth is that we are all from the heart of God, which is love. This makes us love. When we practice putting love first, then we *are* honoring God, for we are doing as God does—loving unconditionally. You see God needs you as much as you need God."

For a moment, a breathless silence prevailed.

"How could that be?" Bill's voice sounded over the din of chatter that erupted. "How could we help God?"

"Bill, it is just like a stew," Victoria said. "If you use healthy, wonderful potatoes, your whole stew is more nutritious and tastes better. But if you have rotten potatoes, your stew is not as good. We are all in the same stew, so the more we practice love as we become unconditional love, the better for all of us. And as we are all one, the better for God."

"I'll need to think about that one," Bud said.

"When we first begin our journey, and the road ahead seems so vast, it is good to have a faithful friend," added Melissa, who had experience. "But don't allow your new friend to run your life; that is not his job."

"Well," Bud continued, "that's not my question. If I talk with the angels, does that mean I'm practicing some type of religion?"

"Oh, I see what you mean," Victoria said. "No. You are practicing spirituality. That's different than religion. Spirituality doesn't come with dogma, rules, or judgment. It is when *you* are in communication with your own spirit or soul and the spirit of God."

"Good," Bud said. "Because Ma is a Southern Baptist, and she would be mighty upset if I brought home ideas from another religion."

Victoria nodded in recognition, with a slight smile. Then she invited the angels in again, so the students could continue to practice communicating with them. The afternoon was filled with love and miracles, and by closure, each participant was overflowing with joy and fulfillment. As Victoria gave each an angel pin to wear, she asked everyone to sit quietly in silence and hold the space for the individual blessings. As she went around the circle, each person rose to receive her or his angel pin and blessing.

She stood before Bill, and he rose to meet her. She looked deeply into his eyes and said, "I bless this angel pin, that it may remind you not only that God loves you but that you are safe to let go of your ego will and allow your divine will to lead. When you have any doubts, touch this angel and remember today. God is with you, trust that in all you do."

Bill nodded gratefully. "Thank you," he barely whispered as he took the pin and immediately put it on his shirt.

Before Bud, she said, "Remember you are the divine son of God. You are precious in his eyes, and he loves you. Touch this pin if you forget or if you need a boost."

Tears welling up in his eyes, Bud gave short, repeated nods. Victoria held his hands a little longer as he received his pin. She could feel his overwhelm from all the new experiences and the intensity of the love. This entire day was like nothing he had ever experienced before. She heard the awakening of his inner voice. If he practiced listening to it and the angels, his life would be forever altered.

"Val, let this pin remind you that the divinity is in *you* too. As you learn to love and accept yourself completely, you will know faith. Touch this pin to recall the love felt here today. It is yours forever."

Val took Victoria's hands between hers and looked deeply into her eyes. "Yes, I'll try to remember," she said, nodding.

As she held Aaron's hands between hers with the pin, Victoria said, "Aaron, this pin has been blessed to remind you that you are never alone. You are always assisted and lifted. All you need do is remember. Bless you."

Face flushed, as if a secret had been revealed, he nodded. Victoria remembered the first time she had really felt supported and knew his vulnerability. She gave his hand an extra squeeze.

"Oh Melissa, dear faithful one." Their eyes locked in a loving gaze. "Letting go is not a loss but a gain. Think of it as reclaiming your true spirit and allowing the spirits of the past and future to take their rightful places. The past is history. The future is a mystery, and the now is a gift; that's why it's called the *present*. Touch this angel when you worry about the past or the future. Let it help you come back to real time."

Melissa let out a sigh of relief.

"Mary," Victoria said, continuing around the circle. "Touch this angel pin to remind you that you are perfect exactly the way you are. You need do nothing but allow God to work through you."

Mary's eyes welled with tears, and as she looked into Victoria's eyes, she smiled, closed her eyes, and nodded, breathing in the blessing.

With a gentle smile, Victoria made eye contact with Jerry. "Your journey has begun. Touch this angel pin to remind you that there is only one path for you—the path with God. Bless you. You are courageous and strong. You are a way-shower, and your life will be filled with adventures, some difficult, some easy, but all for the highest good."

And so she continued, offering each individual a special personal prayer. At the end, she said, "Let us all stand and hold hands for our closing circle song and prayer." They sang and swayed to John Lennon's song "Imagine."

. . .
Nothing to kill or die for . . .

Imagine all the people
Living life in peace

You, may say
I'm a dreamer,
But I'm not the only one...
I hope someday you'll join us
And the world will live as one.

Energy raced through their hands as they sang. With a triumphant gesture, all hands went into the air on 'And the world will live as one!'

Looking around the circle, with a beaming grin, Victoria said the closing prayer: "Dear God, thank you for the opportunity to be in service in this manner. Now, each of you take a moment to imagine a world so united that all the religions, races, and classes of people can become as one, as we did today in class. Imagine a world with no prejudice or hate. Imagine your heart so open, your trust so great that fear eludes you. Imagine life as grace.

"Squeeze the hand to your right in thanks and blessing for that person's contribution for this miraculous day. Squeeze the person's hand on your left in thanks and blessing for that person's contribution for this miraculous day. Now thank yourself for taking the time, making the drive, saying yes to yourself and your spiritual growth. Namaste. Get as many hugs as you can." And everyone giggled.

CHAPTER 13

Let Go

*B*ill and Mary chatted excitedly as he gave her a ride home from class. "Something seemed to break loose today," Mary said. "Like a big door opened. I feel a new sense of life and excitement I haven't felt since before I was married," and she burst into tears. With her face in her hands and head bobbing, she took little gasps of breath as the crying progressed, and then it stopped as suddenly as it had started. With a big sigh, she looked over at Bill and noticed how deeply and lovingly he was listening.

With this sense of support and encouragement, she continued, "It's like I lost myself after I got married. There was no me left. Today I got part of me back." She wiped her tears, sat up a little straighter, and sat dazed in her new revelation. To her surprise, Bill didn't jump in to save her. He kept holding the space for her. The silence was sweet between them. They were in grace.

Bill gave her a big hug when he dropped her at her house, and whispered, "It's a new time for you now." And he squeezed her just a bit tighter.

Back in the car, he smiled to himself in anticipation, and a sort of excitement filled him. It was a new time for him too. He skipped through the front door, and upon seeing his wife, a renewed flush of love flowed through him. "Barbara," he said, as if he were seeing her for the first time. He kissed her sweetly on the cheek. He had lived with this woman for nineteen years, yet he realized in that moment that he really did not know her at all. But how could he have known her when he barely knew himself? He was just a jumbled mass of "should of." What was really beneath all that, he was about to discover!

On the dining room table lay the family album he had been working on for several weeks. It included a genealogy chart from three generations back. He wanted to learn his family's history and share the legacy with his wife and daughter. Funny that he should be working on the physical roots of his family at the same time he began to explore his spiritual roots, it occurred to him now.

That evening, he added a few more photos of his grandparents and held the album warmly to his chest before turning off the light. Ah, dear memories and so much love.

Once in bed, he rolled over and hugged his wife and gently kissed her on the lips. "I love you," he whispered in her ear. "Thank you for being you." Gratitude filled him, and he drifted off with a sweet smile on his lips.

"Fire! Fire!"

The scream shook him from a sound sleep. Eyes blinking, he heard the screams again.

"Fire! Fire!"

He bolted out of bed. It was Jenny, his sixteen-year-old daughter! He ran into the hall toward her bedroom, but there was so much smoke that he fell to the floor and crawled to open her door. The flames burst into the hall. Diving beneath them, he choked. "Jenny, where are you?"

"Dad, I'm on the roof. I'm okay. Get out!"

He crawled back to the hall.

Barbara had made it down the stairs and toward the front door. "I'm down here!" she called.

But he couldn't see, and tumbled down the stairs. "Ouch—ohhh." Then he lost consciousness. His wife was calling to him, but he couldn't hear her.

As she shook him, he came to slightly. "Bar..bar..ra," he mumbled.

"Oh, thank God!" she could barely manage a whisper. "Put your hand on my shoulder, and we'll crawl out together."

They reached the door just as the flames rolled down the stairs. Miraculously, Jenny appeared, and they pulled her to safety. Gasping for air, they lay in a heap.

Then sirens wailed and three fire trucks arrived. A woman firefighter dashed over to them and helped them to safety. She wrapped each them in a heavy blanket. Crying and trembling from shock, they huddled together, holding each other up. Helpless, they watched the flames devour their home.

"My house," moaned Barbara. "All those years of memories. All that work to make it just right."

"The cat," Jenny cried. "Did you get the Button? Button, Button! Come Button!"

"No, I didn't see her," Barbara replied.

Jenny, throwing off her blanket, dashed toward the house. A firefighter caught her by the arm. "No way!" he said. "You'll get killed in there!"

"But my cat. My cat!" she cried, struggling to get away from him.

"We'll try to find him," the firefighter said. "Really. Now, go back into the safety zone."

"My photo album!" Bill cried. "Our family history up in flames. Oh NO! I forgot to pay the house insurance! O God, please. Our things, the album, the cat, our memories." Crying uncontrollably now, he pulled away from his wife and fell to his knees.

"Is this the reward I get for doing your work all these years?" Angrily he shook his fist at the sky. "Thanks a lot, partner! Thanks a lot!" Head in his hands and his entire body convulsing, he wept and wept and wept.

Where was God when he needed him? Nowhere to be found.

Then suddenly, like a twinkling of an eye, he stood up, and with hands outstretched to the sky and head facing up, he proclaimed. "I let go of all of it." Instantly, a calm swept over him, and he felt grounded and supported all at once. "It's yours." He gestured to the sky. "Take it, God."

He calmly walked over to Barbara and Jenny and took them into his arms. "What is, is," he said. "God, I give thanks that my family and I are safe." Now let's find a place to sleep tonight. There's nothing more we can do."

Barb and Jenny stopped crying. Just as abruptly, the fire died down, as if on its own. Soon the trucks pulled away. The firefighters roped the area off and warned everyone to stay away. Then the chief, a big guy with a bowed-legged cowboy walk, dressed in a beige fireproof jumpsuit, came up to Bill. "Well, sir, we did the best we could." Turning to Jenny, he said, "I am sorry, dear; we didn't find your cat. Please wait till morning before you go in, and I hope you can get some sleep." He gathered up the fireproof blankets, gave a little tip of his helmet, and walked off.

"Thank you," Bill said after him. "Thank you."

Beverly came over from across the street and offered them her house for the night. She came out with blankets and wrapped each of them up and led the way to her home. "Bill and Barbara, please sleep in the guest room, down the hall to the right. And Jenny, I've pulled out the hide-a-bed in the den for you. Would any of you like a cup of coffee or tea?" she offered.

"Maybe some tea," Bill murmured. "Yes, some tea would be nice."

"I think I'll just retire," Barbara said. "I'm exhausted."

Bev already had the tea water ready. "What kind what you like?" she asked.

"Chamomile. Thanks."

Jenny flopped hard on the hide-a-way bed, and with an exhausted sigh, fell right to sleep.

Bill gratefully sipped the tea. Bev nodded to him and left him alone to ponder the events. The sun would be up soon.

The sky was unusually bright in the morning. Bill arose quite cheerful. After breakfast, the family walked over to their house, which was charred almost to the ground. Nothing could possibly have survived. As they entered where the dining room used to be, Bill couldn't believe his eyes. His photos were saved under a fire blanket, not even water damaged. Then he heard a soft meow. As he lifted the blanket, their cat walked out unscathed!

Jenny swept him up in her arms, kissing him, crying, "Thank, God. Thank, God! You're all right!

Bill walked over to his desk, which was miraculously intact. He opened the drawer where the bills lay. They too were undamaged, and the insurance bill wasn't due until next Friday. They were still covered! What a miracle! Most of the rest of the house and their belongings were totally destroyed. Barbara cried, and Bill hugged her tightly.

"Dad," Jenny said, after seeing that none of her things had been saved, "how is it that Mom's and my stuff burned and your stuff is fine? You got some connection to God you've been holding back on?"

"No," he said, dazed. "Suddenly while the house was burning, and I couldn't stop crying, I just let it go, and gave it all to God. That's when a calm fell over me. I let it go, and it all came back to me. Now, that's a miracle in action! I can barely believe it myself. It is what I learned in my workshop yesterday. *The power of letting go isn't a loss, but a gain.* I've had it backwards all these years. Well, I'll have a great sermon this morning! Which reminds me, what will you wear? I guess I can put my robe on over these clothes."

"I think I'll pass this Sunday, if you don't mind," Jenny said, almost in unison with her mother.

"Barbara, you will need to come. The word will have already spread, and our congregation will be bringing us food and clothing. I'll need you to help organize all that."

"All right," she shrugged.

CHAPTER 14

Break Out of the Loop

*T*he sun shimmered through Running Bear's bedroom blinds as it began its ascent. She rolled over and stretched her arms above her head and her legs straight out, and wiggled her fingers and her toes. Drawing in a slow, deep full body breath, she stretched her limbs to the sides.

"Ah, yes! A new dawn," she giggled with zeal. And it was Sunday, no less—the quiet day. Running Bear knew exactly what she wanted to do, and after she called in the directions and completed her morning ritual of gratitude and intention, she headed right toward the forest. A force pulled her, so she expanded her field of perception in anticipation.

As she approached the forest, three crows squawked and flew three lariats over her head, then nodded for her to follow them. She had to trot to keep up with them as they led her deep into the forest. The trees whizzed by. Then the crows swept down and up again, did three more lariats, and were gone.

She stood perfectly still to perceive where they had deposited her. At first she could only sense shimmering, glistening energy. The light swirled in rays of glittering yellow and gold, with streaks of gleaming purple and green. As her heart chakra expanded, she lost all sense of her physical body. She was radiant vibrating light, just like everything around her. Shaking from the coursing energies, she slowly walked forward a few steps, then made a deliberate and slow circle. Everywhere she looked, lights of energy sparkled and danced. It was pure, radiant joy and love.

"Yes!" She exclaimed. Arms in a victory V, she spun in a circle. "I'm in the Magic Grove of the Matriarchs!"

She had only heard about the Magic Grove of the Matriarchs from the elders. It was a place in a higher dimension, where few were ever allowed. It was the template of what Earth beings would evolve into.

Everything was shimmering glistening light and love. It was always here, but one had to go through an energetic gate to enter. Now, palms open, with cupped fingers, she felt the air and peered even deeper into the swirling energies. Very slowly, she began to see the majestic Magic Grove of Matriarchs take form. With her face straight up to the sky, she could barely see the top of the trees. They towered three hundred feet plus, with branches reaching out a hundred feet or more. The Magic Grove was the template for the redwood trees.

Then she realized that she was standing in the center of a circle of the matriarchs. Luminous, etheric, they bowed to her one by one. Running Bear bowed deeply to each in response. She sensed that she was not breathing, or not breathing herself, but being breathed by the greater infinite force. Her field expanded and contracted on its own and in complete entrainment with the forest.

She sat in the center of the circle to listen. For a long time, just silence and this magical breathing. Then she noticed that she was not only being breathed, but also lightened and expanded. The matriarchs were raising her vibration so she would be more attuned to them. Higher vibration creates higher consciousness, which creates greater awareness. She reached her hands to the Earth as she was becoming so light she was losing her sense of place. And then it all disappeared again into shimmering, glistening energy. Her head began to swoon, but she pressed her hands to the Earth.

And as if from the bowls of the Earth, an *Om* rose up. Gradually, the sound radiated throughout the forest, the waves expanding from a pebble tossed in a pond. It became so intense that she felt her head would burst. Phew, just in time, it backed off some. Then another wave of intensity flowed through her. Each time, Running Bear's field expanded and rose, then leveled, then expanded and rose.

Running Bear sat upright and strong, hands still firmly placed on Earth. She trembled as the song of the matriarchs emerged like a flower from its bud. It was the song of pure joy. The song of rapture. And the forest became even more luminous. Then laughter and playfulness danced across the forest floor and flowers swayed and trees undulated.

The Voice said, "This is the truth and possibility for Earth. Nothing more or less. For it is wholeness. It is sacred and radiant. It is the isness. And it is possible. Hold nothing less in your intention for Earth."

Running Bear bowed deeply. Nodding her head, she knew all at once what their mission was. "Yes," she replied. "I am grateful to come here and meet you. Humbly, I ask what do you see as Sid's, and Joseph's, and my next step?"

"Carry this field of energy back with you, and it will transform you."

Running Bear bowed, and as quickly as this gate of love opened, it closed, and she was standing in an ordinary—albeit, still powerful—forest.

For a long time, she sat very still, feeling into her experience and grounding the high vibration she donned. Then she expanded her field through the grove of trees that surrounded her, then throughout the entire forest. Now, she breathed it one hundred miles out, then a thousand, then ten thousand. Each time, it grew more powerful and rich. Everything in its path soaked it up.

When she opened her eyes, the crows were circling above her again. She rose slowly and followed them. They guided her deeper into the forest, did three more lariats, and flew off.

Sensing her location, she discovered that she was back in her favorite location of the forest, surrounded by huge Sitka spruce. She tuned into the matriarch of this forest and asked permission to create a medicine wheel.

Grandmother Tree bowed to her, and Running Bear felt her smile as she recognized that her radiant field of love was higher than ever before.

"Yes, of course," Grandmother Tree replied. "I will set it deep into my roots and Earth to help raise consciousness."

Running Bear dropped her energy deep into Earth, connecting to the heart of Mother Earth. She breathed the Earth energy up through her, and slowly and deliberately called in the directions.

"Mother Earth?" she asked now. "May I collect the stones necessary to create a medicine wheel?"

"Yes, they are ready."

"Thank you," said Running Bear.

Now, she expanded her energy to the Overlighting Deva of the stone people. "Welcome Overlighting Deva. Thank you for coming to speak with me. May I gather some stones to create a medicine wheel?"

"Yes. It is our honor. I see several bursting to be part of the wheel."

As she gently walked on the forest floor, she listened keenly with her clairaudient sense. Over to the right, she heard ever so faintly, "Take *me*." She walked over to the East and found a beautiful rounded rock. "Would you like to be part of the sacred medicine wheel?" she asked.

"Yes," came the sweet reply.

"What direction would you like to hold," Running Bear Eagle asked.

"The East."

And so it went, until she had gathered all the needed stones. She bowed reverently to the stone people as she placed them in a pile. Next, she tuned into the head matriarch tree and asked for the best place to build the circle. After clearing the designated spot, she gently placed the stone people in their appropriate positions, forming a perfect circle.

From a distance, she heard footsteps. Stopping all her motions and dimming her breath, she cupped her ears in the direction of the sound. She listened carefully and tuned in energetically. There were two people, two young males. As they approached closer, she knew both: Bud and Jerry.

Bud called out, "Hi, there!" To Jerry, he whispered, "That's the woman who saved me from robbing the Plaid Pantry and brought the dog back to life!"

"Welcome," Running Bear Eagle called and waved to them.

They walked over. "What are you doing?" Bud asked, jumping right in.

"I'm creating a medicine wheel," she answered. "And this must be?" she asked, looking at Jerry.

"Oh, sorry. This is Jerry."

She extended her hand to Jerry. "I'm Running Bear Eagle." She invited them to sit down with her and said to Jerry, "Nice to meet you. You picked a perfect day for a hike. How did you find this particular grove of trees?"

"We were listening to our guardian angels," Jerry said. "We wanted to find a place where the energy is really high so we can practice what we learned in Victoria's angel class."

Running Bear gave a knowing nod.

As Jerry and Bud excitedly described the workshop, Running Bear Eagle tuned in with her high sensory perception to the time and place of the event. This quantum perception channel collapsed all the barriers to time and space. She felt the tremendous release the participants experienced and the incredible love that was present. Witnessing the grief that was lifted from people, she was grateful.

"I still can't understand how I knew my guardian angel was there, when I really couldn't see her," Bud said, head slightly cocked and turning a newfound stick in his hand. "It was like she was in another dimension." His eyes turned vacant.

"She was," Running Bear Eagle replied. "Angels vibrate or live from the fourth dimension on up."

With wide questioning eyes, Jerry asked, "What does that mean?"

"The world consists of different dimensions, or vibrations," Running Bear explained. "What you see here in the third dimension—your solid body, the solid trees, plants, and rocks and fluid water—is only about three percent of what really exists. There is an entire energetic world around and through the solid and fluid world. Einstein discovered that in the higher dimensions, there is no time and space. Everything is now. The past, present, and future all collapse into each other. Almost impossible to imagine, isn't it?"

"Yeah!" Bud and Jerry chorused.

"It is only in the third dimension where we live that time and space are separate. The perception of separateness actually rules our thinking and the way we look at things… unless we know better." The corners of her lips turned up in a knowing smile. Her eyes twinkled, lighting up her face.

They sat for a moment digesting this.

"How many dimensions are there?" Bud asked.

"I am familiar with the twelve octaves, with twelve dimensions in each. That's two hundred and forty-four. But there may be more."

Shaking his head in bewilderment, Jerry went to more solid ground. "So, what is a medicine wheel?" he asked.

"For the native peoples, it is a sacred altar made in the shape of a wheel, made of the sacred stone people."

Jerry tilted his head like a dog confused by his guardian's command, but kept Running Bear's eye.

She continued, smiling slightly, "The medicine wheel was transported from one homesite to another as the tribe migrated with the seasons. More importantly, it determined how we look at the world. The medicine wheel helped us understand the universe and ourselves."

"You lost me there," said Bud.

"The circle has no beginning or end. Look . . ." She borrowed Bud's stick and drew a circle in the dirt. "The circle is round, with no edges or lines. It is all inclusive. The Earth is round also. Everything on Earth is in the sacred circle. So the medicine wheel represents all life and all the relationships therein."

Jerry leaned over and reverently traced the circle with his finger. "Oh, I get it!" he said as he straightened up. "There is only one sacred circle that the medicine wheel represents. Therefore, there is only one of us." With his eyes squeezed shut, he tried to grasp what he had just said.

"Yes," Running Bear said. "That's what the phrase—"

"—'We are all one' means!" Bud exclaimed.

"Exactly!" Running Bear said.

Everyone laughed and simultaneously reached for each other's hands. Running Bear felt the electricity of discovery and wonder run through the current.

After a few moments, they gently released their hands, and Jerry asked, "So, how does this change how we think and act?"

"A good and very important question," Running Bear said. "If you perceive things as separate, as something you can compartmentalize, then it removes you from the consequence of what you do. For a while, only. Ever fly over the farming lands? When you look down, everything is divided into squares."

"That's so we can divide it up and sell it?" Bud said, nodding his head.

"Precisely. Science wanted to discover how to *control* the material world, not how to live *with* it. So it took ownership and used it for its own personal benefit. For example, look at this tree. Many people look at a forest and see how many board feet it will make and how much money it will bring in the marketplace. They see the tree from the frame of reference of 'how can I use it?' A developer would look at this forest and see how many houses and shopping malls he could create. And he'd feel absolutely brilliant when the plans were complete, or when he was able to purchase it. See, ownership in this model means 'I am in control. I can do whatever I want.' The value of preserving this forest for the birds, rabbits, bears, and lions is lost on him because he is asking a different question."

"And what do you see, Running Bear?" Bud asked in rapt attention and with an open heart.

"When *I* look at this tree, I see a wise, ancient spirit. When I am *very* quiet inside, I can hear her spirit talk to me. This tree here is the matriarch." She nodded to the matriarch—Grandmother Tree--a majestic hundred-foot Sitka spruce that stood proudly like a mythical giant. "That means she basically rules this grove of trees. The devas, or nature spirits, consult with her."

"What viewfinder, then, are you looking through?" Bud asked.

"I am looking at the world through a relationship lens," she said, "knowing and acknowledging the pure divine energy, or spirit, of *every* entity and its relationship to everything else. Even the rocks."

"Yes, you called them the stone people. How does this all fit together?" Jerry asked.

"The indigenous cultures see the world as circles, with no beginning and no end; just a continuation of life. The Earth is a circle, the moon is a circle, and the sun is a circle. Animals stake their territory in a circle. The seasons are circular. We are born into the physical world from the spiritual realm. We move around in circles throughout our lives, and then we are born again into the spirit world, completing a major life circle."

Jerry stood up and paced around the trees, kicking at the dirt. "Okay, but I still don't see the difference. I could see the world as a circle and still figure the board feet here, but I'd build my development in the shape of a circle."

"Yes, good." She chuckled softly. "And that has happened. But there are two aspects at play here. It's not because you *see* the world as a circle, it is because you are part of the whole circle. You are connected to everything else. The second aspect is that your developer is still looking through the 'how do I make money' viewfinder. 'Maybe people will buy more homes if I put them into a circle,' he thinks. He does not see the forest as teeming life. He is dead to the rapture of the community that already lives here. He could not clear-cut if he heard or felt the spirit and voices of the tree people. For if he felt or heard them, he would recognize that he was raping himself."

"You mean there is no separation between me and you and that tree?" Jerry asked, looking back and forth from Running Bear to Grandmother Tree to Bud.

"Exactly. You see the three of us sitting here; we look like we are three separate beings. But if you tune into the energetic vibration, you will see that our energy fields are all connected, overlapping even, and literally disappear into each other."

"Wow," Bud exclaimed. His eyes dazed off to the right of Running Bear's head, just enough to actually see the energy fields. "You're very green... and purple, Running Bear!" And then he rolled on the ground and laughed and laughed and laughed, as if he had finally gotten the joke of his life. Jerry and Running Bear were swept in and laughed as hard as Bud.

"The other difference," Running Bear continued when they had all stopped laughing, "is that the native peoples understood that spirit, or the energy template, also called universal life force energy, came first, then matter. Spirit is the *primary* substance to life *not* secondary. Without it, there *is* no life."

She popped up and rather skipped over to a flower. Nothing made her happier then sharing the great mysteries. "Look at this flower bud."

The boys dashed over excitedly and leaned toward the flower.

"Now, if you blur your eyes again just enough, you can see the energetic matrix around it in the shape of the flower to come. The energy blueprint comes first, and then the flower grows into it."

They leaned toward it to see.

"There it is! I see it," Bud exclaimed. "Oops, it's gone now. How do I keep seeing the spirit around the bud?"

"It takes practice to hold the vision, but as fast as *you* have seen, it won't take long," Running Bear encouraged. "Look at this tree," she continued, as she danced over to the matriarch of the forest, who rustled her branches.

Bud's and Jerry's eyes glued to her.

"And this bush." Kneeling and peering into the bush, she whispered so as not to disturb his nap, "That cricket.".

Then hopping up, she leapt over to a large boulder. "Come over here and look. The rocks all have a spirit or energetic field around them. *The people* recognized this and knew they had the same field around themselves and through them too! They understood on a very visceral level that everything comes from the same source. So, when we honor the trees, plants, and animals, we honor ourselves. As we listen to the spirit of the wind, fire, water, and earth, we listen to ourselves—as we are made up of those same elements. These practices keep us tuned into the greater picture and the greater rhythm."

Jerry's head was cocked, but his eyes were steady on Running Bear. "I can't see your field," he said frowning.

"You're trying too hard, Jerry. Close your eyes and ask to see. Now look to the left of my head and blur your vision. Relaxing is the key."

Jerry closed his eyes and took a deep breath. Slowly opening his relaxed eyes, he proclaimed, "O my god, I see vibrating energy all around you! Is that it?"

"Yes. That's universal life force energy."

There was a potent silence as both boys got up and blurred their vision, first on a tree, next on a rock, then a flower, and so on. Running Bear smiled at how quickly they opened to it.

Jerry looked at Bud in total wonder. "Did you see that?" he whispered. A scampering rabbit stopped still in his tracks. The boys, both barely breathing, saw a very still energy field around the frightened rabbit. They nodded and smiled in acknowledgment.

Running Bear watched as they discovered the interconnection to all life.

They looked at each other in amazement as they saw only each other's energy fields. Their physical bodies had totally disappeared. Heads shaking in disbelief and wonder, they burst toward each other into an embrace of full recognition.

Running Bear smiled and gently closed her eyes, nodding to give gratitude for the awakening.

There was a long silence as the boys absorbed their revelation and sat in the magical energy all around them.

Then, about one hundred yards away, Running Bear heard a rustle in the bush. She listened with her clairaudient sense and realized it was Sid and Victoria.

The boys were deep in thought and were quite startled when Victoria and Sid approached. Bud jumped straight up.

"Oops! Sorry to startle you," Victoria said with a smile and twinkling eyes. Then turning to Running Bear, she said, "Fancy meeting you here. I wanted to show Sid my favorite hiking area, and I'm not surprised that you have discovered it also. It's a magnet when you tune into it."

Running Bear nodded and bowed slightly to the matriarch tree.

"That's how we found it!" Bud and Jerry chimed in together.

"We were practicing what you taught in class. It's amazing!" Bud continued.

Running Bear Eagle rose to give her friends a hug.

Together, Victoria and Sid's energy fields formed the shape of a glistening pink heart—the human symbol of love. The sight made Running Bear feel warm all over.

As Victoria set down her backpack, Bud and Jerry popped up to give her a hug.

"What's going on?" Victoria asked Bud.

They all sat down in circle.

"We've been talking about the different ways to view the world," Bud began. "Running Bear says we are all one, from the same source, and therefore we are all connected, and the world is full of circles." He stretched a circle in the ground with a stick. "That's the only part I get. But my world isn't like that. *Money* is everything. Without it, I can't get out of my drug-infested neighborhood. Without it, I can't eat or buy clothes. It was different with the Indians. They made everything by hand. They didn't need money. But the world is different now. Money rules, and there is no way around it!" His face contorted in pain.

Victoria took his hands in hers. "Yes. You are trapped in a circular hell, but the trap is inside you, not just outside you. If it were just outside, no one would get out, but many do. You're trapped in the way you see your situation."

"No!" He jumped up and pushed her away. "It's true: money rules. Without it, I'm nothing, and I'm stuck! This is all crap!" He stomped away and burst into tears. "Oh great," he mumbled. "Here I am crying again!" And he dashed into the woods.

Running Bear instinctively held out her hands to Jerry, Sid, and Victoria to create a connected circle. She closed her eyes and beamed love to Bud. They all followed her example. After several breaths, their breathing became one and fell into harmony.

Several moments later, Jerry broke the silence. "I felt the same way Bud does—trapped in a cycle of helplessness, not knowing which way to turn. Thank God, I wasn't also trapped in poverty. But I still almost killed myself from despair. It doesn't make any difference. Trapped is trapped."

Each nodded, and Victoria squeezed each hand she was holding, and they let go. Then she pulled her rim drums from her pack. Running Bear Eagle smiled and took one. Victoria began to play, *ba-bum, ba-bum, ba-bum.* The beat of the heart. *Ba-bum, ba-bum.* Running Bear Eagle joined her and added a half note to the rhythm. Their playing continued, and Sid and Jerry swayed to the beat. Running Bear sent the sound of the drums to Bud to call him back.

When Bud arrived, he was calm. He joined the circle and began to sway with the beat. Then he began to drum on his thigh. *Da dada.* Running Bear Eagle handed him the drum and showed him how to hold it. He took it and at first blended in with Victoria. But then as if something took over his hand, he pounded a hard and angry beat, feverishly hammering the drum. Gradually, he fell back into harmony with Victoria, who kept the pulse when he fell out. The drumming continued for a while, then tapered off into silence. Sitting still in the silence, they absorbed the vibrations from the drumming. It was sacred.

"Again," said Bud, "this sacred presence." His head bowed and his shoulders became limp in surrender.

"Mother, Father, God, thank you for this sacred and poignant time of realization of our interconnection," Victoria said. She kneeled on Earth and touched her head to the ground, slowly and with such love.

Victoria's gesture brought tears to Running Bear Eagle. With women on the planet such as Victoria, there was hope for Earth's survival, she thought. She knew the Magic Grove of Matriarchs was at work here.

"Why did the drum calm me down?" Bud asked. "It's not like anything is going to be different when I get home today."

"Because we were drumming our own heartbeat. The drum brought us back to our bodies and our breath. The ancient cultures of Native America, Africa, Japan, Korea and others used the drum to amplify the rhythms they felt in their own bodies and the rhythms they felt in the Earth and throughout the universe. I'll show you what I mean. Feel your pulse in your neck."

They all put fingers to their necks.

"Now listen in the spaces," Victoria said.

Bud, Jerry, and Running Bear lay down on the ground. Listening, Bud began to tap the beat on his leg. Sid brought his breath to the spaces. Jerry joined in his own rhythm, and finally Running Bear Eagle did so with hers. They were similar but unique. Victoria drummed the heartbeat on her rim drum. *Ba-bum, ba-bum.* She held the pulse, or foundation rhythm.

Standing, she began to step the pulse, and everyone joined her. Then Bud began to clap out another rhythm: *ta ke*. Jerry joined in with Bud's clapping, and Victoria chanted the syllables *ta ke ti na*. Each stepped the heartbeat with his or her feet, clapped the second rhythm, and chanted the syllables *ta ke ti na*. Sid could not coordinate the clapping but maintained the step and chanting.

"It's okay if you fall out of rhythm," Victoria explained. "Always come back to the base beat of the drum with your feet. That's your foundation."

Just at the right moment, Victoria changed the chant to another rhythm, and everyone followed along: *ga ma la, ga ma la*.

The music they created built to a peak and then naturally became softer and softer. "*Hum ba lay a, hum ba lay a*," Victoria sang, and everyone responded back: "*Hum ba lay a, hum ba lay a*."

Sid and Joseph harmonized the tune.

Bud tilted his head to listen more deeply. In between their harmonies were more tones and different inflections that added depth and richness to the tune. But where were the harmonies coming from? Bud's eyes suddenly popped open. "The angels are singing," he whispered in awe. "The angels!"

"I hear them!" said Jerry, wide eyed. "Angels—listen—so sweet—so—translucent!"

"*Hum ba lay a, hum ba lay a, hum ba lay a, hum ba lay a…*" The tune was intertwining, interconnecting, radiating.

The entire forest swelled and contracted to the rhythm. The ripples of vibration spread for miles around. "*Hum ba lay a, hum ba lay a*."

Then slowly it faded away. The stillness was full and poignant.

Each person, when ready, lay down on the ground. Running Bear felt the entrainment of their breath. Each was alchemized to another dimension of unity.

Bud said, "I'm sinking into the Earth," and gently began to tone.

The tone pierced through Running Bear, and she burst into tears. Regaining her composure, she joined Bud. Soon they were all toning Earth Mother's vibration. And then they fell into a deep profound silence. For several moments, they lay in a blissful state. Their bodies tingling with energy. Heads vibrating.

"Gently bring yourselves back," Victoria suggested softly. "And when you are ready, sit up."

Slowly, each of them came to sitting position, eyes glazed and shoulders slumped in relaxation. She let the silence penetrate before she continued. "How do you feel?" she asked.

"Deeply connected to my source of life," Sid said. "As if I am Earth."

"In oneness," said Running Bear.

"Like I am here but not here," Jerry added. "I'm bigger, lighter, broader. I feel empty and full all at once. Oh, I don't have words for it!"

Everyone laughed.

"I was home again," said Running Bear, eyes flooded of tears. She rocked back and forth. "It was full moon." She lifted her head skyward and waved her hands to the moon. "And the women were drumming and chanting around sacred fire. So much love. Sisterhood. My heart danced." She bowed her tear-streaked face and kissed Mother Earth. "Thank you, Mother. Thank you."

With wide, questioning eyes, Jerry asked, "Were those other harmonies really angels?"

Victoria, Sid, and Running Bear laughed and chorused, "Yes!"

Bud, with eyes at half mast, muttered, "I melted into the Earth. I could feel her heartbeat. Then I heard a tone. The more I listened, the louder it got. It was speaking to me. Then *I* began to tone it. It was me. My vibration. I could feel my insides rearranging, a new level of being. I... I... can't explain. Like I found a new pattern inside me."

"What happened?" Jerry asked, sitting cross legged and leaning forward into the circle. "How can drums, clapping, and chanting change us like this? It is not of this world."

Victoria, Running Bear, and Sid grinned.

Sid replied, "The magnificent part is it *is* of this world, but a part of the world we have forgotten. We just tapped into the inner rhythm of ourselves. Once you know your own pulses, you know yourself. It is a doorway to the inside. The Buddha used the doorway of the pulse of the breath to draw people back to themselves. Back to center. These drums draw us inward also." There was a pause. "If you become anxious or frightened or agitated," Sid added, "remember today and hear the drum. Breath with the drum, and your body will come to center again. Then you can better deal with the situation in which you find yourself."

Running Bear was lying stomach first on the ground. With her head in her hands, she nodded to Sid, "There are rhythms everywhere in life because everything is made up of the vibrations of energy. If you train yourself, you can feel and hear the vibrations and tones playing continuously in and around you. When we, as a society, disconnected from our internal rhythms, we disconnected ourselves from source. That is one of the main reasons that, in only one hundred plus years of industrial revolution, we have poisoned our planet and ourselves. The drum can bring us home again."

"All life naturally gravitates to harmony," Victoria said. "Listen now to the crickets. Listen to how they fall out of rhythm with each other, then fall back into harmony."

"I didn't even hear any crickets till now!" Jerry said, shaking his head. "They're chirping all around us."

"It's interesting that the only creature that can keep from falling naturally into harmony is the human," said Victoria. "The human can intentionally stay in chaos, or out of rhythm. But believe me, it takes more energy to stay out than to resonate with Earth. When you keep yourself in chaos or out of balance so long, you lose your inner rhythm and balance. That's what happened to our entire culture. We don't know what our balance is personally or in our society. The output, of course, is the murders, rapes, suicides, obesity, anorexia, drama triangles, rampant disease, poisoned air and water, and a sick planet."

"Yes," Running Bear said. "It is the circle again that must create a spiral to keep our evolution going." With a stick, she drew a spiral in the dirt. "There is momentum gaining in the spiral as you go down." She started at the top of the spiral and went around to the left. "The chaos brings you up and around to push you to the next spiral, or level of life. This is the formula for evolution. The spiral is the energetic symbol for what happens in the evolutionary process." She completed the circle and then looped down and then up to create the next spiral.

"This is the spiral of life," she continued. "Now, here is another mystery of life. If you do not have the energy or awareness to lift into the next spiral, you will fall back and repeat the *same* circle again and again and again. By that, I mean you will continue to repeat the same behaviors—making money, losing it; attracting people in your life who leave you or hurt you; unable to stop drinking or taking drugs; and the like. I call it getting stuck in the loop. You keep going around and around the same loop."

She drew several very large spirals on the ground. She began to walk around the first rung, then beckoned Bud, Jerry, Sid, and Victoria to join her. As they walked the spirals, she said, "Now, think of something you would like to spiral out of. As you walk through the upward aspect of the spiral, feel it shed off of you."

Bud felt his poverty and slumped under the weight. Then he intended to shed it and felt a surge of energy propel him through the upward circle of the spiral. As he continued upward, his breath relaxed and he felt lighter. On the next spiral, he saw himself well employed and enjoying it. A smile burst across his face.

Sid felt the great suffering of humanity and crumbled to his knees. Fighting back the tears, he collected his breath and rose with a fierce determination. With each step, he labored down the spiral's decline. His mind flooded with sights of human poverty, illness, disease, greed, distortion. After a hearty inhale, he thrust the air from his lungs. And then again and again. With each powerful breath, he became more buoyant. Moving upward on the spiral, he set his mind on joy. With each step, his panting slowed. His eyes gazed straight ahead, with the same determination he felt under the Bodhi tree over twenty-six hundred years ago. He envisioned people of all races healthy and whole and happily cooperating with each other. He saw the leaders of all nations talking and laughing together. As he neared the top of the spiral, his shoulders relaxed and a smile began to emerge. One more step and he would crest the spiral! When he reached the very top, he broke into a huge smile, threw his arms in the air and exclaimed, "Yes! It is done!"

He walked over to Running Bear's blanket and sat quietly with Bud and Running Bear. Soon Victoria joined them.

"I feel so much lighter now," said Jerry. "I shed off the feeling of the great burden of our challenge to save our planet. I can only just do my part."

Everyone nodded in agreement.

"I feel lighter too," said Bud. "But will this break the poverty cycle I'm in? How do I break out for good?"

"The first step is to be aware that you are in the loop," Running Bear said. "Done. You see that now. Next is to identify the actions you keep repeating."

Bud's eyes drifted up to the left, remembering.

"What are your patterns?" she asked.

"Well," he said, "I never have enough money. Then when I get a job, I get fired soon after. The boss is always some idiot who tells me to do one thing and then changes his mind. So I can never do anything right, and he fires me."

"Yes," Running Bear said. She knew this pattern well. For her, people were caught in the same vicious cycle of victimization.

"At school, I'm not so smart. I didn't do my homework and they kicked me out," he confessed.

"Yes," said Running Bear, "but not for being dumb. They kicked you out because you got caught stealing money out of your teacher's wallet."

"How did you know that?" he said, shrinking back like a rat trapped in a corner.

"I see a pattern here," interjected Victoria. "You want something, but you won't work to get it. You feel like other people have more and take advantage of you, so you steal, because if it really boils down to it, life owes it to you. How am I doing so for?"

Bud blushed. "Well, I guess," he said, bowing his head.

"So, in your mind, are you the victim of your situation?" Victoria asked.

He nodded his head vigorously. "Yes! That's what I mean. I can't get out!"

"You can't get out if you keep repeating the same actions," Victoria said. "Isn't it obvious? They don't work. You aren't getting back at the world, you are digging your own grave deeper."

"What's the second step?" Bud said and turned to Running Bear. "I see the behavior now. I'm so stuck, that even when you *gave* me the three hundred dollars, my buddies stole it from me. I can't win for losing!"

"The second step is to make an *intention* to break out of the cycle and create a new spiral," Running Bear replied.

"Okay, I'll do everything I can to create the spiral. What's three?" His posture straightened and eyes brightened.

"Make an effort to apologize to anyone you hurt, as long as your apology will not hurt them further. This is the amends part," Running Bear said.

Victoria smiled.

"Whew," Bud said. "Now, that could take a long time. I don't think I can do that."

"Just start by making a list of all the things you have done that may have hurt someone. You will know what to do," Running Bear said, breaking Victoria's stream of thought.

"In Buddhism," Sid said, "we call it *right action*. You are making right what you wronged. Revenge only sinks you deeper into the loop."

"Yes," Running Bear said. "Revenge must be healed by all the Earth's people. My people need to stop blaming the White man for destroying them. For if we continue to stay in blame, we remain victims. And what that really means is the White man *still* has control over us!"

"In Buddhism, throughout the ages," said Sid, "the focus has moved from the mental aspect to compassion for all things great and small. Buddhist teachers today teach kindness and compassion and acceptance for all life." He nodded to Running Bear to continue.

"The Native Americans honor the spirit in all things, which brings respect and kindness to all two-leggeds, four-leggeds, and all things that fly and crawl and swim and are planted. The Native Americans," Running Bear said, "have realized that if we are to share this planet, we must begin to teach the native ways to non-natives. For the White, American, and European cultures have so disconnected from the pulse of life, they have poisoned themselves and our home."

"And," continued Running Bear, "if your heart leads you to something, then having skills and information will assist you to create it. The Indians did not just pray for the deer to fall over and die for their dinner. They prayed that the Great Spirit would give them a deer whose passing would strengthen the herd and their tribe. Then they went with a high level of skill and shot the appropriate deer with their bow and arrow or a spear. They were trained, skilled hunters. They used their minds, skill, and spiritual guidance to assist them. Then they gave thanks to Great Spirit for the food and clothing they would create from the deer's body. So, do you see the balance of it?"

"Man, my head is swimming," said Jerry. "The head, the heart, right action, spirits everywhere. Life isn't anything like I thought it was!"

"And yet," said Bud, "it really is simple. If I am quiet enough and listen to my heart and my own pulse, I will at least be heading in the right direction."

"Yes!" chorused Running Bear, Sid, and Victoria simultaneously.

"And just practice, practice, practice!" concluded Victoria. Everyone laughed and then simultaneously joined hands. "Thank you, Great Spirit, Mother Father God, for this glorious day so filled with love and new understandings. May we all hold these truths deep within us and put love first. Namaste." She squeezed Sid's hand, and the squeeze went around the circle. "It's time to leave." She rose and hugged Bud and Jerry and Running Bear Eagle.

She collected the drums and mallets, then hesitated before putting the second drum into the pack. "Bud, would you like to borrow this drum? You seem to have a natural affinity toward it."

"Really?" he asked, amazed.

"Sure. Return it the next time I see you," she said, handing it to him. "If it gets out of tune, heat the skin up with a hairdryer. Namaste." She smiled and jaunted off with Sid into the forest.

"I think it's time for me to go too," Running Bear Eagle said. She collected the stones she had gathered and placed them under Grandmother Tree for another time. Hugging Bud and Jerry, she too disappeared into the woods.

"Let's split," muttered Bud. And they headed out of the forest. Bud headed home to the opposite side of the town from Jerry.

"I'll call you," yelled Jerry to Bud as they got farther apart.

"Okay!" responded Bud and turned the corner, out of sight.

As Bud walked along, he began to tune into the rhythms all around him. The background noise was a white noise of cars roaring and the undertones of people speaking. But as he listened more keenly, he began to hear new rhythms. *Chic-a-boom, boom. Chic-a-chic-a-boom. BOOM, BOOM.* And so it went as he walked in the circle of pulses.

Suddenly he realized he had walked to the Plaid Pantry that he had attempted to rob a few days earlier. By some angelic nudge, he found himself walking inside.

The owner recognized him immediately and started to press his newly installed alarm button.

Bud raised his hands above his head and said, "I didn't come to rob you. I came to apologize." He couldn't believe his own words and looked around for who was really talking. "I'm learning a new way to live, and the first step is to right my wrongs," he heard himself saying. "So I've come to apologize to you for scaring you and your customers and for hurting your dog."

By this time, the dog had raced out, but instead of attacking Bud, he lay down on his back, tummy up, and whined to be patted. Amazed, Bud petted him and whispered, "Thank you, little dog, I feel you have forgiven me. Now, if I could just do that for myself."

The storeowner stayed protecting his cash box and watching carefully. The boy wasn't armed today, except with a rim drum. *Could that be the new weapon?* he thought.

After petting the dog, Bud just looked at the storeowner. "Well," he stammered, "that's all I have to say. I'm sorry."

As Bud started to leave, the man called out to him, "What happened to you? Where's the Indian woman?"

Bud turned around. "That day changed my life. The Indian woman showed kindness to me, and since then, I have learned that I'm trapped in this hellhole because of the way I view my life. It's hard to believe, but what I've been doing has only made things worse, so I'm doing somethin' different. I didn't plan to come here, but suddenly here I was, so I know it is my angel guiding me."

"Where's the Indian woman?" he asked again.

"I don't know," Bud answered honestly.

The man walked to the other side of the counter. "What's the drum for?"

"For me to beat the rhythms of my heart on. And the other rhythms I hear within me and around me." He got really quiet and listened to his own pulse again and began to beat the drum to it. Then he brought in the pulse he was picking up from the man. When he brought in the pulse of the dog, the beat came to harmony.

The dog felt the difference in Bud and knew this was good. The man could not contain himself and began to tap on the counter. After a while, the drumming faded, just as it had done in the forest, and they remained in the heightened silence for several moments.

Struck by the sacredness, the storeowner heard himself say, "Well, you know I need some help around here. My last assistant quit after the robbery. Would you like to try it? It's minimum wage to start."

Bud looked at him for what seemed forever. He could not believe his ears. Usually he had to fast-talk himself into a job. Someone was actually offering him one?! "Sure. When do I start?" he replied. Still amazed.

"How about right now?" the man surprised himself by saying. "It's slow now. I could show you around. The dog sure likes you." Before his mind could interfere, the man gave Bud a tour of the store and explained that he would need to memorize where all the items were. He showed him the storeroom, where deliveries came in, how the cooler was loaded, and the like. "A lot to learn," he said. "But I'll be here to help you." Hesitantly he walked over to the cash register. "I'll show you that later. For now, learn the stocking. There is a load that was just delivered. You can begin to unload it now."

"Do you have a time card for me to fill out?" Bud said, very businesslike. "And do you need my social security number and stuff?"

"Well, sure," the man said and went back to his office to get the paperwork. "This kid is going to keep me straight. I usually just pay these kids under the table," he mumbled under his breath.

CHAPTER 15

Clarity

*J*erry arrived home to find his mother cooking Sunday dinner, which was unusual for her.

"Hi, mom," he called out as he entered the house and headed to his bedroom.

"Hi, Jerry," she replied. She was fixing his favorite meal, spaghetti and meatballs.

Jerry came down to the kitchen after a while. "Cool, spaghetti! My favorite. What's the occasion?"

"Nothin'. I just had time today and thought you might like it."

Time? Jerry thought. *She never has time. She's always in a hurry. It's always, 'hurry up, hurry up, I don't have time.' Something must be up. I wonder what she wants?* He shuddered.

Jerry sat down at the kitchen table and watched her for a while. He felt a nudge on his left side, gentle. "Mom," he began. "I am sorry about the river incident. I know we haven't talked about it. I felt so hopeless. Dad leaving and all. All the promises broken. There just wasn't any hope for me. I couldn't see a way out. I didn't mean to scare you. I'm really sorry."

She kept on preparing the meal while he talked. "Oh, that's okay son," she replied half conscious.

"NO!" He jumped up and walked over to her.

She leaned away from him, but kept chopping an onion.

"Mom." He caught her eyes. "It's *not* okay. I almost killed myself!"

His hands flung up in the air and he spun around. "When I saw the tunnel of light," he said, gesturing to the sky, "it pulled me to come. I almost followed the tug!" He slapped the counter and stomped back to his chair at the kitchen table.

He waited for her to respond, but she kept chopping, her eyes watering from the onion, and staring blankly. He closed his eyes and bowed his head. Emotions were mounting inside of him. So much had happened in such a short time. Remembering this afternoon, he took a deep breath to settle the surging energy within him and connected his heart and mind and higher self. He heard the beat of the drum and Victoria's voice: *Ta ke ti na, ta ke ti na*. He tapped his foot. He dropped his energy into the heart of Mother Earth. Click—he was connected.

A calm washed over him, and he began again, softly at first. "Mom, Victoria showed me another way. She said I had made a pledge to help heal the Earth, and that I could make a difference if I stayed alive to help. That we need all the voices for Earth that we can get. I didn't know what that meant, but I'm starting to now. So, mom, it's not all right. Did you hear me? I'm apologizing!"

She turned her gaze to him, her head shaking. "Oh. Yes . . . yes," she stammered, "I hear you." She set down her knife carefully on the counter and went over to him. Kneeling down to his level, she tenderly took his face in her hands and looked him in the eyes. "I . . . I love you, Jerry." She pulled him close. "I love you, son." Tears streamed down her face and when her hug tightened, she murmured, "Don't ever leave me!"

"I'm sorry, too, Mom," he barely whispered.

"I think I stopped listening a long time ago. It all became too overwhelming with your dad leaving, not enough money, and then you almost killing yourself." Her voiced choked. "I'm so sorry Jerry!"

For several moments, their shoulders heaved together as they held each other closely, shedding tears of pain, grief, and unbearable hurt.

Then, rather awkwardly, she let go of him and returned to the onion.

Sid and Victoria walked deeper into the woods. Victoria suddenly broke away from Sid and began to skip and leap into the air. "Smell the green," she called to him as she skipped backwards. When he caught up to her, she tilted her head back just enough to be a perfect match for his lips.

He smiled as he leaned toward her to kiss her ever so sweetly. Then he took her hand, and they skipped together through the woods, laughing playfully.

"You know," she said, slowing to a walk, "since I experienced *Ta ke ti na*—the rhythm system we just experienced in the woods—I see everything through the lens of pulse and rhythm. I reexamined different phases of my life within this new paradigm. The day after the *Ta ke ti na* workshop, I could feel my cells rearranging, so I scheduled a quiet day for myself, to get the most out of the experience. The entire day was in a slow *Ga ma la* rhythm, gentle and flowing."

Her hands danced to the rhythm. "Toward the end of the day, however, I needed to hurry to the post office before it closed, and the grocery store. As I was moved into these activities—actually, at the thought of them—I felt myself get tense and irritated, as if now my beautiful day was ruined. Then I thought, no, this is just a fast *Ta ke ti na* rhythm, and that's okay too. *Ta ke ti na, Ta ke ti na,* I sang, and the stress just dropped away. And I sang *Ta ke ti na* all the way to the post office."

She dashed around, lifting her legs like a prancing horse, and made a figure eight. "*Ta ke ti na*," she sang.

Sid couldn't help but laugh with her.

Then she stopped suddenly and walked in slow motion, lifting one foot deliberately, then the next. "*Gaaaa maaa laaa,*" she sang exaggeratedly, trying to keep a straight face. "On the way home, I slowed right down. Then I realized that I've spent ninety-five percent of my life in a fast *Ta ke ti na*. That's out of rhythm for me. I need more *Ga ma la*. That's why I've burned out six times in twenty-five years. I get so excited about the work, that my natural rhythm is buried somewhere in the adrenaline. Suddenly, I'm sick or seriously injured. As the years progressed, each time I burned out, the ante went up."

Sid nodded, listening intently.

"*Ta ke ti na* helped me realize I need to listen to my inner pulse and follow it."

"I can relate to that," Sid said. "I finally learned about the middle road after starving myself, then feeding myself into another kind of stupor. Funny isn't it? The easiest way is often the hardest."

"And it is all in the rhythm," Victoria mused. "Once we truly know our own rhythms, we truly know ourselves."

He leaned over to kiss her. Gently stroking her face, he kissed her again. Body touching body, they merged, not knowing where one began and the other ended. Then synchronistically they linked arms and skipped out of the forest, singing "*Ga ma la, Ga ma la....*"

CHAPTER 16

Right Action

"*Ta ka ti na, Ta ka ti na, Ta ka ti na,*" Bud sang softly as he stocked the shelves. Hefting a heavy box, he sang, "*Gaaa maaa laaa.*" Realizing it was lighter than he thought it would be, he muttered to himself, "Wow, I'm done already. Guess I'll go back and tell the boss."

The storeowner was waiting on some customers when Bud surfaced for another assignment.

An elderly woman on aisle two saw Bud and screamed. "Call the police, Mac, he's back! Over there!" She pointed toward where Bud was standing. She dropped her shopping bag and ran for the door, her hands over her ears, bracing against the sound of gun fire.

Startled, Bud leapt higher than the first shelf, and while airborne, flew around the corner and ducked down.

Mac dashed out to catch Mrs. Nowak's arm. "Anna, Anna, don't be afraid. He works for me now."

"What? Are you nuts? He shot your dog!" She pulled away from him and started to run with a little hobble.

"Anna, let me explain." Mac turned and saw Bud walking toward them, with the dog happily beside him. But Mrs. Nowak was heading for her car.

"Mrs. Nowak," Bud called to her, "sorry I frightened you." He stayed his distance, then kneeled to pet the dog.

Mrs. Nowak looked around and saw the dog licking Bud's face.

"I'm learning a new way to live, and Mac hired me, so you'll probably see me again. I hope we can learn a new way to think about each other."

With one eye on Bud, she looked at the storeowner.

He nodded.

Shaking her head, she walked back into the store, every cell alert, and completed her shopping.

"Did you finish stocking the shelves?" Mac asked Bud, after Mrs. Nowak had left.

"Yes."

"Let me check."

To Mac's amazement, not only were the shelves stocked, but the produce was in orderly rows. The boxes were broken down, ready for recycling, and the cooler was spotless. "I'm very impressed. No one has ever done such a good job, not even me. Now I'll show you how to use the computer." He could not believe what he was saying.

Mac explained how to calculate the stock with each entry. Then he demonstrated the various transactions that could be made, and had Bud practice.

At first, Bud was a little clumsy. He had never been on this side of the counter before. It was strange and exhilarating.

After a few mock sales, he had learned how to make a transaction and correct a mistake. He had just begun to feel more comfortable when his first test arrived.

In walked the policeman who had responded to the robbery. After he collected his items, he walked to the counter.

Bud smiled, but his knees quaked. *Will he recognize me?* he wondered.

As soon as Bud had that thought, the cop said, "Mac, what's going on here?"

Mac smiled shyly. "He'll tell you."

Breathing deeply and connecting to Earth, Bud replied, "I realized the other day that if I kept doing what I was doing, I would end up in jail or dead like my brother. The Indian woman and her friends helped me see another way to act, so I am practicing it now. I came by earlier today to apologize to Mac, and he hired me. That will be twenty-five dollars and fifty-two cents please."

He had been checking the items through as he spoke, mastering two totally different rhythms at once. But he was too scared to notice his accomplishment. However, it did not go unnoticed by the policeman or Mac.

Startled by the response and then the request for money, the policeman reached into his pocket and pulled out a twenty- and a ten-dollar bill. He was watching to see if Bud gave him the correct change.

Bud counted the change as if he had been doing it his entire life. "Thank you," he said and nodded his head.

The policeman nodded, gathered his groceries, and walked out. About half way to his car, he turned briskly, with determination, and headed back toward the store.

Bud watching him, frozen.

But instead of going into the store, the cop made a large loop back to his car, almost as if another force was guiding him.

Bud gasped.

"Well, I guess you passed that test," Mac said. "I can't believe he didn't take you in."

Bud looked at him wide eyed, shook off the tension, and walked over to the magazine display counter to straighten it out. "Phew," he said inaudibly. "That was close!"

At the end of Bud's shift, Mac said, "I learned something from you today, Bud."

Bud stood very still, hardly breathing, eyes matched to Mac's.

"I learned not to judge," Mac said.

Bud visible relaxed.

Looking down, Mac muttered, "Maybe I can change too." Then looked right into Bud's eyes as he shook his hand. "Thank you, son. Thank you." And he went back to the computer.

Bud walked home in the twilight, shaking his head. *Maybe they were right*, he thought. *Maybe I can break out if I see the situation differently. It really is my choice.*

Bud had remembered to phone his mother, so she wouldn't worry. She was pleased by his consideration and had dinner waiting for him when he got home. "How did it go Bud?" she asked when he walked in.

"Well, Ma," he replied.

"No trouble or nothin'?"

"Well," he repeated almost otherworldly. Then he shared with her his new way of viewing life and what happened at the store.

She stiffened up during the cop part of the story. "Wow," she exclaimed when he had finished talking. "All I can say is praise the Lord. The Lord *is* watching over his sparrows today!"

For the first time, Bud appreciated that song. *Maybe God really does care—if I care*, he thought.

Dinner was delicious, and the conversation light and fun for the first time since Bud's brother was killed.

CHAPTER 17

Things Aren't as They Seem

everend Bill had a little skip in his walk as he approached the
church. With a twinkle in his eyes and a smirk like a kid who just
discovered a hidden chocolate bar, he approached the church about an
hour and a half before the service, hoping to have a few minutes alone.
But Mrs. Briggs, his assistant, was there and hobbled over to him and
enveloped him her ample arms and full-figured body for a big hug.

"I am so glad you're all right!" she said rapidly. "Thanks for the call
last night. I would have hated to learn about the fire on some electronic
media!" Then she stepped back and gazed at him. One eyebrow cocked
upward and the other down. "You don't look mad or upset. You look
rather pleased with yourself, actually. What's up?"

He looked at her as if for the first time. His awareness was greater
and his perception deeper today than ever before. He realized how truly
devoted she was to him and the church. A slow smile emerged on his
lips, and he extended his right hand to her, placed his other hand over
hers, and said, "Mrs. Briggs, thank you for the excellent management of
our church and of me for over twenty-five years. I don't think I realized
how dedicated you are and how lucky I am to have you by my side,
running this church until just now!"

"Oh...ah," she stammered, head tilted to one side. "You're
welcome, but...but...what happened last night? You're...you're quite
different."

He took her arm like an English gentleman, chest erect, head tall, and escorted her to a chair in the counseling space in his office. He sat adjacent to her and leaned forward, with his hand on his chin and his eyes narrowed, as if he were about to reveal a top secret. "A real miracle occurred last night." he whispered, shifting his eyes back and forth as if looking for an undercover spy. "I've been waiting for a sign my entire life that there really is a God. I know that sounds ridiculous coming from a minister, but I've had my doubts. Last night..." He paused and the twinkle in his eyes and his smirk reappeared. Straightening up, he said, "But, you will hear all about it during my sermon this morning!"

She smiled and nodded her head. "Well then, I'll be *there* instead of in the office catching up."

Mary peaked her head in to say hello. "Good morning! What's up? I feel some excitement here."

Mrs. Briggs rose from her chair, winked at Reverend Bill, and gave Mary a big hug. "He's had a miracle. Sermon should be good today!" she said and walked back to her office.

Mary scooted into her chair and leaned way forward expectantly. "Yes?"

"Oh, you'll hear all about it this morning," Bill said. "Now, what can I do for you?"

"Now, that's a first!" she blurted out. "Oh, sorry, that just slipped out. I mean..."

"No problem. It *is* a first, and I apologize for that. Things are going to be different around here from now on. Let's get ready for the service. Is David the sound man here?" He linked their arms, and off they went to the sanctuary.

The congregation responded to the new energy, and the excitement spread like wildfire. Everyone was wide eyed and breathless during the house-burning scene. Many cried at his plea to God, and some gasped during his proclamation of letting go of the house and all their possessions. Murmurs of "Oh my!" "I couldn't do that," and so forth rumbled through the crowd. But all was dead silent as he described his family walking through the burned remains of their home the next morning.

"And as I lifted the fire blanket over the dining room table, the cat rushed out and leaped into my arms, nearly knocking me off balance! Jenny cried out, 'Button! Button!' and grabbed her from my arms, hugging her tightly. Then, very slowly, I lifted the blanket completely..." He ducked his head as if lifting a blanket. "My photos weren't burned! They were in perfect condition. Neither the fire nor the smoke had touched them."

The entire congregation leaped out of their seats and applauded uproariously. "Wow!" "Yay!" rippled through the crowd.

After some time, Bill nodded for them to be seated. "Let go and let God. It's true. May God bless you all," he concluded, to another round of uproarious applause.

After the service, Mary took Bill aside. "I'd like to ask Joseph to come and speak to the congregation. I believe he will add to this new energy you created today. I feel a big change coming. What do you think?"

He paused to feel into the suggestion. "Yes, great idea. Confer with Mrs. Riley and Joseph to make the arrangements. The sooner the better, so we can keep the momentum going." He turned and walked toward his office, then as if nudged ever so gently, he stopped and came back to Mary. Looking into her eyes, he said, "Thank you, Mary. Thank you very much." He took her hand affectionately and squeezed it.

Mary's face lit up with a beaming smile, "You're welcome, thank you back!" She gave him a quick hug and dashed off to find her husband and kids.

CHAPTER 18

New Joy

There was new life to be born at church, and Mary was going to be part of it.

The next thing she was going to do was to get a new job. She hated the Welcome Wagon. Joseph was right: enough of doing things because she thought she should. She wanted to do things she loved.

In the want ads, she found a listing for a conference planner. Five years' experience was the minimum. She didn't have five minutes, but something would happen. While putting her resume together, she asked herself, *What have I done that uses the same skills as a conference planner?* First she created a list of the skills a conference planner would need, which she got from the job description. Then it was easy to list the skills she used in her Welcome Wagon Job: organizing church functions, not to mention the management of her home. She sent the resume and a cover letter out immediately and envisioned herself having a connective, interactive interview.

But now what to do about her husband, who did not want "his" wife working outside the home. *Oh, well,* she thought. *I'll just ask for what I want. God will show me how.*

As it turned out, her angels assisted her along the way, and the conference-planning job was hers. The interviewers and Mary clicked at first sight. It would be her first real job out of the home, and with a handsome salary to boot. Wouldn't Joseph be impressed!

Without even thinking, she drove right to Joseph's after the interview. She was excited and knew he would share her joy.

"I took your advice, Joseph, and got another job," she blurted out as soon as the door opened. "I'll be planning conferences. They hired me with no experience."

Joseph smiled and invited her in, "Congratulations, Mary!" He gave her a warm hug and pointed to the couch.

She sat in what was becoming her usual seat.

"I start next Monday, but I haven't told my husband yet. You're the first person to know. I just came straight here from the interview." She twisted her hands in her lap nervously and looked up sheepishly, waiting for a response. But Joseph said nothing and continued to listen. "I'm a little nervous about telling my husband. He didn't even know I was looking for a job," she hedged.

"Yes?" he prompted.

"Well, he doesn't like me to work away from home, but I don't like the Welcome Wagon anymore, so I got this job." She paused for a long time, getting the courage to say the rest. And finally, while Joseph just beamed her with love, she said, "That's how he controls me... There! I said it. Oh Joseph, I've never verbalized that before. But when I hear myself say it, I know it's true. He's clipped my wings, and now it just isn't right for me. What should I do? I thought maybe I just won't tell him, but I know that after a while he'll wonder where I am, and I'll be working some weekends. He'll be so angry." Tears welled up. She slumped like a burst balloon. The excitement of the accomplishment had vanished, and was replaced by the terror of her husband's response.

After pausing, Joseph leaned forward and said, "When you tell your husband about your new job, tell him with kindness, not the tone of 'gotcha bucko.' Understand that when he feels he is not completely in control of you, it is not safe for him."

"But I can't make him feel safe anymore. I can't play the perfect obedient wife. There is more in me than that. It's my turn to express myself in new ways. Maybe the "Me Too" movement has reached me too!" She erupted into tears, hiding her face in her hands. "I feel trapped!" she yelled, slapping her hands in her lap. "Trapped like a rat in a cage. Just running around doing tasks."

"Mary, "he said gently, taking her hand, "your feeling situation is not much different than your husband's. Our partners are always mirrors for what is inside of us, only in a different set of clothes. You also need to control a situation to feel safe. Do you think you don't manipulate him?"

There was a long pause. She rolled her eyes, then put her chin in her hands. With eyebrows crunched, she looked down and shifted uncomfortably in her seat. "Manipulate him? Me? What do you mean? He's always bossing me around, and I'm terrified that the dinner won't meet his expectation or that I have missed sweeping something up—" She stopped suddenly and looked up at Joseph, curious.

Joseph nodded. "Yes? What's your part in this play?"

"Well, I withdraw from him when he hurts me or doesn't do what I tell him," she said and burst into tears again. "One time I didn't talk to him for a whole week," she said between sobs. "I was so mad! He was nicer after that, but not for long. Oh Joseph, is this my fault too?"

Joseph enveloped her with love. "There is no fault here. Seeing our part of the situation is always painful," he whispered gently. "But this is another example of how connected we are to each other."

"I always felt it was my duty to be the perfect wife," she said, now composed, knowing how old-fashioned that sounded. "But I realized after the angel class that what I was doing was a disservice to both of us. Me pretending to be someone I wasn't just perpetuated the façade. It isn't an authentic relationship. Yikes! What a mess." Shaking her head, she looked questioningly at Joseph.

He was still listening intently, continuing to raise the vibration of the conversation with love. He nodded.

"What should I do now?" she asked.

"What do you think, Mary?"

She reflected. "Tell the truth, I guess."

"Yes," said Joseph. "That's a good place to start, because it will clear the energy and open space for something new to be born."

She rose with new determination, then slumped. "What if he doesn't like the new me?"

"That's a possibility, Mary," Joseph said, "but you will never know until you try."

She nodded and headed for the door. Turning back to Joseph, she said, "You're a godsend, Joseph. Thank you again." She gave him a little hug and smiled.

"Thank you."

As she skipped down the walkway to her car, Mary hollered over her shoulder, "I'll keep you posted!"

Joseph smiled and waved a goodbye.

At home, after the kids were in bed, she sat adjacent to her husband's chair on the corner of the couch. Though a little nervous, she felt Joseph with her, and that gave her strength. She sat erect and looked right at her husband. "Jim, I am beginning to grow inside. I feel like I am finally growing up," she began.

Jim put down his newspaper and gazed at her as if for the first time and said, "I'm listening."

She could not remember a time he had actually stopped reading or stopped whatever he was doing to listen. The room was energized. She took a deep breath and continued, still holding his gaze. "For many years, our relationship has been very parental. I don't mean with the kids; I mean with each other. With me sort of mothering you, and you fathering me. I feel ready now to create a more mature relationship, one where we come together and honor each other's unique strengths." She paused and waited for a response.

"Go on," he replied.

"Well, I recently learned there is a higher purpose to our marriage than earning money and raising kids. There is a divine purpose. The purpose God has for us as a couple." She paused, again watching him closely for any signs of anger.

He turned bright red and began to raise his hand.

She did not cringe but instead sent energy through her feet into the Earth to connect. She immediately felt the support and gave a deep relaxing exhale.

Clinching his fists. Jim gave a hard swallow. "Well, I . . ." he said, but then stopped, as if something had overcome him, and said quite calmly, "Go on."

"Healing our past wounds is one purpose, so that we don't repeat what our parents did. We can look at our relationship in another way."

"But our parents did just fine, look at us!"

"I'm not happy living our parents' lives. I want more out of life than just being a homemaker. The kids are both in school now and I...I'm, sort of in a new school myself." She couldn't believe what was coming out of her mouth. She recalled Reverend Bill saying that when the disciples asked Jesus what they would say when he was gone, he answered that he would tell them when they got there. *Surely* he was speaking through her now.

"I don't understand about wounds in a relationship," Jim said. "But I can see you seem very different tonight. You're calmer and more confident than I ever remember. So I want to hear what you have to say."

The energy in the room felt angelic, like in class the other day. Mustering her courage, Mary continued, "I believe, we can ask for different perspectives on the situations we face." She was quite centered now but didn't have a clue where she was going with this. Her thoughts jumped around, and she said, "I realized the other day that I'm afraid of you—afraid of your anger and afraid you will disapprove of me." Wow, she hadn't realized that until just this minute! Continuing quickly so she wouldn't lose her nerve, she said, "I also realized that when I feel hurt or want to get back at you, I withdraw from you."

He took a double take and lowered his eyes. "Like when you have a headache right before bed? Is that what you mean?"

"Yes, perhaps. I just want to feel safe with you," she blurted out and burst into tears.

Clumsily, he reached for her hand and looked into her eyes. "You don't feel safe with me?" he asked. "But that's my job, to make the entire family safe. How could you not be safe? I make plenty of money. We live in a lovely home. I come home from work every night at the same time. I don't understand?"

"I...I don't feel emotionally safe," she continued. "Yes, the house is bolted up, and we have an alarm system, but my heart isn't safe. It's afraid of your disapproval or your scorn and ridicule." She seemed to hear Joseph's voice now, saying, *It's hard to see our part in it.* So she said, "Just like I was with my father." What? She hadn't realized that before either. Her father?

His eyes went back and forth rapidly, as if scanning a document and desperately trying to read it. He said very tentatively, "You don't want me to treat you like your father treated you?"

"Right. I want us to be two adults supporting each other's inner growth, the development of our souls, not just feeding our bodies. I didn't even know I could have inner growth until recently. But now I understand that is what I've been yearning for. An authentic relationship where—"

"But," he interrupted, "then what is my role, if not provider and protector?"

Her eyes softened. She was introducing new thoughts and perspectives to both of them, ideas she didn't understand yet herself. "You're still a provider and protector, but maybe on a higher level now, including our emotions. Not that you protect our emotions or your own, but that you *respect* them."

"What does that mean?"

"I don't know, I am learning as I go along. I guess our relationship would have a new basis, a foundation of rigorous honesty that includes acceptance of our fears and insecurities. We would no longer cover them up with anger or withdrawal. As it is, you get angry, and I withdraw."

There was long pause as they both digested this.

"I think that is the key," she said. "I would feel much safer if that were the case. I think I am saying 'the truth will set us free.'"

They talked late into the night about deep, untouched feelings they had never expressed. He was afraid that he wasn't good enough and would not be able to meet her expectations, just as he felt with his father. They laughed at times and cried at other times. Both realized a miracle was taking place. They honored each other as if they had just met. And in fact, this was a first meeting of their hearts on such a deep level. About two o'clock in the morning, they made love, and each was satisfied.

"Oh Jim, did you *feeeel* that? I felt our souls merge above our heads in the shape of a heart! Phew! I feel like I am floating." Mary snuggled closer to him and kissed his cheek.

"I'm vibrating all over. It feels so strange," he said and lifted up onto his elbows to look at her. "Mary, you're glowing. I mean it. There is a pink halo around you."

"*We* did that. We united like never before. Wow!"

Entwined in each other's arms and legs, they fell into a deep, euphoric sleep.

As the sun poured in through the window, Jim stirred and rolled over and whispered in Mary's ear, "I could stay like this forever. I'm not quite sure what happened last night, but if this is the beginning of something new, I'm in."

They both laughed, gave each other a quick kiss, and begrudgingly got out of bed.

"Okay," Mary hollered to the kids downstairs. "We'll be right down!"

After Mary got the children off to school, she prepared for her new job and suddenly remembered she had totally forgotten to tell Jim about it.

CHAPTER 19

The Hard Truth

*J*oseph's shoulders were tight up under his ears, his heart pounding, and his gait a little brisk as he entered the church. *Breathe*, he told himself. *They won't kill you tonight.*

"Joseph!" Mary exclaimed. "You're here! Welcome. I think everything is ready for you." She dashed over and hugged him tight. "I'm sure," she whispered in his ear, "they will love you, just like we do."

Joseph gave an audible sigh of relief. "I needed that. Thank you, Mary."

She was so different from when he first met her, when she seemed so unhappy, frightened. Now her inner power and joy permeated everything she touched.

"Let me show you to your seat," she said, jarring him out of his thoughts.

"Yes...yes, of course," he stuttered.

"I have a glass of water for you at the podium. Will you need anything else?"

"No, thanks Mary. That's perfect," he said, looking around.

"Okay let's do a sound check." She took his arm through hers and gently stroked it, then gave him a reassuring squeeze, as she guided him into the sanctuary.

They paused at the entrance to take it all in. It was quiet, but the atmosphere was energized with anticipation. Behind the alter, on the furthest wall, hung the cross representing his crucifixion. The tongue-and-groove redwood it was mounted on within an inset vaulted ceiling gave a warm feeling to the church. The wood pews had the same reddish tone on the cushions that blended with the carpet. All of this created a welcoming feeling.

Mary led him to the podium and adjusted his lavaliere microphone. "Sound check, please," she called up to the sound man.

"Hi, Joseph. I'm David. Have you ever used a microphone before?"

"Ah, no, not really."

"Okay, no problem. Just count to five with the volume you will be speaking at."

"One, two…" He startled when he heard his voice coming from the other side of the room. "Oh!"

"It's fine. It's always a little shocking when you first hear your voice from another part of the room. Keep counting. I'm setting the bass and tenor ranges."

"Three, four, five," he continued, breathing to relax himself.

"Check. That'll do it. Thanks."

Mary took him to the front-row pew and motioned for him to be seated. Checking her watch, she said, "I'll be back. I'm going to greet our guests. And Reverend Bill will be along to introduce our opening music and then you."

Joseph sat quietly, reflecting that all of this was being created in his name.

The organ began to play a lively melody. And guests flooded in to the smiles and hugs of Reverend Bill and Mary.

"I can't wait to hear this man. He must be pretty special to have an event on Friday night," said a middle-aged woman with perfectly matching shoes and handbag.

A group of teenagers with nose rings, triple-pierced ears, and torn jeans huddled outside excitedly until Reverend Bill waved them in. "Wow, I've never been in here before," one said. "Feels different than the church my family goes to."

One of his buddies pulled him toward the sanctuary. "Come look at this…"

A young couple in their twenties approached the church arm in arm. "Reverend Bill has sure been introducing new ideas lately. My stomach is a little nervous tonight. I'm feeling something life-changing may happen tonight. I bet this man Joseph will just blow us away!" She tapped her husband's arm excitedly.

Sid, Victoria, and Running Bear Eagle arrived together, laughing and smiling in anticipation.

"Welcome!" Reverend Bill and Mary exclaimed together, and hugged them heartily. "Joseph's in the front-row pew on the left. He'll be happy to see you."

Running Bear led the way. "There he is," she said, speeding up.

"Ah, thanks for coming!" Joseph greeted them with a warm smile and hugs all around.

"Won't miss this for the world," chorused Sid and Victoria.

Running Bear sat next to Joseph. She leaned close to his ear and squeezed his hand. "Be gentle on them."

He gave her a slow smile and whispered back, "Not a chance."

They both laughed.

The sanctuary filled to overflowing, and ushers dashed about, bringing in extra chairs.

Bud and Jerry scooted in just as Reverend Bill was approaching the podium.

"Phew, we made it on time," Bud whispered to Jerry as they slid into a seat in the back row.

"Yeah, expect something magical to happen," replied Jerry.

"Welcome everyone to our very special event tonight," opened Reverend Bill. "Let us pray."

The audience silenced and bowed their heads.

"O mighty God, bless this opportunity for us to open our hearts and minds in a whole new way. Help our prejudices melt away to the glory and power of Christ. Amen."

Heads rose in anticipation.

"And now, all the way from Portland, Oregon, star tenor of the Portland Opera Company, Anthony Abelli!"

The audience jumped up and applauded as Anthony dashed onto the stage. His dark wavy hair bounced as he crossed the stage in his black fitted suit pants and white tuxedo jacket that complemented his strong, slender body. He shook Reverend Bill's hand and squeezed his shoulder affectionately. Then he slowly and deliberately turned to the standing ovation and bowed deeply to the audience. The applause exploded with hoots and hollers.

After several seconds, Reverend Bill motioned the audience to be seated, and with a huge smile and twinkling eyes said, "Anthony will open our program with a rousing rendition of "Dream the Impossible Dream."

The overture began softly, and a hush fell over the audience.

> To dream the impossible dream . . .
> To run where the brave dare not go.
>
> To right the unrightable wrong . . .
>
> This is my Quest to follow that star . . .
>
> And the world will be better for this,
> That one man, scorned and covered with scars,
> Still strove, with his last ounce of courage,
> To reach the unreachable stars!

The audience sprang to their feet in applause. And Anthony bowed several times, with an elated smile, then ran off the stage, waving.

Reverend Bill came back on stage. "Thank you, Anthony," he said. "That was terrific! Please come out for another bow."

The applause continued through two more bows, and then everyone caught their breath.

"Now for our featured guest," Reverend Bill continued. "I would like to introduce a man of humble means, an artist, he calls himself. I believe he is an artist, though not of canvas and oils. His canvas is life and his oils are the human souls he touches with a loving brush stroke.

My life has begun to transform since I met him. It was as if he gently turned me in a new direction. And with the help of your comments lately, that direction has freed me and allowed me to love and minister more deeply than in the past twenty years. I have been honored to wear the clerical robe. He teaches me that no one needs 'the robe' to be richly in touch with God. Please welcome with an open heart, Joseph."

The applause was thunderous. Jerry and Bud gave each other high five, as Sid squeezed Victoria's hand.

Joseph calmly walked onto the stage. In silence, he looked out at the audience with such great love that many wept. Some shifted in their seats, while many sighed as if relieved of some great burden.

Then gently he began. "Thank you, Reverend Bill and Mary, for making this gathering possible." He nodded to each of them in their perspective seats in the audience, then continued. "Yes, let us dream the impossible dream." His voice built slowly. "The dream to live in love. To reach the unreachable star, the star of inner peace."

Applause broke out again. The electricity rippling through the crowd was now permeated with divine love.

"Tonight I am going to speak about how to live in love, *really*, and be peaceful inside. But to do this, your perspective on life must change first. So we will start with the great illusion of separation that has plagued humanity for thousands of years. There are many myths. By that, I don't mean untruths, but stories in our culture that have shaped who and what you are. These archetypal stories are the basis of your belief system. In other words, you are imprinted with these beliefs, and you don't question them.

"One of these archetypal beliefs is that you are a victim, and need to be saved. You believe there is a power greater than you that will come and scoop up your wretched form and bring it out of its misery. You have much proof for this belief, for the Bible is full of the stories of being saved from the enemy. In Judges Chapter 1 it reads:

> Now after the death of Joshua it
> came to pass, that the children
> of Israel asked the LORD, saying,

Who shall go up for us against the
Canaanites first, to fight against
them?

And the LORD said, Judah shall
go up: behold, I have delivered the
land into his hand.

And Judah said unto Simeon his
brother, Come up with me into my
lot, that we may fight against the Canaanites; and I likewise will go with
thee into thy lot. So Simeon went
with him.

And Judah went up; and the
LORD delivered the Canaanites and
the Perizzites into their hand; and
they slew them in Bezek ten thousand men. (KJV)

"So, in this passage, the Jews started out as the victims of the
Canaanites, who were the persecutors. Through the power of God,
Judah became the rescuer or savior. 'And the Lord delivered the
Canaanites and the Perizzites into their hand; and they slew them in
Bezek ten thousand men.' So, the Jews became the persecutors, and God
the rescuer. Thus, the Jews were saved from the enemy.

"There's another passage in Judges Chapter 4:

And the children of Israel again
did evil in the sight of the LORD,
when Ehud was dead.

And the LORD sold them into the
hand of Jabin King of Canaan, that

reigned in Hazor; the captain of
whose host was Sisera, which dwelt
in Harosheth of the Gentiles.

And the children of Israel cried
unto the LORD: for he had nine hundred chariots of iron; and twenty
years he mightily oppressed the children of Israel.

And Deborah, a prophetess,
The wife of Lapidoth, she judged Israel at this time.

And she dwelt under the palm
Tree of Deborah between Ramah
and Bethel in mount Ephraim:
and the children of Israel came up
to her for judgment. . . .

So God subdued on that day
Jabin the king of Canaan before the
children of Israel. (KJV)

"There are two messages here. One, if you displease the Father,
or God, you will be punished. 'And the children of Israel again did
evil in the sight of the Lord when Ehud was dead. And the Lord sold
them into the hand of Jabin King of Canaan.' But also a message
that the very one who has punished you will be the one to save you.
'So God subdued on that day Jabin the King of Canaan before the
children of Israel.'

"This puts you into a catch twenty-two. The very one you trust and
love and are devoted to is the one who will hurt you if you step out of
line. Several belief constructs come from these two teachings, of which
there are many more examples."

"Wow, really?" someone said softly to himself. "I never understood it like that."

Jerry turned to Bud and whispered, "That's what we were talking about in the forest with Victoria and Running Bear."

Murmurs of "Oh my" and "Really?" cascaded through the audience.

"These beliefs reside deep in your abdomen, where your first chakra is, and rule the way you act toward yourself and others. Let us look at the first pattern that is created. It is called the *drama triangle*. You may have heard of this before, but listen to how it effects your life at its very core. The triangle has three parts. Each person moves from role to role quite unconsciously. The roles are the victim, the persecutor, and the rescuer or savior. The Jews are victims of the Canaanites in *both* examples. Also, they are the victims of God, who has punished them for something they did to displease him. The Canaanites are the persecutors, as is God. Then the Jews plead to be saved, and God sends them saviors: Judah and Simeon. In the second story, he sends Deborah and Barak. Then God moves from persecutor to the savior of the Jews. In both situations, the Canaanites move from the persecutor role to the victim role."

There was a rumble of disbelief in the room.

"This story," Joseph continued, "is so engrained in your consciousness that it manifests in every realm of human existence, from early biblical time to the present. In Victor Hugo's *Les Miserable*, a story from the 1800s, Jean Valjean is a victim of poverty, steals a loaf of bread to feed his sister and her seven children—he's the rescuer here—is caught, and is sent to prison for thirteen years (now the victim). He gets out of prison, hard and sullen, and steals a kindly priest's silver, now the persecutor. When brought back by the constable, the priest in turn *gives* him the stolen items, *plus* two silver candlesticks, so that he may use them to begin to lead an honest life. The priest is now the rescuer. Now Jean has been saved and goes out into the community and brings it great wealth and helps the poor. He is now the rescuer. He has played all three roles: victim, persecutor, and rescuer.

"Now, moving forward in history, we see that, in most movies, there will be a victim, persecutor or antagonist, and protagonist or hero/

savior. Remember those terms from English Lit? Good against evil all play into this construct. The antagonist/persecutor is the evil one. The *Star Wars* movies make the aliens the antagonists and Star Fleet the protagonists. The aliens play the evil role persecuting Star Fleet, only to become the victims of the Star Fleet, after some thrilling, high-tension fight. So the victim, Star Fleet, becomes the persecutors of the aliens and the rescuers of the Star Fleet. Think about it. You think you are evolving, but you just bring your old story into your new technology.

"There is so much drama as each party moves from role to role that you do not realize you are playing this game. But go now a layer deeper. How does this pattern translate into your personal life? Do you ever feel like the victim of your childhood, your spouse, your children, your teachers, your minister, the weather, the government, the airline reservationist, the waiter or clerk? Did that car just almost sideswipe you? Who is doing what to whom? If you find yourself thinking 'if only' I had more money, 'if only' my husband watched less TV, 'if only' my son would do his homework, 'if only' I could lose ten pounds, 'if only' I were smarter... and so it goes. Your 'if only' thoughts are an indicator that you are in the victim position. These thoughts put the control of the situation on the object of desire.

"Let me emphasize: *'if only' thoughts are a key to the victim position, as are 'poor me' and 'Why did that happen to me?' and 'I am just not good enough,'* etcetera. These and similar thoughts put the control of the situation on the object of desire. 'The other,' or the persecutor, is in control, for you feel helpless under his grip, just as the Jews felt helpless under the punishment of God. Because God (in the persecutor role) had all the power, only the persecutor can save you.

"So the victim believes that 'only if' the *persecutor* can change—that is, stop drinking, study, be fair, be honest, come home, be environmentally responsible—then everything will be all right. *That's the trap.* You feel that if you just wait long enough for the other person or situation to change and you continue to be your perfect self, the persecutor will change. You put all your focus on being perfect, so God, your husband, father, wife, etcetera—the persecutor—won't attack. And you put the rest of your focus on trying to change the persecutor.

You do this without realizing that you move into the persecutor role also. As you know, you cannot change anyone but yourself, and that is quite hard enough, without trying to change someone else who has great control over you. Why would the other person change and give up such power?

"And of course, being a victim is also a very manipulative role. For as you have seen, you are not the victim for long; you get your revenge. And you become the persecutor. Your husband gets thrown in jail. You put a restraining order on him. You throw away his favorite shirt. You have an affair. You are not honest. And so it goes in different degrees of dysfunction. The pattern is played out subtly in your home; at your office; and in your church, schools, and government.

"Turn to a person next to you, and each of you take a turn to tell the other times you felt helpless or victimized at home, at school, or at work."

The people in the audience shifted focus to the person on the left, and a buzz spread across the room. Mable, a woman in her sixties, had been abused as a child but never spoke of it before. She burst into tears in the telling.

So it continued for several minutes, as Joseph beamed the room with love. The more intense the love, the more people realized how trapped they really felt. Mary and her husband nodded at each other, holding hands tightly for the confirmation Joseph was presenting.

Without saying anything, Joseph raised his right arm into the air and signaled them to come to silence. There was a hush.

"Realizing your part in the drama is very important and the first step to stop blaming others for your discontent. Then you can really begin to change your reality, and therefore your life. You are watching Reverend Bill do that right before your eyes. Now let's look at how your *former* inner thoughts are projected onto the world stage."

Nervous laughter rippled through the audience.

"Some of you will remember Saddam Hussein. Some of you will have only read about him. In 2003, a coalition led by the United States invaded Iraq to depose Saddam. U.S. President George W. Bush and British Prime Minister Tony Blair accused him of possessing weapons of mass destruction and having ties to al-Qaeda. Saddam would not allow any inspections of his weapon holdings, so the tension mounted. Recognize the drama triangle? The United States and Britain take the victim role, and Saddam becomes the eminent threat or persecutor. The flame of fear was fanned and the United States, Britain, and two other countries attacked Iraq with 380,000 troops, leaving 30,000 Iraqis and 172 U.S. soldiers dead. Who are the victims now?"

"Innocent people," shouted someone from the audience.

"Yes, yes," agreed the crowd.

"Then the persecutors pound their chest like heroes for they have saved 'us' from the horrible persecutor—the crazy man, Hussein. Iraqis and many innocent people become the victims of this amplified drama. You feel righteous, for it is in your cellular memory: 'And the Lord said, Judah shall go up; behold, I have delivered the land into his hand.'

"Hussein is just a magnified character of the persecutor role. He was a reflection of your own thoughts. Your thoughts are projected collectively on the world political screen. He was the enemy and therefore threatened your lives. This is from the same template that all political wars are formed, and all wars in your living rooms, your boardrooms, and your streets. It is the exact same story. You blame your wife. You blame your president. This construct is the root blueprint to wife beating, child abuse, murder of the betrayed lover, and the like. For it is the beloved—God, father, husband, lover—who is the rescuer *and* the persecutor."

A man in the back shouted, "He would have killed us! He had the weapons! We had to stop him!"

Heads nodded and a wave of terror spread through the crowd.

"Yes," said Joseph calmly, "that is what you believe. But it never would have happened if the global mind hadn't projected it onto your political screen. I use Saddam as one of hundreds of examples available. For humans have been at war for thousands of years."

"So you think a rapist should be allowed to get away with it?" a woman in the third row shouted. "I was raped, and he was never convicted!"

"Listen to yourself," Joseph said lovingly. "You are living and telling the story from the template I just described to you. I want you to step out of that story and create a new one. You can't fix this template by wars or more hate and fear, because it just keeps recycling itself. Do you want to continue sending your children to war?"

"No! No!" they yelled.

"Do you want to continue to have girls and boys raped?"

"No! No!"

"Then we must create a new template, a new mythology, a new way of being together."

Bud stood up. "He's right. I changed the way I viewed my life and went back and apologized to the store owner I tried to rob two weeks earlier. It was a miracle. As I was walking out, he hired me! I changed my template, and the story changed. Joseph's right!" He sat down, quickly realizing what he had just said, and tucked his head, afraid someone would turn him in now. But instead the audience went silent for several very poignant seconds.

Joseph was just about to speak again when a woman in raggedy clothes, with hair askew, leaned on the pew in front of her for support to hoist herself up and said with tremor in her voice, "Oh, oh. I see now. Our inner thoughts create the thoughts in the global brain, so we are actually perpetuating the drama triangle. Yikes!" And she sat down, rather gingerly shaking her head. "I'm gonna stop that right now," she mumbled to herself.

"Okay," Joseph began again. "I think you are getting it. Do you want to hear one more piece to the story?"

A chorus of yeses erupted.

"How does this show up in how you treat yourself?" Joseph continued. "There are many layers to this answer, only one of which I will address. In most of the Judeo-Christian religions, you are taught that you are born with original sin. You start out the victim and the stage is set. You do things to hurt yourself. Each person experiences this at different levels. Some do not take care of their physical bodies. Others actually abuse their bodies with excess food, drink, dangerous sports, misuse of money, overwork, compulsive sex... and the list goes on. You feel dirty and must be cleansed and saved, *or so you believe.*

"Many stories reinforce the belief that you need a savior, that you are a helpless victim. In the era when those archetypes were created, the human species was developing the victim archetype, for it was an important part of your soul's development. If you have not at one time played the role of a victim, then you can't fully appreciate being a *victor* and being fully present and one with divine love. But there is hope. For now it is the time to move out of this controlling drama, as an individual, as a family, as an institution, as a country, and as a planet.

"Now is a new time. Also, in the global mind is the story of the empowered human. Some spiritual leaders name the next step in human development the Divine Human or Human Noeticus or Universal Human. No matter what name you settle on, these leaders see the continuous evolution and advancement of your species from Cro-Magnon man, who buried his food with his dead, to Homo sapiens, to Homo universalis. You are at a similar stage to the fish that crawls out of the water to become the reptile, or reptile that grows wings to become a bird.

"How do you get to this next stage? Is there a model? Where do you begin? You have been working on it since the last astrological age, two thousand years ago. Buddha, Jesus, Krishna, and the other avatars modeled *Homo universalis.* They founded the great religions. But you will not need religion as you know it now, because you already have the information. It is locked in the ancient scriptures, if you read between the lines. The universal laws have been kept secret because, as a species, you were not mature enough to handle the information. But you are on the evolutionary curve, and it is time now for the mysteries to be revealed.

"You do not need the second coming of Christ. Nor do the Jews need to wait for their savior. The second coming was not about Jesus coming back and saving you; that wasn't his message in the first place. It is about *you* becoming the Christ."

The crowd rustled, and murmurs of "Blasphemy" and "Now that's going too far" arose from the audience. Reverend Bill perked up and leaned forward.

"Now is the time to step out of the loop of the drama triangle that has you gripped by the throat. Now is the time to awaken to your true possibility. Now is the time to allow your God seed to germinate. *Now* is the time. You are moving from an age of physical mastery to an age of symbolic and spiritual mastery. You have advanced in science with computers, nanotechnology, cybernetics, and space travel. The planet is hooked up through computers and telephones and satellites to become one planetary organism electronically. These communication systems have become the planet's nervous system.

"What do we do?" someone shouted from the back.

"Many of you are already doing it. You are allowing love to come into your cells and bring light to the many wounds inside. And of course, one of your biggest challenges will be personally breaking out of the drama triangle. For as each of you breaks out of the drama triangle, you will begin to project the victor model into the collective unconscious, and soon it will be so filled with unconditional love that a critical mass will occur. Your God seed will sprout throughout the lands, and your wars will stop and your religions will become unnecessary, for you will *embody* the characteristics of the religions. You will not need the dogma."

"Yes!" and "Oh my!" called out the audience.

"And all the religions and all the nations will stand as one body and one mind. Your famous Beatle, John Lennon, knew this, but you weren't ready to hear the message, so you killed the messenger. How do you break the drama loop? Jesus paved the road out of the drama triangle. Christ is an archetype of love. He is larger than the cycle of victim/persecutor/rescuer. He modeled how to get out of the drama triangle. Though Christ appeared to be the victim of Romans and the savior of the people, he never responded like a victim, for he knew there was a larger divine plan. And most importantly, he did not persecute anyone. *You see, once the persecutor is out of the picture, the cycle is broken, and this literally shatters the entire structure.*

"*He did not persecute anyone.* Christ did not attack any people or nations. He blessed and loved his betrayer. He never spoke against the Romans or the Pharisees or the priests. Nor was he here to just save the

Jews. Christ's message was for *all* humans. *The savior is within.* And what will save you is *unconditional acceptance and love for yourself.* He did not come to save you from your sins, for you have not sinned. You are learning how to live within the universal laws, and many times you miss the mark. *He came to show you that love heals all wounds.* His story demonstrated that life is eternal, that you will never die, but are born again into a higher level of life.

"The resurrection is the story of Jesus, not the crucifixion. YOU can resurrect yourself from your little self to your divine self. Your true self. Stop persecuting others, and most importantly, stop persecuting yourself. *Once there is no persecutor, there can be no victim and with no victim, no need for a rescuer.* Then you are free!"

There was uproarious applause. The room was electrified.

After a long pause, he asked, "Are there any questions?"

"So, let me get this straight. You think we were stuck in the victim archetype because it is basically imprinted into our DNA?" Victoria asked.

Joseph smiled and nodded. "Yes. It has been so deeply programmed in you that it is in your DNA."

"Has everything we've been taught, wrong?" asked a young man with a nose ring.

"No. That was the level of learning you were at. Now move to the next level; it is yours for the taking. Did you stay in third grade all through school? No, you moved on to the fourth and fifth and sixth and on up. Earth is the school of your soul. Your soul needs to graduate third grade. So let it."

An angry elderly woman from the back of the room raised her hand.

Joseph nodded to her, knowing what she was about to say. She would voice the thoughts of many.

"What you say is blasphemous. Christ came to save us from our sins, for we are sinners and need to be saved."

"Then be saved now and move on," he replied in the most loving manner. He walked all the way to the back of the room and placed his hand on her head and said, "Be forgiven now of all your sins and realize the true beauty deeply within your soul. You are a beloved child of God. Be now an adult woman of God."

His light was so radiant and his love so strong, that the entire room was transformed. A huge collective sigh was released. Then he returned to the stage, paused, then raised his right palm and said, "The impossible dream is possible. Inner freedom is possible. At the core of this shift is forgiveness. Now, inhale, and with your exhale, forgive everyone for whom you carry a grudge."

"Ahh." "Ohh." "Ooo." The sounds of forgiveness rippled through the audience. "I feel like I can fly!" someone shouted out in glee. Others echoed the feeling: "Me Too." "I'm as light as air!" Then the entire room broke out into a clamor. Everyone was talking at once.

Joseph raised his hand, and everyone resumed their seats. A hush fell over the room. "Forgiveness. Now make a shift in the perspective with which you see the world. To have a shift, you must let go of your old repeating story—the story you wake up with each morning, the story you repeat tirelessly to your friends and family. See the world with new eyes.

"Everyone stand up and spread out from each other. Draw an imaginary line on the floor. Now step behind the line. Behind the line is your old story. The other side of the line is you in the new story. Stand in the old story and feel it. Now, with the conviction of a newlywed, vow to begin to live the new story. See yourself five years from now doing and feeling exactly the way you want to feel. Place that image on the other side on the line. Now, when you are ready, only when you are ready, step across the line into the new story."

Many people were deep into themselves. Then several bursts of joy were emitted throughout the room, as one by one, each person stepped into their new story.

"Now, feel how this feels," he continued. "Take it into every cell of your body. Breathe it in. Now take another step forward, but take the new story with you."

They stepped forward more quickly this time, as if they were getting the hang of it. "Yes!" one woman cried out. "Yes!" And everyone broke into peals of laughter, for they were all feeling the same emotion of freedom and possibility and excitement all at once.

"Please be seated. At the back of church is a bowl of small rose quartz crystals. Before you leave, please take one and put it into your pocket. And when you forget, touch it and remember you are victorious. You are creating a new story for yourself and for the planet. Feel again what you just felt here. Own it. Thank you." Joseph bowed low and deep, with such humility that many wept.

The audience jumped to their feet in uproarious applause.

Joseph bowed deeply again and paused, looking out at the audience to fill each person with the radiance of divine love. Then, as if floating and yet with complete deliberation, he walked lightly across the stage and down to his seat.

Reverend Bill raced across the stage to the center and said, "What did I tell you? We *can* change our lives and therefore the world. Thank you, Joseph, thank you." Tears were running down his cheeks.

There was a long pause, electrified with awe and wonderment. The hush was so deep, people's breath slowed. Shoulders relaxed and minds emptied.

Reverend Bill, composed, gazed out at the star-struck audience and said, "To close our program, three members of our choir will sing 'Imagine,' by John Lennon. Please welcome Michael, Rachel, and Sandy."

After a hearty applause, the piano began and the trio sang.

> Imagine there's no heaven
> It's easy if you try
> No hell below us
> Above us only sky
> Imagine all the people
> Living for today . . . Aha-ah . . .

The audience stood up and joined hands and sang along. The entire congregation swayed to the music, and Mary wept as she sang.

I hope someday you'll join us
And the world will be as one.

Victoria leaned into Sid's shoulder and squeezed his hand.

Bud looked over to Jerry with a huge smile and nodded.

Their joined hands rose into the air in an exclamation of joy on the last phrase of the song. "Yes!"

Michael, Rachel, and Sandy bowed to the applause, and Reverend Bill said, "Joseph is right, the time is now to become and to live as Christ lived. I give thanks to each of you for joining us tonight and hope you will accept this gift personally and change your life now. Thank you, God. Amen."

Joseph had slid out to the vestibule to greet the guests, who formed a line to greet him. The first gentleman shook Joseph's hand vigorously.

"Thank you, Joseph," the man said, with a shaky voice. "My life changed tonight, and I commit to make this my top priority."

Joseph embraced him, and the man slumped into his body, pulling in the love.

"You lied," said elderly woman who had spoken angrily from the back of the room, now donning a little smirk. "Christ *is* back, and he's you, and we *are* saved." She clumsily hugged and squeezed him with new might and determination. "I am so glad to be alive and witness this. I missed you two thousand years ago, but not this time!" She skipped away ever so slightly—as much as her body could manage, that is. Then she briskly turned around, and with a huge loving smile, caught his eye and winked.

Some wept with joy. Others were speechless and amazed. Joseph blessed each of them as they came through the line.

When the room was empty, Victoria, Running Bear, and Sid ran up to him, each waiting their turn for a hug.

"Wow! They were transformed, Joseph!" Victoria said. "And now may your humble friends escort you home?"

Joseph laughed and winked at her. "Thanks."

They walked a while in silence, taking it all in.

"What next, Joseph?" Running Bear asked.

"This will ripple out and accelerate the evolution. With Facebook, Twitter, and other electronic media, it will go virile," Joseph replied.

When they arrived at Joseph's house, Sid shook his hand and squeezed Joseph's shoulder. Their eyes met, and each nodded to the other knowingly and embraced.

As Joseph hugged and kissed the rest of them and said goodbye, they each whispered to him, "Thanks, Joseph."

"Now the work will really begin," he said. "Let's meet at our sacred place and discuss a plan for the next step."

Everyone nodded in agreement.

CHAPTER 20

The Power of Forgiveness

The next morning, Reverend Bill's phone rang wildly, with people calling about Joseph's speech and the changes already occurring in their lives.

"Reverend Bill," one woman shared breathlessly, "you won't believe it, after everything you heard from me over the last twenty years, get this: I no longer resent my parents and husband. It's a miracle!"

"Such a weight is lifted from me," another exclaimed, still in awe. "I never realized how heavy and burdensome holding on was till now!"

"Things sparkle now when I look at them," giggled another. And on it went all day.

On Sunday, parishioners were still all a buzz. Those who missed Joseph's talk wanted to know what to do to shift *their* perspectives and forgive those who hurt them. Reverend Bill said he would get back to them with a plan. He congratulated them all for their revelations.

Hanging back from the crowd at the church, Jerry and Bud were already talking about the how.

"He said the key to the next step is forgiveness," Bud said. "So, what can we do to speed things along?"

Mary heard them and piped in. "I think Joseph would say, 'start with yourself.'"

"Meaning what?" replied Jerry.

"Meaning do your own searching moral inventory. Forgive those who have harmed you and whom you have harmed."

"Of course," said Bud, and laughed. "Sure, no problem. Mary, I have no idea how to do that."

Mary smiled.

"Jerry, I have an idea," Bud said. "Let's get together next week and work together on this. Mary, could we use the church, say, Thursday evening."

"I think so. You could use the small room adjacent to the kitchen. But I'll ask Reverend Bill to make sure."

Bud and Jerry were beaming. After hugging each other and Mary, they set out for home. Everyone felt a new exhilaration and hope.

The next day, Mary consulted with Reverend Bill about the room on Thursday for Bud and Jerry. Their conversation was in earshot of several people at the church. Bill thought it was a great idea and silently decided to join. He could use some support on his own forgiveness work.

Thursday seemed to come along quickly, and ten people came to the informal gathering.

"What's going on?" Bud whispered to Jerry. "Why are all these people here?"

"Beats me. Oh look, Reverend Bill is here, maybe he knows."

With questioning eyes, Jerry and Bud approached Reverend Bill. "Do you have another meeting scheduled tonight? Should Jerry and I go to another room?" Bud asked.

"Oh, no," said Bill. "We are all here for the forgiveness meeting. I think it's a great idea."

Breathless, Bud and Jerry scurried to set up chairs for everyone.

Mary walked in, tugging her husband along. They found a seat in the circle of chairs, and George sighed in resignation.

Taking Bud aside, Jerry whispered, "What do we do? Neither of us has ever run a meeting, let alone on a topic we don't understand ourselves. Geez, I wish Victoria were here."

"Let's think," Bud said. They paused a moment, then Bud blurted out, "Let's do what she would do. I'll focus on her and remember the angel class." He paused, then said, "Okay, she started with a prayer and a song. Maybe we can improvise a song and pray that a prayer comes through."

People were settling down in the chairs and glancing over at Bud and Jerry.

"Take a deep breath, Jerry," Bud whispered.

They pumped each other's fists. Both turned toward the group, like a singer to an eager crowd. Slowly and with new attention, they walked to their seats, one on each side of the room.

Jerry began. "Welcome. What a surprise. Bud and I planned to come here tonight and figure out how we could support each other in forgiving those we have hurt and those who have hurt us. It looks like we will have lots of support."

"Let us say an opening prayer," Bud offered. "Reverend Bill, would you lead us?" Bud was so relieved he had come. He didn't know a thing about praying himself, let alone out loud.

Bill smiled, "Thanks, Bud, but I think it would be more appropriate for you or Jerry to start us off. This is your meeting."

Bud lost his breath for a second, and his heart skipped a beat. He closed his eyes and saw Victoria. She had led from ancient inner knowing. So, he stood up and took the hands of each person beside him. Everyone rose and joined hands. After a couple of deep conscious breaths, he prayed silently. *Dear God, please speak through me.* Little did he know that was exactly what Victoria prayed before she spoke.

Then he prayed out loud: "Oh mighty God, we gather together to begin the work of forgiveness. We ask that you guide us, so that our work will be filled with love. Amen."

Everyone chorused, "Amen."

Jerry smiled. *Good job*, he thought, and then said, "We were excited by Joseph's talk the other night, but Bud and I are completely new to this work. We just took a class from Victoria—boy, I wish she was here!" There was an empathic giggle around the room. "She opened with a song and check-in, so—ah—let's do that."

There was some rustling around. No one was sure who would sing and what a check-in was.

Reverend Bill clapped out a beat with his hands, then began to sing.

The Lord's got the whole world in his hands. In his hands. The Lord has the whole world in his hands.

Bud joined in, tapping the rhythm on his thighs. Mary dashed to the kitchen and grabbed some empty pop bottles and wooden spoons and passed them around. People began to tap out the rhythms and join in with the singing.

Reverend Bill kept repeating the first verse because most people knew that one.

The Lord's got the whole world in his hands. In his hands.

The Lord has the whole world in his hands.

Building to a crescendo, he sang,

The Lord has the whole world in his hannnndddsss!

Everyone laughed with joy.

"Wow!" Bud said, with wide eyes of amazement, a giggle, and a little bounce in his chair. "That was great!" When the laughter had softened to sweet sighs, he said, "We learned about check-in from Victoria's angel class. It allows everyone to introduce themselves and state why they have come tonight. When you are done speaking, say 'ho.'" *Where did I get that*? he thought. "Who would like to begin?"

"I will," said Mary. "I am Mary, and there are many things in my life that I have kept buried inside me. Many unspoken hurts. Tonight I commit to forgive them. Ho."

Jerry nodded to the person on Mary's left. "Let's go around in a circle. You're next."

"'My name is,'" Mary nudged him.

"I am George, Mary's husband. I've never done anything like this, and I'm a little nervous."

People tittered and shifted in their seats.

Bud remembered that Victoria always gave everyone a chance to think about what they were going to say, before it was their turn, so that they could relax and listen to each other. "Before we continue around the circle, close your eyes for a moment and decide what you want to say when it's your turn," Bud offered. "Then you can relax and listen to each person as they speak." He gave a big exhale.

Everyone closed their eyes to reflect—why *am* I here? After a moment, they began to open their eyes. Shoulders dropped, one by one, around the room, and a calm settled in.

"My sense is," Jerry began, "that we need some guidelines to make this space safe for all of us. So, I will begin, and if any of you have a guideline you need to feel safe, please say it out loud. Let's agree that we will all use the word 'I' when speaking, instead of 'you.' It helps us own our feelings. And let's agree to commit to honesty and respect for others. Let's not judge each other or ourselves. Just let the truth come forward." He stopped for a moment and waited for someone else to join in. He was relaxing into it now.

Mary said, "Let's not give advice unless the person asks for it twice. Everything said here stays here." She paused. "Those are the guidelines I remember from Victoria's angel class."

Reverend Bill added the last one. "Let's speak and listen with our hearts. I've really been practicing that." He smiled and rocked his head with glee.

"Any others?" Bud asked. There was silence for a moment. "Okay, now let's continue our check-in." He nodded to the woman sitting next to Mary's husband.

"I didn't completely understand what Joseph was saying, but it felt right, and I don't think I have ever felt so much love in one place in my life. So, I'm here to try and forgive and forget." There was a pause, and she jittered.

Bud assisted her gently. "Ho?" he said, looking at her.

"Oh, yes," she giggled, embarrassed. "Ho."

A gentle nervous laughter rippled around the room.

And so it went. Some people were curious about the process. Some just had come as if led from a deeper, quieter space.

"Well," began Bud after everyone had finished. "Now the hard part. What do we do next?"

The woman in gray piped up. "I'll start. I have been doing the Twelve Steps for years, but I am still resentful. I can't seem to let go of my parents' neglect. I think of all the lost opportunities. My dad was an alcoholic, my mother was a raging enabler, keeping the perfect house with the perfect children. It was all a lie. After the divorce—I think I was six, but it's all a blur—it felt like my dad just disappeared. I lost both my parents at once. Mom was so stressed she never knew where I was or what I was doing. She was angry and depressed all the time. At that point, I became the male figure of the family. Anyway, I have done years of counseling. I understand the dynamics. I know why it happened. I know the gifts that have come from it, but I can't seem to let the pain of the neglect go." She was near tears at this point, and there was silence in the room, rich with love.

Mary, moved by an inner force, got up and walked over to her and sat at her feet. At this unsolicited act of kindness, the woman burst into tears.

Rising to stroke her head, Mary offered words so loving and so forgiving. "You deserved better. You give so much to so many others. You should have had parents who were more caring and loving. I feel your pain of neglect." Mary wept quietly. Looking up, she motioned for the participants to gather around, just as Victoria had done in the angel class.

Mary continued, "As you feel your head being lovingly stroked and your hands held and your back supported, allow this to reach you deeply. Let this be for all the times you weren't loved or held when you needed it. All the times your family was not there when you needed them. Let this time fill those times so they may be forever changed."

Reverend Bill began to hum a hymn as he wrapped his arms around her other leg. People sat at her feet, on either side of her and behind her. She wept softly, and Mary repeated over and over, "Let this time be for all the times you needed to be held and never were. For all the times no one was there to listen or play or understand. Let this be for all those times. You *are* loved. You *are* appreciated. You *are* loved. You *are* appreciated. You *are* loved. You *are* appreciated." Her words blended into the rhythm of Reverend Bill's humming.

After some potent moments, the woman opened her eyes and saw Christ standing in the center of the room. He smiled at her and said,

"Be healed now, as it is your time. You have much to offer others. Your service has been sporadic at best because there is still a part of you that was dying not living. You chose your parents so that you could learn how to truly love yourself, for you had to find your way through the loneliness and pain. I am the light. Be now lifted." And he vanished. Trembling all over, she wanted to yell out, "Did you see that?" But she knew that Christ had come just to her, with his special message. She felt the pain of the neglect melt away. She wiped her tears with a cloth handkerchief and sat with a radiant, peaceful, smile. Then she took a long deep sigh. Finally, she was free.

She looked into the eyes of each person around her and patted their tender hands.

As their eyes connected with hers, there was a recognition that they were all interconnected. They were all part of this web of life, and needed each other. Each gently released their touch and drifted to their seats.

A deep hush prevailed. Then a unified sigh.

There was more. Quietly and slowly at first, she said out loud, "I am sorry for the pain I caused and the judgment I held of you, mom and dad and brother. I apologize for the times I was not there for you when you needed me. I was too full of my own pain to help you with yours. It seems we did the same thing to each other." And she burst into tears again. "Please forgive me. Please forgive me. Please forgive me." She was crying, but this time in remorse instead of self-pity.

A slender woman in a blue-print dress from across the room blurted out, "I see it now! His cruelty to me was just a reflection of the cruelty I did to him in more subtle ways. I judged him so. He could never do anything right. Though I didn't say it, and *thought* I was supporting him, he must have felt my disapproval and struck out the only way he knew how. Probably he was expressing himself the way he did with his unaccepting parents." Then she began to cry and release years of bottled-up pain.

There was no time for the group to go to her, for someone else began. "My God!" he said in realization. "That's why my wife had an affair! I see it now. She thought I never loved her. She would say that, but I did love her and could never understand why she did not feel it." His speech quickened. "She felt that she never did anything well enough. I was better at everything than she was, or so she thought. Oh my, all these years I have held onto such anger for her cheating on me. Goodness, thank God she found someone to accept her." He was crying now for the first time since he was a small boy. "I judged her as I judged myself and ruined our relationship and then blamed her. Yikes!" Hands over his face, shoulders pulsing, he sobbed uncontrollably.

Another man burst out, and between deep gasps of breath, said, "I would come home from work and sit in front of the television all night. Though my wife was in the same room, often I would not speak to her. There was a wall around me, so thick that no conversation but monosyllables were grunted. At dinner, I insisted the television stay on so nothing could be discussed. I would just complain about those damn stupid politicians ruining the world. I felt so alone, but that was all I knew how to do. She would try to make dinner special and romantic in the beginning of our marriage, but I could not respond, so she gave up and just endured the silence. Then one day, about ten years later, she filed for divorce, and I was shocked. How could she do that to me? I had taken care of her all those years. How blind could I be? All these years, I blamed her for leaving me. I even tried to get her back. But she had stiffened like a corpse. Oh Janet, please forgive me." With his head in his hands, he cried softly.

Next, as if he would burst, Bud started. "No one was there for me. Ma had to work because Pop left when he learned she was pregnant with me. Each day, she went to work. Each day, she came home. Each week, we had just enough money to eat and pay the rent. But that took all her energy. She couldn't help my brother when he got into drugs. Drugs were his escape out of a hard life. But instead of freeing himself, it killed him." His voice escalating now. "They shot him in the back. They shot him in the back! In the back!" he screamed. Then, as if the air went out of the balloon, he stammered, "He was three payments behind to the dealer. It got all mixed up. Didn't even give him a chance. Just blew him away!"

Tears racked his body. His fists clenched, and his eyes squeezed shut to stop the pain and tears as they gushed out in torrents. He was muttering now. "I wasn't any help. I got in trouble in school. Ma, Oh Ma, I'm so sorry. I didn't realize until just now how hard you worked. How you struggled to keep a roof over our heads. How devastated you were to lose your oldest son. And how frightened you must have been for me. Ma, Ma, forgive me!" Rocking back and forth, he cried, "Please forgive me. Please give me another chance. I'll make it up to you!" Head in his hands and shoulders throbbing, he sobbed.

The energy in the room was electrified. No sooner had he finished, than Mary began. Turning to her husband, George, who cringed, she said very calmly, "George, all these years I have been your obedient wife, keeping our home clean and lovely, raising our children, waiting on you hand and foot, for I thought that was my role. But I realize today that I did it out of duty, not out of love. There has been an impulse in me to grow spiritually and intellectually beyond my household duties. I blamed you for suppressing me, so when I got a job, I didn't tell you about it. A housekeeper has been cleaning the house and making the dinner before you get home, so that I can go to work." She paused to gather strength and took a big breath. "I was afraid to tell you because I thought you would disapprove and make me quit. But I won't quit my job; I'll quit our marriage first." Her arms were folded across her chest, and she glared at him in defiance.

The room froze.

Mary's body shook as if something had escaped. She breathed and there was a palpable shift in the room. Her eyes lifted to meet George's. Biting her lower lip, she softly, almost inaudibly, said, "Please forgive me."

George, eyes blinking rapidly, looked straight at her. He tilted his head and gazed up at the ceiling remembering. "I had noticed that some of our things were put in the wrong place, but I ignored it. Right under my nose, and I slept through it oblivious."

Mary stiffened in anticipation of his rebuke. But none was apparent. Instead he said. "Mary, please forgive me for not paying attention to your feelings, to your softness. To your vulnerability. It scared me until now. I see that it is your strength, not your weakness. Please forgive me for ignoring you for so long."

He reached over and took both of her hands, with tears streaming down his face. "Mary, will you please forgive me?" Humbly, he bowed his head and kissed her hands. "So, soft. So kind," he wept.

Everyone was breathless. So many marriages mysteriously fell apart after ten or twenty years, or went cold. This was Mary and George's story, but this was their story also.

Mary, feeling more confident than ever in her life, calmly replied. "Yes, George. I forgive you. I love you." But that was as far as her aplomb could take her. Crying, she hugged him with such love and acceptance that everyone in the room reflected her glow.

The wave continued.

"Yes, that's it!" Reverend Bill exploded. "All these years, I have been managing this church out of duty, not love. I was doing it for God instead of doing it with love. That's why I resented the workload and got so mad when people did not fulfill their obligations. They were acting out my feelings. Oh God, forgive me for I know not what I do. My intention was honorable but maybe driven by the fear of not being good enough in your eyes or in anyone's eyes." He looked around the room with the most pleading eyes. "Please forgive me, if you felt judged or unloved or not good enough in my presence. Please forgive me."

One by one, around the room, each person from the parish said, "I forgive Reverend Bill. Please forgive me for judging you and expecting you to be God instead of human."

Spontaneously, each person took the hand of the person next to them and stood up, and someone from the choir began to sing,

> Surely the presence of the Lord is in this place.
> I can feel the mighty power and the grace.
> There is a holy hush around us. I see glory in each face.
> Surely the presence of the Lord is in this place.

Sitting down again, as if on cue, the woman in the gray began to pray. "Oh glory is to God. I came here tonight thinking I would

Union of the Masters

probably just talk about the wounds one more time, but instead I saw and felt them from the inside. It was as if I finally got beneath the pain, and with just a little space, my intention, and the grace in this room, that old bitterness, that old resentment, was deeply imbedded after all these years, but tonight it was lifted by the grace of God. Thank you, God. Thank you, God. Thank you, God." She wept.

Then Mary said, "I came here hoping to forgive George for all his hurtful ways, but what I got was the bigger picture. I saw my part in the story—the way I was burying my feelings, not having clarity. I have spent twelve years blaming him, and in five minutes of taking positive responsibility, it was healed. I learned about the depth of forgiveness today. Wow!" she exclaimed, shaking her head in disbelief.

George, squeezing Mary's hand, began softly and slowly, then picked up momentum. "I have resented this church for years, for I saw a hypocrisy between the words said and what I felt when I was here. Today I know why. This is the house of God, not the house of perfection. We are all trying our best with the tools we have. I also learned tonight that some of my husband and father tools are antiquated. I vow to learn how to update them. I vow, and you are my witnesses," he said, looking around the room, "to listen to my wife and children with my heart not in a 'fix it' mentality. Tonight I begin anew. Thanks for bringing me, Mary, even though I did not want to come." And to Reverend Bill, he added, "Thanks for making this imperfect place available."

Everyone smiled through tear-streaked faces.

Another man said, "I think my blaming and anger have kept me alive all these years because my hurt was so deep. When I felt it, I thought it would destroy me, so I stuffed it and pointed at Janet. Now I know that only drove the pain deeper and made the resolution impossible. I am the one who suffered. I felt so betrayed, but what I learned here tonight is that there is no betrayal. I ignored her for ten years. *I* betrayed my vow to her. *I* was the betrayer, not Janet. Or maybe we both were. I don't know and I don't care anymore. I am free!"

These realizations seemed to amaze him and the others around the room, who had also been raised to give their power to a higher authority without realizing the cost.

175

Then a woman who had not spoken, but was madder than fire was hot. "I can't forgive. You speak of such trite things: cheating, not listening, neglect. Those are nothing compared with the beatings and daily rapes I endured from my father. He made me promise not to tell or he would kill me. He would have, too. He was the meanest man. I can't forgive him. I won't forgive him. I won't let him off! He violated his own blood with glee!" She was hysterical by now.

Bud glanced at Jerry with a "now what?" look of desperation.

"May I make an observation?" Mary asked.

The woman glared at her and was about to say no, when she thought better of it and replied with a nod.

"Are you sure?" Mary was practicing not giving unwanted advice.

The woman's rage had dissipated about two notches, and she said, "Go ahead. I've heard it all anyway."

"My company is helping to organize a peace day at the United Nations," Mary began. "I read some documentation of Mahatma Gandhi's peace work and his spiritual practice. Gandhi was asked after his land was destroyed, if he hated the people who did it. And Gandhi replied, 'They have taken so much from me, why would I give them my mind?'"

Silence fell upon the room, but it was a silence filled with anticipation.

The woman screamed, "NO! I can't forgive him. NO! If I forgive him, I won't have my support group. They are all the friends I have. No! I finally have a family. I could lose them too!" She cried uncontrollably as the group gathered around her.

Wow, Bud thought. *Things sure do get complicated.*

She kept crying, "NO! NO!"

Everyone was silent, but each remembered his or her own struggles of letting go and being alone. As they loved her and accepted her pain, they loved and accepted their own pain. After some time, her screams became sobs, and her sobs became peace.

"What do I do now?" she whimpered.

No one had a clue. Bud wished Victoria was there again.

Then with a revelation, Reverend Bill said, "You need do nothing. Surrender your will to God and allow the good to come in. Your support group has helped you come this far, now put your focus on some creative project that helps others. The altruistic side of you will give you great pleasure and support so you can continue your healing and spiritual growth."

"I'm not creative," she mumbled, still hiding her face in her hands.

"Maybe not as a painter or sculptor," Reverend Bill said, "but you are made of creative energy, you have creative energy running through you all the time. It is what keeps you breathing. Listening is creative. Cooking is creative. Music, writing, singing, all are creative. As a matter of fact, everything we do is creative. And," he said after a pause, "You have us. We will help you shine your light."

The woman opened her eyes to be met with ten pairs of adoring, loving eyes. She looked from one to the other, breathing it in. Her eyes questioned, but *their* eyes did not falter; they sent only love. The eyes she met reflected the love buried in her. They gave her the courage to bring her love forward. Her eyes grew from longing to loving. She was able to love each person, as they loved her. Smiling she said, "Childbirth was easier than this!"

Everyone laughed and knew the miracle was at hand.

"This *is* a birth," Mary said, "and it's yours."

There was a group sigh, and once again everyone joined each other's hands together and began to sing,

> Surely the presence of the Lord is in this place.
> I can feel the mighty power and the grace.
> There is a holy hush around us. I see glory in each face.
> Surely the presence of the Lord is in this place.

Bud began the closing prayer. "*It is* amazing grace!

But he was crying too hard to continue, so Jerry continued. "Amazing grace in this place. We came to forgive, and we have forgiven and been forgiven. We have seen much more than we even knew was there. Thank you God. Thank you God. Blessed be."

"Amen," answered the group.

"Get as many hugs as you can," Reverend Bill concluded, and everyone laughed.

Each person felt so grateful for their own healing and for being part of everyone else's, that as they hugged each other, they gave deep, heartfelt thanks to each other.

As the woman in the gray hugged Bud, she said, "You may be new to this work in this lifetime, but you are an ancient sage. Your light will bring peace and healing to many, no matter what you do. Thank you for leading us tonight."

Bud squeezed her tighter in response, for no words could choke out.

Mary and George left holding hands. They had a new life to begin, and they were going to do it together.

After everyone had left, Reverend Bill helped Bud and Jerry put the chairs away. They were silent as they worked, breathing in the presence of love.

Jerry went over to Reverend Bill and said, "Thank you for coming tonight. We had no idea such as event was even possible, yet alone probable. What a miracle." Jerry hugged Reverend Bill with greater appreciation for the difficulty leaders have.

"We are all just doing our best," Reverend Bill replied.

Jerry pulled out his iPhone and motioned to Bud. "Let's call Victoria!"

"The phone is ringing!" Jerry said excitedly. "Hi, Victoria." He was so thrilled, he did not know where to start, so he just blurted out, "Bud and I came to Reverend Bill's church tonight to practice the forgiveness Joseph was talking about. We thought if we worked together, we might do better."

Bud was jumping up and down. "Hurry up! Tell her what happened!"

"When we got here, there were ten people who wanted to join us. We didn't know what to do, so we prayed that you were here. Then the words and prayers and everything just came to us!"

By this time, Bud was beside himself. He grabbed the phone away from Jerry and put Victoria on speaker. "Miracles were happening all around the room. It was like magic, and we owe it all to you."

Jerry said, "I came to forgive, but I think I just wanted to complain some more about the adults ruining the world, the way adults complain about politicians ruining the world. Then something wonderful happened. We saw the other side of the betrayal. I can't explain. All I know for sure is that if it hadn't been for you, none of this would have happened." Tears were welling up in his eyes now.

Bud added, "You would have been proud of us, Victoria!"

They both listened as she spoke.

"That's an amazing story," she said. "I am so sorry I missed it! And *yes,* I am *very* proud of you. You let God flow through you without being interrupted by your thinking, or judging mind. That's the space to create miracles, and you facilitated it. Way to go!" She bowed to them silently.

Bud and Jerry were both jumping up and down, nodding their heads in excitement. Bud stammered into the phone, "We're sort of blissed out and speechless about what happened. Thanks for showing us the way, Victoria."

"Thanks," Jerry called into the phone.

"Thank *you,*" said Victoria. "Thanks for following your hearts! You two are fast learners. Hallelujah! Bye for now."

"Bye."

Bud handed the phone back to Jerry, and they proceeded toward the door, where Reverend Bill was waiting.

"Good night, gentlemen. You are a blessing."

That was the first time anyone had called either of them a gentleman or a blessing. Life certainly was changing. Bud and Jerry hugged, gave a little hop, and headed toward home in opposite directions.

By Sunday, news about the miraculous forgiveness evening had spread like a whirlwind throughout the church community. Participants were visibly more at peace with themselves, and others were eager to share their own revelations. The new energy created a deeper sense of commitment and love throughout the service. There were so many questions and requests to experience the forgiveness, that Mary organized another meeting for the following week. The meetings eventually became weekly gatherings.

CHAPTER 21

The Plan

*E*nergy was mounting, and there was an urgency for Joseph, Running Bear, and Sid to meet in council with Grandfather Tree and Mother Earth. Just before dawn, they gathered at their usual site and stood in circle to listen to the dawn of the new day.

Afterwards, Running Bear called in the directions, and Sid prayed with sublime illumination: "May all beings be filled with loving kindness. May all beings live without fear. May all beings live from the recognition of interconnection. And may *we* have deeper compassion for the struggles of this dimension and help all beings transcend suffering. May we have strength and insight. May we connect with our hearts at an even deeper level. May it be so."

"And it is so" echoed around the circle.

Joseph began after their brief check-in. "Speaking at the church group brought back a lot of memories for me—not all of them good. When I was in body before, the church and the state were one entity, so the ruler spoke with divine authority. It was hard to defy that. Now, in the United States, right-wing fundamentalist Christians have infiltrated the government, politics, and the Supreme Court system—in a brilliantly executed scheme, I might add. But the founding fathers of this country explicitly wanted to keep the church and state separate to avoid abuse of power."

Earth shook the branch in the center of the circle and added, "The rampant polarity of thought and hate is not just in the United States. It's all over the world, with demonstrations and hateful fear of immigrants." She shuddered again. "I feel it in my body. It is a like a child in horrible pain with no apparent way out."

With her head down, straining for a new insight, Running Bear said, "Yes, yes. We, as a humanity, are trapped, or so is our perception. But, of course, it is one's perception that creates one's reality. Now is the time for real unification of the mind, body, and spirit. But we have always said that. Do you think we are closer now to the next step in the evolution of humans?"

"Yes," replied Joseph, nodding. "Democracy encouraged the common people to empower themselves—that's the American dream. And in two hundred years, the United States became the greatest world power and leader in innovation, production, and environmental issues. But that is changing now. The U.S. is losing trading power, allies, and market share. Why? Because the focus on the self and the ability to duplicate businesses across the globe took the focus away from the 'highest good of all' and shifted it to 'what can I get for me, *my* family, *my* group.'"

Sid stood up and started walking around the circle. He thought better when he did this. Then he spoke very thoughtfully. "When humans disconnected from their true Buddha nature—the connected self—they filled the void with consumerism. It started out slowly, and during the Great Depression that was from 1929 to 1939, people were desperate for food and clothing. There wasn't a moment to rest and take a breath before they went right into World War II. Before President Franklin D. Roosevelt brought the U.S. into World War II, he was preparing the country and aiding the allies financially and with arms. This helped build up the U.S. economy again.

"Then with the industrial revolution and the ability to duplicate clothes, and cars, and everything, the hungry got hungrier. Their desire, greed, and clinging became a vicious cycle and perpetuated itself."

"Yes!" said Running Bear. "I knew things had gotten out of hand, but to be here and see how crammed store shelves are with cheap plastic goods, synthetic fabrics, and disposable products is shocking to say the least and truly heartbreaking!"

"Not to mention the exponential shopping made available online," Sid added.

"People need more and more to fill the void. Of course, you can't fill it with stuff. There is only temporary relief with shopping, sex, drugs, alcohol, and food. It does not feed the soul," Joseph continued.

Grandfather Tree swayed some branches before he spoke. "Consumerism has gotten so out of control that we are literally dying from toxic waste. Our manufacturing and trash are killing us slowly but surely. None of that was necessary, yet all of it was necessary to bring consciousness to the crisis of survival to force a change."

"That's it," Running Bear interjected, popping up. "There isn't the needed urgency to facilitate global change. We need all the countries to work together!"

There was a poignant pause, as everyone soaked in her electrified energy. The *urgency* wasn't there.

"So, how to make it urgent for those leading and deeply hypnotized by their monetary power? How do we unify the urgency?" asked Sid, still pacing around the circle. "It's odd, isn't it? There are so many climate summits, but few strides are being made. People are demonstrating, and some companies are moving away from fossil fuels, but you are right, the urgency isn't there. And urgency is the only thing that will turn the tide. We need to do something that will unify everyone to realize the urgency and come together."

Mother chimed in, "We need to unify not against something—as we did during all the wars across my body, but *for* something—for a healthy planet and healthy, happy residents. For all of us—the two legged, the four legged, those who crawl or fly or swim, and those who are planted. Can't forget you, Grandfather!"

Everyone laughed as the spark ignited.

"Maybe the three of us could present before an assembly of the main institutions' leaders—that is, political leaders, business leaders, education leaders, and religious leaders. These institutions created the first chakra tribal beliefs that people are living their lives from. When the first chakra beliefs are brought into the consciousness of oneness and connectiveness, then the remaining beliefs will fall in line more easily," Running Bear offered.

"Yes, that would unite the leaders, and their energies would then connect with the grassroots efforts already working around the globe. Conversations are happening in towns and on the media. People around the world want a change—a deep, core change in perspectives. More authentic fairness, empathy, and compassion are yearned for throughout the world. We need a new look at ethics and level of responsibility to ourselves; each other; future generations; and our home, Earth. *Together* we need a to create a list of *global*, unified priorities," Running Bear concluded.

"I believe the momentum for a conference like this has already been laid," Joseph added, smiling ear to ear.

"We could physically demonstrate the theory of oneness," Sid said, with a little hop to his step.

Joseph jumped up, getting excited. "And then guide them into a ritual of forgiving each other."

"We could encourage them to embrace Earth in all their policies— from the pulpit to industry," Running Bear chimed in, now really jazzed. "I can see it now: a worldwide ceremony honoring Earth, to put her above all else. We can encourage them to commit to saving themselves by saving the Earth."

"We will have to find some way to explain how everyone will make money in the process," Sid added, laughing.

And they excitedly planned their strategy.

CHAPTER 22

Putting it All Together

W hen she heard about their plan, Mary went right to work on obtaining an opportunity for Joseph, Sid, and Running Bear to speak. Surprisingly enough, there was an environmental conference scheduled a month later. Through some artful negotiations by Mary's boss, who was the president of an international conference company, the leaders of that conference were convinced to invite religious leaders, education leaders, business leaders, and heads of states to participate in a Real World Conference to Save the Planet. Now it was just a matter of whether the new guests would accept the invitation.

Mary scheduled the plane reservations, with Victoria and herself included. Reverend Bill thought it was a grand idea and notified his fellow ministers, rabbis, and priests in the area and asked them to spread the word. He shared with the clergy the miraculous healings that had occurred since Joseph showed up in town. He was beginning to wonder if this wasn't Jesus coming back, as the Bible promised. But he didn't want to scare his friends off, so he kept that thought to himself. As the news of the Conference to Save the Planet spread, many of the clergy and their congregations decided to attend. The organizers of the event were quite amazed at the response and had to find a larger hall to accommodate the gathering.

Another surprise was the response of the business leaders, who were usually resistant to anything environmental because it meant capital outlay and a delay in manufacturing. But there seemed to be an aura of excitement about this conference, and in poured the yes replies.

Meanwhile, Bud and Jerry were washing cars on Sunday afternoons to try to raise enough money for their airfare and hotel accommodations. Then, after one of the now-regular forgiveness meetings, a tall gray-haired gentleman, about sixty-five years old, approached them about their conference plans. "Bud and Jerry," he began, looking down and rocking from foot to foot, "I am still reeling in gratitude from the release I had at our last meeting."

Bud and Jerry nodded, holding him in love.

"I hadn't been able to forgive myself for cheating on my wife, who died soon after she discovered my betrayal. But now I feel we are both released from that hurt and pain. Thank you again. I heard about the trip to Washington for the Conference to Save the Planet. Are you boys washing cars to earn money to go, plus going to your regular jobs?"

"Yes," they said simultaneously.

"Would it help if I matched whatever you raised?"

"Yes!" Bud and Jerry leaped into the air and grabbed each other with glee.

As the man walked away with a smile, Jerry gave Bud a high five. They finished putting away the chairs from their meeting with renewed zeal.

Meanwhile, Sid had stopped by Victoria's after the council meeting to share the news. As he walked into her office healing space, she was busy writing on a flip chart, probably preparing for another class, he thought. She was wearing her favorite sea-foam green sweat outfit. The sun glistened through the window, giving her hair a beautiful golden glow. He could tell she was deep in thought, as she wrote with her pen on the chart. Figuring that he would not disturb her, he began to turn around and leave.

"Not so fast," she said, "just let me complete this thought, and you will be glad you didn't leave."

They both laughed.

She wrote a couple more phrases on the flip chart and then, as if in slow motion, turned around and danced over to Sid to give him a hug and kiss. "So glad to see you," she muttered in between kisses.

Stroking her head gently, Sid replied with a satisfied sigh. After a moment of silence, he ventured, "What are you up to?"

"I am preparing a class on the similarities in Christianity, Buddhism, and Native American religions. It is time for us to shift our focus away from the differences; we have that part down."

He nodded.

"Wanna hear what I have so far?" she asked.

"Sure," he replied, interested in what she had come up with this time.

"My thesis," she began, "is that the religions are basically aiming for the same end goal: unity with God—be it the Great Spirit in Native American religions, the higher mind, the Atman in Buddhism and Hinduism, or God. The goal is the same: 'going home,' as the southern Gospel singers proclaim. But the journey is quite different and depicts the different frame of reference of the culture from which it originated. The first chakra tribal beliefs mold the paradigm, or frame of reference, from which the tribe sees the world. These paradigms were quite different in the infancies of the religions, but as time progressed, they came closer together. Most people still believe that theirs is the only way, however."

"Precisely what our council has been discussing," Sid replied.

She nodded. "The human species has evolved enough mentally, physically, emotionally, and spiritually now to unify the creative consciousness permanently, not just occasionally. I think the important aspect people and leaders of religions miss is that the beliefs are *not* frozen; they form and evolve through time and history. The Jews realized that there was only one God, and through the years, the concept of one God has grown to one source for all, not just the chosen ones. The Christians stopped scarifying the lamb to appease God. The native cultures stopped scarifying the maiden to the same end. We *have* evolved and we *continue* to evolve, though many want to freeze their beliefs in their own time frame because it seems safer. Do you see what I am getting at?"

"Sure. Religions have been evolving through time. As people change and evolve, so do the religions. That accounts for all the spin-offs and small spiritual groups that have cropped up," Sid said. "Which I think is great, of course, as Buddhism is a spin-off of Hinduism—of sorts."

Their eyes met in acknowledgment.

"Yes, people are discouraged," she continued, "with the terrible history of religions and are trying to find a spiritual home. We are looking for our lost tribe that had love, trust, and honesty at the base of it and people with like minds. Many of us are adrift. I believe if a person does not have a spiritual practice of some kind, a huge part of that person is undeveloped. We are after all, *spiritual beings in a human experience.* If the soul isn't nourished, you can never find true happiness."

"What's your thesis?" Sid asked.

"That if you believe you are separate from others, not only in your physical form but the way you think, believe, and act, you will create a reality that proves that difference. The reality is we all feel somewhat different, because we are all unique. At first, we were bound together by our tribe. The tribe gave us our roots, beliefs, our religion, our art, rules to live by, support, companionship, security, protection, our goals, skills, and ambition. The tribe was our lifeline. As time progressed, however, the family and cultural community or nationality replaced the tribe," she continued. "In America, a melting pot of world cultures, our primary family became even more important. But now the structure of the family has changed. The extended family—grandparents, siblings, cousins—live all over the world. Though it still takes a village to raise a child and support an elderly person, mostly our former support is not in our homes or even our neighborhoods. Yes, we can connect by telephone, text, email, Facebook, twitter, FaceTime, Snapchat, Instagram, and so forth, but the hug or hot chicken soup needed when we're sick, the gentle touch, and the breath are not there as before.

Sid nodded. *So true*, he thought. He walked over to the flip chart where she was still standing and looked at what she was writing. She put her arm around his waist, and he snuggled closer.

"As a species we need each other," she continued, kissing his cheek. "We need to touch, to love, to help, and to support." She gave him a little squeeze. "We need to receive that support as well as give it. It is part of who we are. In the search to fill in where the clan, the family, the community left off, we have created support groups for everything: grief work, alcohol abuse, weight loss, men's circles, women's circles, and the like. These support groups replace the connectiveness we had in the tribe and the community. They replace the moon circles each month. They replace our families. So the need for churches and spiritual groups is extremely high now. Because of our need to connect, we are forced to rely on people outside our tribal community." She paused, thinking. "A woman I know, for example, to this day cannot feel support from anyone other than her family, because in her eyes that is all there is. Many support her, but she cannot receive it. The disbursement of our families and the culture avails a huge opportunity, as it *forces* us to broaden our perspective and change our paradigm about how we really are connected. Therefore, the concept that we are all from the same Source or Mother, that we are all brothers and sisters, that there really is only one tribe, becomes easier because we must trust outside our intimate, safe circle for the first time in a very expanded way."

"Really, we are reexamining our spiritual roots," Sid added, stepping a little to the left. "For if we explore our cultural roots, there is always a spiritual or religious side that grounds us further."

"Exactly," she replied, pointing her pen at him. "And in this time of disruption and rapid change, many are running around madly searching for their truth and some spiritual connection, a home base. 'To whom do I belong? What are life's rules?' Everything is challenged. The bad news is that, in this breakdown stage, many are living helpless futile lives. The good news is that before another form can emerge, the old must break down, and it is. It is no coincidence that the former religions are falling in disfavor or changing radically to survive.

"The old tribal beliefs must be changed. We can no longer believe that our particular tribe is best and only *our* god will save *you*," she said. "That belief has to be transformed to be able to embrace the idea that we all come from one source and that there is really only one tribe. This new tribe has many colors and vibrations, but it's all one tribe from the same source. So, in this course, we will explore how what used to seem so different to us and strange really has some fundamental similarities in it."

She paused and looked into his eyes, so alert and full of love. "A cup of tea?"

"Sure." He smiled and went over to put the water on, while she added something more to the flip chart. After the water boiled, he took her favorite mug—brown and sage-green pottery—put in her favorite herbal tea, and brought it to her.

"Thanks, Sid. Ah, my favorite cup and favorite tea." She leaned over and kissed him gently.

"I like your premise, and I think you have a book here." He sat on her wicker client chair and leaned back.

"Really?" she replied, surprised.

"Yes. There is enough information, actually for more than one book. Volumes have been written on the interpretations of my work, and probably even more on Christianity—just for starters."

"I will have to think about that... As I was saying, if you look at the Judeo-Christian faiths, Buddhism, and Native American spirituality, you can see how they have really come together," she continued. "Each religion holds the vibration of the subculture and the land from which it was derived. Thich Nhat Hanh is a Vietnamese Buddhist monk—do you know him?"

He nodded in affirmation, as he didn't want to interrupt her again, and gestured for her to continue. Thich Nhat Hanh, or Thay, had influenced millions of lives, and he was grateful that his work had such a pure voice in this time.

"Okay, then, Thay says study your faith deeply so that you may study another's faith deeply. I think what he means is that if you understand the spiritual principles your faith is based on, you will more easily see those same principles in other faiths. The only barrier, then, is the language. This is what he says in his book *Living Buddha, Living Christ*." She picked up the book and opened to page 55 and began reading.

"'When Jesus said, 'I am the way,' He meant that to have a true relationship with God you must practice His way. In the Acts of the Apostles, the early Christians always spoke of their faith as 'the way.' To me, 'I am the way' is a better statement than 'I know the way.' The way is not an asphalt road. But we must distinguish between the 'I' spoken of Jesus and the 'I' that people usually think of. The 'I' in His statement is *life* itself, which is the way. If you do not really look at His life, you cannot see the way. If you only satisfy yourself with praising a name, even the *name* of Jesus, it is not practicing the life of Jesus. We must practice living deeply, loving, and acting with charity if we wish to truly honor Jesus... *When we understand and practice deeply the life and teachings of Buddha or the life and teachings of Jesus, we penetrate the door and enter the abode of the living Buddha and the living Christ, and life eternal presents itself to us.*"

They paused for a moment to let the passage sink in.

She reread the last italicized part: "*When we understand and practice deeply the life and teachings of Buddha or the life and teachings of Jesus, we penetrate the door and enter the abode of the living Buddha and the living Christ, and life eternal presents itself to us.*"

"Yes." Sid nodded. "Right on."

Victoria laughed. "Sid, you're getting the lingo."

He looked up from his tea and smiled coyly.

Shaking her head, she continued. "That is the essence right there, *the deep daily practice.* I believe Native American Indian spirituality and Buddhism build the practice into everyday life. That is why so many White Americans seek out their teachings and practices. Many of the Christian churches have forgotten the *practices.* They teach more to the intellect and less to the body. The simple practice of calling in the spirit of fire before lighting a candle reminds us that we are all interconnected. And there are the Buddhist practices of mindful eating and waking meditation." She gave him an exaggerated bow.

"If the teachings do not manifest in the body through action, they are worthless. We quickly lost our sacred rituals when science became God. And now there is an apparent need in our culture to return to sacred life," she continued. "You taught and practiced compassion. Christ taught and practiced love, and Running Bear taught and practiced creating a relationship with all relations, another aspect of our interconnectedness."

She walked over to the flip chart and wrote out:

Putting it all together
Compassion

Love

Relationship

"Oh my, they are all heart chakra qualities. I hadn't realized!" she exclaimed. "These three religions have all come to the same place. There's no need any more to keep the tribes separate.

"Hmm," mused Sid, looking at Victoria with wonder, "you always find a way to bring it back to love. You know, you are quite ingenious." He walked over to her and gave her a sincere kiss of gratitude, then said, "Sorry, I couldn't help myself. You're so radiant when you are teaching what you love. There it is again: love!"

"Yes, she laughed. "The Beatles had it right in the sixties: 'Love, love, love!'" After a unified breath, she said, "So, where was I? You great distractor, you!"

They both laughed. Something they did so well together.

"Something about not needing separate tribes anymore," Sid encouraged.

"Oh yeah. Each tribe has a different language, or at least lingo," she continued. "They have different foods and rituals. And the study of sound has shown us that each group has a different vibration to it. If you enter a culture or subculture that resonates differently, you feel foreign. The basic rhythm of the tribe is different and therefore strange to you. The language has a different vibration. The traffic and city noise is different in New York than London or Hong Kong. Notice the difference between the desert, the mountains, and a little town. It is not just the terrain that is different; the entire vibration of the area is different. And that vibration permeates the land, the animals, the people, and the thoughts. This is another aspect of why the tribe has such power over us. The tribe members' vibrations are similar. Being away from that vibration can be frightening."

"Yes, I can relate to that. The vibration here in the United States in modern times couldn't be more different than in rural India 2600 years ago!"

"I bet," Victoria said, trying to imagine. "My thought is that once you entrain to the new rhythm, you attune to the culture and feel more at home. Was that true for you?"

"Yes, that's what I've done since I came here. Not only is it 2600 years later, but I am in a completely different country."

"I hadn't thought of that," reflected Victoria. "You seem to feel so comfortable with yourself. Was it because you relaxed into it knowing there is no separation?"

"Yes, plus we are on a very specific mission here, and I am with dear friends." He smiled at her. "But go on."

"So, the problem is when you resist allowing the new vibration to become part of you, because it scares you. If we could only get past that and realize we are from the same source. Just because I am different doesn't mean I am better or worse."

"Is the key problem, then, the first chakra belief that you are only safe if you stay within your own tribe?" Sid asked.

"Yes," she continued. "And centuries ago that was true, for sticking with the tribe made the tribe strong. But now sticking with the tribe and making other tribes wrong makes us all weak."

"Once these concepts are expressed, what are you going to focus on?" Sid asked.

"I'll continue to give concrete data to help those who have not yet developed polysensory awareness, which immediately connects us.

We will explore the similarities of religious rituals of the Buddhists, Christians, and Native American Indians," she answered.

"But the rituals are all different. And each religion has many sects."

"Yes, another example of the power of the Tower of Babble, she replied. "Even the unifying concepts were splintered into many fragments. My work is to put Humpty Dumpty back together again."

They both laughed. "Right," said Sid, "with a new heart and a new suit of clothes."

"Yeah. With One Heart." Victoria smiled.

They paused for a moment. Yes, one heart for all living things.

"In gluing Humpty, we will focus on the rituals' similar intentions," she said. "For example, each religion has rituals and practices to support its beliefs. All the religions I am aware of, and these three in particular, have rituals for cleansing and purification. Because of the immensity of the topic, I'm going to stick with Buddhism, Christianity, and Native American religion. The ritual may look different, but the underlying intent is the same."

"Before you continue, how are you defining ritual?" Sid asked.

"Good question, I'll start with my favorite definition from Jean Houston, *The Search for the Beloved*, page 42." She picked up the book and read, "'The ritual comes from the Sanskrit *rita*, which refers to both art and order. Like all real art, ritual provides organic order, a pattern of dynamic expression through which the energy of an event or series of events can flow in an evolutionary process toward larger meaning or a new stage or level of life.'

"Joseph Campbell describes myth as the greater story of your life as it connects to the universal story. A ritual is the enactment of a myth. And by participating in the ritual, you are participating in the myth. And since myth is a projection of the depth wisdom of the psyche, by participating in a ritual, you are being, as it were, put in accord or in alignment with that wisdom, which is the wisdom that is inherent within you anyhow. Your consciousness is being re-minded of the wisdom of your own life. Campbell discovered similar themes in all religious mythology. Crucifixion, resurrection, purification, conscious awareness expanding. And from Thomas Healki's book *Creative Ritual*,

'Every society has engaged in religious ritual. In this way, the ritual worker—shaman or priest—has kept alive the Inner Reality of life, itself, in the hearts of the people. This Inner Reality is the source of life. It doesn't matter what you term it—Christ, Krishna, Cosmic Power, Divine Principle, Atomic Equation—it is all the same thing... Ritual is an integrative process that attunes the psyche to natural force. In ritual, the inner mysteries, the divine principles, can be explored and made manifest in the life of the individual.'"

"Those are great definitions," Sid responded. "I kind of like your definition best, though-- 'ritual lifts the veil of unknowing and allows the practitioner to be aware of spiritual forces, the doorway to higher dimensions.'"

"You remembered!" Victoria smiled.

Sid nodded.

"Therefore, ritual can be life transforming. So many people perform rituals in their churches for years, not really understanding the power rituals can have on their personal lives. Once a ritual becomes boring or rote, the doorway closes to the other side and the reptilian brain center that is activated by ritual isn't getting the current it needs for stimulation."

"What rituals are you going to discuss?" Sid asked.

"The four most common rituals: rituals for cleansing and purification, rituals for communication with the higher powers, rituals for offerings, and rituals for unity. Many of the rituals overlap; each actually brings one closer to God. But for the sake of discussion, it's easier to divide them up. To demonstrate the power and significance of ritual, we will do rituals from New Thought Christianity, the Apache nation, and Buddhism."

"The next logical question, then, is why do people want to open the doorway to the spiritual realm?"

She smiled at him. "Yes," she replied nodding. "Some people think opening the doorway is the most ridiculous thing they ever heard of. Life is what you can see and touch and that keeps them quite busy enough, why complicate the issue?

"Because?" Sid prompted.

"Because we are spiritual beings in a human condition," she continued. "Our purpose of life lies within us; the doorway helps open us to ourselves. It is like an incredible treasure hunt, and the pot of gold at the end of the adventure is us. It is the unique and individual story of the Holy Grail. The Holy Grail is the search for the god within. The search for the beloved, as Jean Houston calls it. It is when we open that doorway, that life becomes so full and rich."

"Ritual will do all that?" he questioned. "You must remember, I left all the Hindu rituals out of my teachings."

"Well," she looked at him impishly and walked over and ruffled his hair. "We need them back!"

The both laughed and hugged again.

"Okay, go ahead. You know I'm teasing you. Which is so easy to do!" He escorted her back to the flip chart and winked at her.

"Okay then. I lost my train of thought." She paused. "Oh yes, ritual is the beginning. Intention, practice, and inner healing are the journey. The awareness of ritual and intending that the journey be sacred give it more power and significance—combining spirit and matter as one."

"It also heightens its purpose, and allows the universe to assist in grand ways," Sid added.

And they talked late into the night.

CHAPTER 23

Oneness

*B*efore anyone could believe it, it was departure day for the exciting trip to the Real World Conference to Save the Planet in Washington, DC.

Everyone met at the church to take the two-hour shuttle to the Portland, Oregon, International Airport. At final count, thirty had joined the party. The parking lot was full of people and luggage and was abuzz as everyone spoke at once. They dashed from one person to another, greeting each other excitedly with hugs, "Wow, don't you look great?" and special hand squeezes and exclamations of joy. "Can you believe we are really going to a World Conference to Save the Planet?" "It's unbelievable!" And so it went as more folks arrived.

Mary and George were giggling, holding hands, and sneaking kisses. Each listened with their hearts now instead of their heads. George realized how much he had missed of his family life. He hadn't known what was in their hearts, but that was changing now. Mary felt like an eagle gliding on the updraft. She could hardly believe she helped put this trip together. George had gotten some time off work to join them. This was the first-ever time he had rescheduled his calendar to support her.

Jerry spotted Bud and exclaimed, "Dude, cool leather shoes and suit!"

Bud put his leg out to show off his shoes and replied, "First ever for both! Can't think of a better occasion to change my image!"

They both laughed.

"And you look pretty rad in your new suit and shoes too," Bud said admiringly.

"Yeah, it's a little uncomfortable, but I'll relax into them," he said, wiggling his tie to loosen it. They gave each other a high five and huge smiles. With a jaunt in their steps, they rolled their luggage toward the shuttle, where the crowd was bustling.

With a graceful bounce in his stride, like an antelope gliding through space, Sid approached the group, his relaxed black slacks and white jersey flowing. Shimmering gold light filled his energy field. And then a grin burst across his face, radiating pure joy, when he saw Victoria approach.

The breeze gently lifted her hair from her delicately sculptured face. Her steel-blue gray Indian dye accordion skirt billowed behind her. To honor Sid, she had taken special effort to find this skirt, which was handmade by a woman from Calcutta, Indian. A steel-gray rayon short-sleeved top fitted her slender body, and a black cloth belt accented her small waist. Her gold necklace danced as she hurried toward Sid, her gold earrings shaped in the sign of the ancient Greek key glistening in the sun.

Sid was mesmerized by the sight of her. "Ah," he sighed, "beauty in movement. I love her so."

Time slowed as she approached. Each stride lifted and lowered her gracefully. Their lips met, luggage dropped, and their bodies merged.

"Home at last," whispered Victoria.

Then quite nonchalantly, they walked in synchronized rhythm toward the shuttle. She pulled her luggage with her right hand, holding Sid's hand with her left. Their energy fields merged and formed a glistening pink heart.

Sid and Victoria saw Joseph approach in his ethereal, mystical manner. Was it an illusion or did his feet never touch the pavement? In his usual causal, natural style, he wore a wheat-colored blousy shirt over loose pants that were tied at the waist with a cord. Around his neck, hung a gold Star of David that bounced as he glided forward. He drew both of them into his arms. "Hello, my two dear illuminated friends!"

They kissed each other's cheeks in greeting.

Running Bear wasn't far behind, walking in her deliberate, grounded way. Each foot fully felt the Earth beneath her. Her loving smile glowed as she approached her friends. She wore her favorite long brownish-tan cotton dress, which fell gently to her ankles. The print on the dress was subtle but apparent: scenes of mountains, streams, and deer grazing blended into the fabric with tans, black, and sunset orange. She was truly one with Mother Earth.

Joseph swept her up into the air and kissed her cheek lovingly.

She returned the gesture with a rich hug, then kissed Victoria and Sid.

This was the moment they had been waiting for… for thousands of years. Their hands joined spontaneously to form a circle. A symbol of no beginning or end. Their eyes locked in acknowledgment and wonder. It was happening!

Approaching the shuttle, Reverend Bill, adorned in a new, fine, navy-blue suit, white shirt, and red tie, raised his right hand to quiet the crowd. The group silenced immediately. "It all went so fast, and here we are, ready to embark on a historical journey across the United States to do our part to bring a deeper awareness of our intrinsic interrelation to ourselves and our world. I have never been so proud and excited about anything in my life. Thank you for standing up for what you hold dear in your hearts and joining us for this transformational Real World Conference."

Everyone clapped and looked around at each other in amazement.

Then Mary stepped forward. With flushed cheeks, she handed everyone an itinerary and briefly reviewed the highlights with them before they boarded the bus. Once on the bus, the group broke out with bursts of excitement, though some still held their breath with anticipation. They were on their way to the airport to fly to help raise consciousness of our interconnection and bring lasting peace and the end of climate change to the world. No one really had any idea what was going to happen. And for most, this was the first time they had ever made such a journey with so little information. But each felt called to join for some inexplicable reason.

Everything went smoothly at the airport, and the flight was breathtaking. The weather was so clear they could see the Cascade Mountains.

"Is that Mount Hood, Jerry?" exclaimed Bud. "I have never seen her before. Wow! Can you see, Jerry?" He pulled his head way back to allow Jerry a better view.

"And on the left side of plane, we are passing Mount Hood, and Mount Saint Helens is coming into view," the pilot announced.

"Yes, Mount Hood!" exclaimed Bud and gave Jerry a high five.

Jerry and Bud looked north. "Look, they're stilled capped with snow," Jerry said. Mary and George came over to view with them.

"Now, keep looking north from the left side of the plane and see Mount Adams, in Washington state," the pilot continued, quite enjoying herself. "I climbed that mountain once."

"Ooo, ahh," rippled throughout the plane.

"I never thought I would ever be in a plane," Bud marveled. "It's so green, and the mountain peaks so white. Earth is SO beautiful! I had no idea."

"And I almost left her," Jerry said, shaking his head.

When the mountains had faded from view, Reverend Bill walked through the plane, making sure everyone was fine. He stopped in front of Joseph's and Running Bear Eagle's seats. "Joseph, you must be quite tired of me thanking you," he said with a huge grin. "But, really if you had not shown up at my church, I would still be resenting my ministry and feeling like God had abandoned me. Now I am exploding with joy and gratitude."

Joseph's eyes met Reverend Bill's with such love and kindness, as he leaned toward him and offered his hand. He placed his left hand on top of Reverend Bill's and said, "I could never be bored witnessing your joy. This journey is as important to me as it is to you. I'm so grateful Mary found me during her Welcome Wagon ministry!"

Overcome with the love, Reverend Bill nodded, as his eyes teared up. He squeezed Joseph's hand before he let it go.

Then, with the warmest, most affectionate smile, he extended his hand to Running Bear. Tears ran down his checks. "And you, Running Bear." His voice broke with emotion. "You brought us Bud and Jerry and Victoria. I never could have imagined that love could heal so quickly and deeply as it did with Bud and Jerry. Bud would still be robbing Quick Stops, and Jerry would have drowned. I never imagined that a Black street kid would lead us in such profound and deep forgiveness." He let go of her hand to get his handkerchief out. After an emotional pause, he said, "I am so ashamed of my lack of faith and my narrow perception of the world." He paused again to wipe his eyes, his hand shaking with emotion. He looked deeply into Running Bear's eyes, but was too overcome with emotion to continue. He bowed his head to both of them and returned to his seat.

To ensure the safety of the flight, Victoria invited Archangels Michael, Uriel, Gabriel, and Raphael to fly with them. Archangel Michael flew at the nose of the plane, Uriel to the right side of the plane, Gabriel on the left, and Raphael as the back. She could feel their presence encircling the plane with shimmering gold light.

She snuggled under Sid's shoulder and gently kissed him on the check. She whispered, "Did I ever tell you that I was told in a meditation that you and I would be together, but this time as man and woman? I never dwelled on it. I acknowledged it and let it go. But I must admit, I never expected it in this lifetime. How I love to be wrong!" They both laughed and kissed again.

"Now on both sides of the plane," the pilot began, "we are approaching more peaks. Here comes Mount Jefferson." Several people jumped up and went to the left side of the plane to see it. "Wow! Next time move more slowly, so we can keep the plane upright," she laughed. Quickly several people moved to the center aisle. "Next Broken Top. Slowly now!" Her voice was light and playful. Then to the thrill of most and the terror of some, she tilted the plane to the left to give a great view of The Three Sisters.

Victoria giggled and peered out the window. "A pilot hasn't done this in decades. What an absolute treat!"

"These are volcanic mountains," the pilot continued, "formed about fifty million years ago by upheavals in the Pacific Ocean floor off the coast of Oregon. The Cascade Range runs seven hundred miles from northern British Columbia, through Washington and Oregon, into northern California. Some of the peaks are over ten thousand feet."

Wows rippled through the plane.

"Keep looking as the renowned Bachelor Mountain is coming into view. It is an internationally famous ski resort."

Bud and Jerry were craning their necks to see. "Look! Awesome!" exclaimed Jerry and Bud simultaneously.

"Have you ever skied there, Jerry?" Bud asked.

"No, I've never skied. Gotta change that!"

"Never seen anything like this!" Bud was off his seat in excitement.

As the Cascade Mountains faded from view, people returned to their seats and settled down. Some chatted quietly, others dozed off. No one felt much like watching a movie after this real show, and they knew more was to come.

Running Bear whispered to Joseph, "That was fantastic. I've never been in a plane either."

"Me either. It certainly is a thrill. Geez, Running Bear, we lived before there was electricity!"

It was a while before the pilot came back on the PA system. "Well, I promised you more, so look out to see the majestic Rocky Mountains. You can view them from both sides of the plane. One view is as breathtaking as the other."

Bud jerked forward from his dozing. "Oh, Jerry, look!" He nudged Jerry on the arm.

"Glory, glory, glory! There are miles of them. Hundreds of jagged peaks everywhere!" Jerry got up to stretch and then leaned across Bud. "Oh my God! Awesome!" Jerry exclaimed. "It's like another planet. So barren. Stark."

"So fierce," added Bud. "Yes, fierce. That's the word."

"Mother Earth," Running Bear half whispered to herself, "your beauty and grandeur are beyond words. I lived in these mountains for lifetimes, but to see them from this vantage point is transformational. Thank you, Mother. Thank you, Mother." And with tears in her eyes, she bowed humbly. Her eyes met Joseph's, and the understanding was instant.

After the great plains and miles of farmland, cities began to arise.

The landing in Washington DC was smooth and gentle, and applause erupted.

Mary registered the group and handed out their name tags. There was an excited buzz in the lobby as over a thousand people registered and greeted each other.

Joseph, Sid, and Running Bear Eagle were seated in the front row with the other presenters. After Mary got her group settled, she sat down next to her husband, squeezed his hand, and whispered in his ear, "My dear sweet George, I love you more than ever. It means so much to me that we are sharing this experience together. Thank you, my love!"

George leaned over and kissed her. "Thanks for helping me wake up. I could have missed all this stuck in my old rigid ways." And he returned the squeeze.

When the auditorium was filled, the organizer of the conference took the stage. A hush fell over the crowd.

"Welcome to each of you who has traveled here from all over the globe for what I hope will be the most productive and transformative Real World Conference ever held. I am Adelita Ortiz. With an amazing team, we have founded the First Annual Real World Conference. Why did we decide to call it the Real World Conference? Though there have been many global conferences and many summits on sustainability or world peace, this is the first one to combine reversing climate change and creating a peaceful planet. You have answered our call, and I thank you for all the research, time, and effort you have put into attending this conference. Millions of children have demonstrated around the world to protest our lack of action about climate change. They understand that if substantial changes aren't made immediately in our manufacturing and production of greenhouse gases, their lives will be in danger and there may be no future for their children. Now is the time to change the trend of decades of stalemate, fear, and denial throughout the world."

Applause rippled throughout the auditorium. Calls of "YES!" rang out in multiple languages.

"Heads of states and local governments from 195 countries around the world are here today. And with them are their top leaders in education, business, and manufacturing. Congratulations!" More applause.

"Environmental leaders from *every* country are represented today." Applause.

"Welcome to the directors of hundreds of nonprofit organizations to protect human rights, woman's rights, LGBTQ community, children's rights, Earth rights, and more. Many of these organizations were funded by their local governments and businesses." The applause reached a crescendo.

"In addition, the world's greatest religious and spiritual leaders are present. And, of course, to record the event and spread the news created here, are journalists from around the world." The applause exploded.

"A little insight into my background will give you some understanding of why this conference was spearheaded. I have dedicated my life to bringing peace to my family, my community, and our planet. My mother tells a story of when I was a little girl. I would stand between my parents if they were arguing and say, 'No. Stop. Love each other.' When a bully taunted another child at school, I intervened. And so it has continued throughout my life. Another determining point was when my parents took my two brothers and me to Mexico. I was about ten years old. My little heart was broken with the poverty we saw. I wondered why I had running water at home, and these children did not. I wondered why they didn't have enough clean water to drink or food to eat, and I did. I wondered why their streets were littered with trash and mine weren't. These questions led me to a degree in anthropology, a minor in psychology, a PhD in environmental sciences, and decades of avid studies and practices of Buddhism.

"Yes, I have learned a lot and been active in many groups, with very little substantive result. What I realized was there will never be peace on Earth until there is real peace and acceptance in all of our hearts. We will not shift our behaviors until we shift our perception. And from a new perspective—a new lens, as it were—we can form new intentions together with much greater possibility of achieving them.

"That brings me to another point. One thing the environmental movement has left blatantly on the sidelines is the power of intention. You can say one thing, but in your fearful heart, intend quite another. The real intention will always win. Intention drives action. It organizes the energy of creation. My parents knew that, and with forethought and intention, named me Adelita, which means noble, strong, and courageous. This name was used for the heroine of the Mexican folk song *La Adelita*, one of the most famous *corridos* to come out of the Mexican Revolution. The song tells the story of a young woman in love with a sergeant. She traveled with him and his regiment. Due to this song, the term La Adelita came to signify a woman of strength and courage, the archetype of a woman warrior. I, too, am La Adelita. But that's not all. My last name, Ortiz, means brave, strong, and fortunate."

The crowd rustled. "Ahh."

"I have needed these qualities throughout my journey. In war we band together against another group. We can't do that now, as we are the enemy. We are the cause of this disruption. So now we must band together for, not against, each other, but for the survival of our planet. We must come together in one purpose and one cause: reverse climate disaster and live peacefully together."

Again, applause broke out.

"We have the science to reverse climate change, and thanks to *Project Drawdown, the Most Comprehensive Plan Ever Proposed to Reverse Global Warming,* edited by Paul Hawken, we have a path that is the most comprehensive plan ever proposed to reverse global warming. During this conference, we will explore what has been done since the *Drawdown* map was developed, how it has been updated, and the effect climate change has on every living being and the planet, herself. Hundreds of thousands of organizations across the globe are addressing climate change. But let's look deeper. As the planet is in chaos from the warming that has already occurred, so are all the beings that live on Earth and in Earth. Countries are in political turmoil. Social groups are in upheaval. Genocide and racial persecution have increased at an alarming rate. And viruses like Covid-19 are on the rise, drastically reducing our physical movement and private space. Our foundational structures have collapsed, and we wonder why we feel overwhelmed, stressed, and fearful. Will this conference solve all the world problems? Probably not. But there will be another great wave to raise consciousness and to create a new way of perceiving our world and living together in harmony and love. To move from perceiving ourselves as separate to knowing that we all integrally interconnected."

Applause broke out yet again.

"We will begin *not* with an update of the science and new advancements, for this intellectual approach has proven insufficient to move people from their rigid perceptions and fear to take enough authentic action to reverse climate change. So today we take another avenue. We will start with our spiritual leaders, who have traveled from places around the globe, as many of you have, to help us align our consciousness with the magnitude of the problem. For it is only in a true and deep shift of consciousness that we will be able to work together to reverse climate change, live peacefully together, and save our planet."

The stage was set for Joseph, Sid, and Running Bear Eagle to present next, but no one could have anticipated what would happen.

"Next, I have the privilege of introducing our first guest," Adelita continued. "Joseph, a man of wisdom and vision for the future. He will tell you about himself and then introduce his two colleagues. Please welcome Joseph."

There was polite applause until Joseph stepped onto the stage. Then a hush fell over the crowd. Joseph no longer wore his slacks and shirt, but wore his simple cloth shroud. He walked with grace and purpose onto the stage. His radiance was transfixing. As he caught each person's eye, they knew instantly that they were loved and accepted. With a deep calm and presence, he stood in silence for another moment.

"Many of you know me as Jesus of Nazareth. Jesus the Christ."

A clamor ran through the arena. Could it really be Jesus? Was this some kind of joke? If it were, someone would pay dearly for wasting time on such a prank.

Hearing the clamor and reading their minds, he replied, "It is true, and by the end of our visit here today, you will feel your time has never been better spent."

That really caused a stir. But before they could continue their disbelief, he proceeded. "I said I would come back, and I have. And this time I brought two very important friends. The first is Siddhartha Gautama. Some of you know him as the Buddha."

The audience gasped.

Buddha walked mindfully onto the stage and stood beside Christ. His aura was also a brilliant gold and visible to the audience. He bowed first to Joseph and then to the audience. "Through understanding, we gain compassion," he said calmly, as jaws dropped throughout the audience. "Today we shall assist you in a deeper understanding of the truth of your purpose and existence on this planet."

Then Christ said, "Now it is my pleasure to introduce you to Running Bear Eagle, an Apache medicine woman. She is a teacher of the divine connection of relationship to all beings large and small."

The indigenous peoples in the audience gave a sigh of relief that they were represented. And many women in the audience noticed and were grateful that there was a woman present.

Running Bear entered the stage, wearing her ceremonial garb. Now, *everyone* was paying attention. As her counterparts had done, she deliberately made eye contact with each person, seeming to say "Welcome, sister and brother." Then she began, "I have returned to teach you the power of nature medicine."

She stepped back and the three stood back-to-back, forming a trinity. They stood silently as the portal of healing, loving light entered the arena and lifted each person's polysensory awareness so they all could see, feel, hear, smell, and taste the subtle energies of the fourth and higher dimensions. As people looked at Joseph, Sid, and Running Bear Eagle, they saw and felt radiance in every cell of their bodies. A huge collective sigh was released.

With quickened breath, Christ, Running Bear, and Buddha heightened their golden fields to form a sphere encompassing the three of them. The sphere lifted off them and began orbiting around the arena.

Suddenly everyone recognized the sphere as Earth. Telepathically from the sphere, they heard, "I am your home. I gave willingly everything you needed to sustain yourself, but you want more. You are me, and I am you. Notice your body is two-thirds fluid. So is mine. Your body is made of carbon-based molecules. So is mine. Your soul is on a journey of growth and development. So is mine. You suffer with emotional pain. So do I. Because we are one, your anger goes right through me like a razor blade."

Obliging their need for sensory experience, she gently sent a razor-sharp pain through everybody present. "You think you own me, but you cannot own another soul. In your assumed ownership, you have tragically mistreated me. Feel now in your body what the pollution of my waterways feels like for me."

She flooded each person's bodily fluids with chemicals, plastic shrouds, feces, poisons, detergents, and much more. People screamed with pain. They spit up foul smelling fluid. Every organ in their bodies ached unbearably. The feeling of being poisoned maliciously surged through them.

"Now feel what you have done to my breath."

They gasped for air, as she nearly suffocated them with gas fumes and chemical burn-off.

"Now feel what you have done to my skin by covering it with pavement, digging into it for your minerals and basements."

It was as if each person were suddenly paralyzed and suffocating simultaneously. As if concrete were poured over them. Their bodies began to overheat, for lack of ventilation from the largest organ on the body, the skin. One man passed out. Another had angina pains. Most tried to scream, **"STOP!"** But their mouths were cemented shut. Many were losing oxygen and becoming dizzy or faint.

"But that is not all you do on a daily basis to do to me." Then she projected to their bodies the pain of birth and death. "You are now killing what I birth faster than I can give birth. How long do you feel you can live in this state now?"

About thirty seconds, was the desperate thought of most of the participants.

"You are correct. That is about what I have left in geological time. *About thirty seconds.* And if your babies were killed at the same rate as you are killing mine, there would not be enough life-force energy to re-species the planet."

She projected into them the painful, tortured deaths of one species after another that their poisons and construction had murdered. By this time, many of the participants were experiencing a virtual death. They were watching and feeling their bodies being poisoned and beaten all at once. The agony was unbearable. Many saw the white tunnel turn black and turn them away. They were left in a black hole—a void so empty and so frightening that all hope was lost.

She waited until each person experienced this death. "Had enough?" she asked.

Yes, their minds screamed.

Earth Mother began to slowly withdraw the asphalt, pesticides, fertilizers, drug, toxins, and pain. "Is this what you mean to do to the source that gives you life? ***Then, stop it now!***" she concluded.

Before anyone had time to catch their breath, Christ began. "No one can talk you out of your beliefs, for they are deeply ingrained in your neurological structure. No matter how many deformed babies are born, or how many children starve to death or are poisoned by the water and the air, you still keep a death grip to your way. So I have no intention of trying to convince you to change. You have learned to love your family and your nation with such vigor that you kill, rape, and maim for them."

To each person, he flashed the image of their beloved child—a son or daughter, nephew or niece. The love each had for this child flowed fully. As each person was deeply in their own wonder of the love for their special child, he changed the child into each person's worst enemy.

For the Arabs, the child was changed into a Jew. For the Tibetans, a Chinese child. For the Greeks, a Turk. For the Irish a Brit, and so on.

At first, they felt shock and repulsion at the appearance of the enemy, so they pulled their love back from the child. But the child was still an innocent child, and they could feel this child's need to be loved. Some participants kept their hearts steadfastly closed, but others were so filled with the love in the room that they could not bear to withhold the needed love. Those who continued to withhold saw the child begin to wilt and die right before them. When they attempted to again love the child, it was too late. They could not reverse the death. Many wept in acknowledgment of what they had done.

Next, he flashed for them times in their lives when they had loved and how that love healed and saved lives. The tension lessened in the room as they witnessed the power of their love. Joseph let them stay in that feeling long enough to be revived and pleased, and then he changed it to times that each had withheld love. And each was able to not only *see* but also *feel* the pain they caused. Many burst into tears. A woman in the mid-balcony screamed out. Each was deep into their own experience.

Now he put them into the middle of wars their countries had engaged in, or were in at that very moment. They were at the front lines or experienced fighter bombs devastating thousands of lives with one push of a button. The agony of war coursed through their veins. Then the most amazing thing happened: as they shot and killed an enemy, they instantly saw the soul of that enemy rise up out of its body, go up into the ether, and come down again as their very own child. The same exact soul, was their flesh and blood!

They were breathless and confused. Their hate, which had so readily poured out, was now confused with the love for their child. How could this be? But the experience was so real and tangible it could not be questioned. Each remembered a nephew, a child, or an adult they did not like. Now it made sense. Spirit was teaching them oneness.

At this point, Christ gave each person the suggestion to ask forgiveness for the hate and murder.

There was a long and powerfully emotional pause.

"Do you know now our intrinsic interconnection?" he projected to them.

But that was not enough. Sid now projected to them starving children throughout the land. These were not just the sad pictures so many had become numb to seeing. Now they were able to feel exactly how the starving baby felt. Many of the children were riddled with parasites and tumors. Their guts were swollen from the poisoned waters. Their bones were weak and fragile and cracked. Their surroundings were filthy as they sat in their own feces. The audience members squirmed and tried to escape the horror, but their bodies were the bodies of the dying children, and there was no release.

With almost no recovery time, Christ showed them a past life of their own in which they had been either starved to death or killed in a horrible manner. Gasps of horror filled the room as the reality came even closer to their own soul experience.

He then placed them in lifetimes where they were the perpetrators—that is, the thief, the murderer, or the adulteress. But instead of just allowing them to witness the events, he put them inside the people they had violated. And then he posed the question "How can you judge another now when you know you have been on both sides of the story?"

After giving the audience only a few moments to recover, Running Bear began. She put each participant inside a tree in a forest that was being clear-cut. Each person felt the tree's sudden terror as the loggers approached. Then the screech of the chainsaw and the laughter of the men as they attacked the trees. They felt the searing pain and the agony of the tree as the chain saw cut them in half. Everything was chaos; their spirits were caught in the trees. They tried to help each other but were unable. All the animals and insects tried to escape, but many were smashed by the falling trees and lost their homes and lives. To complete the job, loggers laid poison down, so the rest of the animals, birds, and insects would all die.

Relentless in her message, Running Bear shifted participants into the bodies of the dying animals, birds, and insects, allowing them to feel the slow, agonizing deaths from poison. Many people fell out of their seats onto the floor, screaming to be released. But she held them there until the reality of their actions was cellularly impressed. Finally, she pulled back the scenes but let the pain linger.

After a short rest, those who had fallen onto the floor dragged themselves back into their seats, but no one had time to protest for Running Bear journeyed them into one more scene. This time it was a scene of people of all colors, religions, and nations living in harmony. She took them to the forest and introduced them to the tree people and showed them how to ask permission to take a tree and how to do it painlessly. Each participant saw the spirit of the tree they wanted to cut join the spirit of another tree or lift to the other side before they cut it down. They saw how to take only a few trees from the forest at a time and never to take the matriarch or patriarch. The forests were free from disease with this method.

She showed them a world where packaging was minimal and all biodegradable. She showed them a world where they could see each other's thoughts and feelings so there were no lies or secrets. They became conscious of their own inner light. She projected a world where each person knew they were a spark of God's love. They felt the harmony and the connectedness. And as each walked and felt this new world, they realized there was no disease or fear. When they thought something, it almost instantly manifested, so no one was hungry or homeless. No one was alone. *No one was alone?* Yes, no one was alone, because each was so consciously connected to the love of creation that there was no abandonment or loss possible. They knew they were inextricably part of the whole, though still unique. Each realized that they were an important piece of the whole cosmology, and without them, there would be a loss for all.

Running Bear introduced them to the energies of the other planets in the solar system and showed them how intertwined the energies of all the planets were and how this affected each of them individually. She showed them what life would be if they could instantly heal themselves from injury or illness. She taught them to walk lightly and consciously with all beings. She showed them the death process and how the soul rejoices with love, as it is reborn into the spirit world.

Then in a flash, she projected them into a spirit that was just ready to be born. They saw the soul council of the infant giving her last minute instructions. Then they felt the miracle of birth, but this time no veil fell over the baby and the baby remembered where she had come from and who she was. Consequently, the room filled with hope and love never before experienced by anyone.

> I call for all the Buddhists to come forward and hold hands around our
> Mother, the Earth. To stand united. I call for all the Christians to put down their swords and stand with each other and the Buddhists. I call for the indigenous faiths, the Jews, the Muslims, all faiths to put down their way and join hands in the uniting of the world.
> I call for all the educators to open their hearts to the each other, their students, the parents, and the educational staff and join hands. I call for all the business people to open their minds and hearts to the truth seen today and join hands to work as one family with Earth Mother.
> I call for all the people to put down their righteousness and their divisive ways, and join the family of life.
> We are all one tribe. We are all one tribe. We are all interconnected. We are all love. We are all love. Never to be separate again. We know the truth now. We are all one.

Everyone was swaying and singing along, "We are all one." Then a most amazing event occurred: they were suddenly not in the auditorium, but standing, with hands linked, all around the Earth, gathering people from all over the globe to join in singing, knowing, and feeling the truth of their existence.

The animals and birds and insects joined the circle. The fish and water beings joined in the singing. The sounds of the whales and dolphins permeated the song and raised it to yet another level of bliss and awareness. Everyone's physical and emotional pain dissolved. The love was so great that they witnessed the deformed regain wholeness; the starving, health. Miraculously, rivers and lakes and oceans became clean again. The ozone layer in the stratosphere was repaired, and the all layers of Earth's atmosphere were revived. Land filled with trash and nuclear waste was restored to health and abundance. The Earth's temperature dropped into normal range.

People who were not ready to live in love gently left their bodies to join the spirit world. They could now choose to reincarnate to another planet that still lived in polarity.

The structures and buildings began to disappear and cities became simple rural communities, equipped with advanced technology and the ability to manifest through thought. People were living their dreams. Artists were painting. Singers singing. Children playing. People were talking with the animals and trees as a manner of course, discussing better ways to live together. The angels and devas were visible and an integral part of all life.

As the singing continued, the love grew and each person and every soul evolved to loving consciousness. Finally, everyone left on the planet was holding hands around Mother Earth. The animals and birds and insects joined the circle. The fish and water beings joined also. The sounds of the whales and dolphins permeated the song and raised it to yet another level of bliss and awareness. Everyone's physical and emotional pain dissolved.

Now this must be Eden, some thought. Others thought, *This is Nirvana*. And they were both right.

'Thy kingdom come, on Earth as it is in Heaven.' The kingdom of heaven had arrived!

After a long, delicious pause, Running Bear brought the audience back to the auditorium, where they stood holding hands for a very long time. There was not a dry eye in the house. No one wanted to release their hands, lest the magic and the bliss disappear.

Finally, Running Bear began a hand squeeze that went around the room. As each person received it and passed it on, they let go. But no one moved even then.

Joseph said, "We are all from the heart of God and intrinsically connected. We always have been. It is the time now to think and *act* from this truth. Touch, speak, and think only with love and acceptance."

Running Bear added, "As you have realized, we are all related, and everything we do and think affects everything else. There is no separation between the kingdoms. You have been blind to the truth. You thought you were separate, but today you know the truth of your interconnection and oneness. Take this new awareness and heightened consciousness to heart and go change the world, that Earth may heal and move to her next stage of evolution with you."

Sid bowed, and Running Bear and Christ followed.

Everyone exploded into uproarious applause. Then, as if on cue, each person began walking up to those they once disagreed with or even worse hated, and hugged and kissed them. They all vowed to see differently and *act* differently. Suddenly, their distrust for each other dissolved, and new ideas on how to reduce production, how to heal, and how to replenish the Earth for everyone's good abounded.

The excitement was so profound that they spontaneously formed committees to create new political, religious, educational, and financial systems. The original agenda for the conference was tossed, and Adelita went with the flow.

At one point, the cell phone lines were so jammed that Joseph gave a special seminar on telepathic communication. As a result, when the participants arrived home, they already knew what had happened and what was to be done. Everyone on the planet got the message; critical mass was finally a reality.

In the days and weeks that followed, business people joined with spiritual people and politicians and formed new agreements. Warring countries made peace and planned how to live together in love. Country boundaries were opened. Money and resources were shared and waste was minimized.

Corporations banned all disposable products, including plates, cups, and plasticware. The interim substitute for plastic that was biodegradable filled grocery shelves. Running Bear taught people how to use Earth's resources sustainably so waste was eliminated.

Developers totally changed their projects from more building to taking down shopping malls and restoring the land back to nature with nature preserves, and more educational centers. Biologists worked with environmentalists and corporations to restore forests and wetlands. Scientists gathered with Running Bear to learn how to create energy from chi instead of oil and gas, or even solar and wind. Plans to create chi energy stations around the world were made.

Everyone was empowered to realize that their soul's purpose was to benefit all beings. There was no need for welfare, unemployment, and social services, as the consciousness of interconnection elevated everyone.

Pharmaceutical and biotech companies released all animals from their labs and joined with herbalists and explored with earnest the medicinal uses of herbs and other plants. Many of their plants were closed, and the land was returned to nature.

Businesses focused on creating sustainable products designed in the life cycle of birth to birth, so no waste was ever created. Landfills were restored.

Thousands of businesses changed not only what they did, but also how they did it. They considered all life in each decision. An amazing joy rippled through the lands. Deaths on Mondays decreased instantly. Suicides, rape, murder, and theft stopped, and those words were lost from the vocabulary of each language and dissolved from the global mind.

Trapped souls in graveyards were released to the spirit world—at peace at last.

The backwoods peoples once in hiding came out to rejoice with the others. Their prophecies were changed from annihilation of the planet to revitalization.

Mary was promoted to vice president of her national conference planning company. She booked Running Bear Eagle, Victoria, Joseph, and Sid all over the world to teach the new skills.

As the human kingdom transformed, so did the animal, insect, mineral, and angelic kingdoms. Each of them advanced to their next level of evolution. Animals no longer ate each other; instead, they too survived on chi. Life spans were planned to eliminate overpopulation. When a being completed its journey on Earth, it moved to its new octave of life in the evolutionary chain.

Communication with other star systems opened, and summer vacations included a trip to Sirius 2, not just Yellow Stone National Park. The National Park system grew, and cities were full of parks and wild life, and people lived side by side with the animals. There wasn't any fear of lions or tigers or bears. Many species, once extinct, returned to Earth to live in harmony.

Automobile companies and the oil and gas industry joined together to create travel stations. "Beam me up, Scotty" became their new tag line. They poured their huge profits into restoring the highways back to nature.

The genius of the movie industry's focus changed from entertainment—that is, sex and violence—to teaching the new skills. For entertainment, people gathered together in their communities and families to sing and dance and hold a positive intention for what they wanted to manifest together as a community. Everyone was an artist, singer, dancer, and lover of life. Greed dissolved, and true communities of love and acceptance flourished.

Allopathic doctors joined with Eastern medicine and energy healers to develop new systems of healing. Schools erupted all over the globe to teach people to heal themselves. Doctors and therapists became teachers.

Accountants closed their offices for there were no taxes, and bookkeeping became unnecessary. Everyone had everything they needed, and nothing was hoarded or hidden or claimed.

Interest in the theater and music grew. Athletics became joyful, for competition was gone and money was eliminated. People played to improve their skill and ability to work together at even higher levels, not to beat someone else.

Life, so interconnected, became sacred and honored. Prisons were emptied and closed. Judges put their robes down and attorneys went sailing.

Peace came to the heart of each person and, therefore, to the planet. There was no need for formal governments, though councils and inter-councils kept information flowing across the lands. After a while, money was disbanded, for trade was unnecessary once everyone could manifest their needs at will.

Epilogue

*I*n a beautiful garden, Christ officiated the wedding of Buddha to Mary Magdalene.

Bud and Jerry became national seminar leaders on forgiveness. Reverend Bill's church grew so large, they had to build a new sanctuary, but this time with Mother Earth calling the shots.

Mary and George's relationship blossomed with continual love, and their children and grandchildren grew up in a safe, peaceful, clean planet.

Mother's fever was gone, and she thrived with clean rivers, lakes, and oceans. The air was clear from pollutants. Cancer became a word of the past. All her children were healthy, happy, and at peace.

At last, the thousand years of peace had begun.

About The Author

*D*eborah-Marie Diamond, M.A. is a pioneer in quantum healing and has helped thousands of people around the globe. After graduate school at the University of Colorado, she studied herbology, western and Ayurvedic nutrition, and acupressure. Realizing that the future of health was in quantum healing, she embarked on an intensive ten-year training with native shamans and medicine women.

Her thirst for self-healing and interconnection, led her to become a New Thought Minister and a Buddhist Insight Meditation Teacher. She is the founder of *Circle of Life Center, Diamond Hands on Healing School*, and *Diamond Mystery School*. With a profound dedication and love for Mother Earth, she has been active in the environmental movement since college.

Deborah-Marie's religion is love, and from that perspective she knows that we are intrinsically interconnected—the fundamental principle of oneness. She exemplifies that living in sacred relationship brings awareness, peace, and health to all beings and the planet. Currently, she lives in Asheville, NC.

www.deborahmdiamond.com